I0823213

Other Books by Kathryn Berla

The House at 758

Going Places

The Kitty Committee: A Novel of Suspense

Dream Me

Beau & Bett

Ricochet

12 Hours in Paradise

La Casa 758

JOHN DOE DOES NOT SUCK

Kathryn Berla

ISBN: 978-1-963832-40-2 (paperback)
ISBN: 978-1-963832-59-4 (ebook)
LCCN: 2025947356

Printed in the United States of America

This book was handcrafted by skilled artisans. No AI was used in the writing or cover design for this book.

Shadow Dragon Press
9 Mockingbird Hill Rd
Tijeras, New Mexico 87059
www.shadowdragonpress.com
info@shadowdragonpress.com

Content Notice:
This book has a strong focus on the topics of anxiety and obsessive compulsive disorder (OCD). As well as vampires.

CHAPTER ONE

"MR. DOE. I KNOW you're in there!" Mrs. Dilliberato jangles her key ring, trying to scare me into opening the door.

Her walking in right now would almost be worth it to see the look on her face... as her eyes adjust to my darkened apartment... as her mind processes what she's seeing... perhaps taking it for a joke at first. Me, lying in my coffin, minding my own business.

She doesn't have the legal right to enter my apartment with my rent just two weeks late. I know that. She knows that. And yet she continues to shake her ring of keys as though she were a rattlesnake coiled to strike.

"I know you're there," she says. "You *owe* me money. You *give* me my money."

I hunch my left shoulder away from the coffin wall. I should have allowed for a few extra inches. If I measure across my shoulders when I'm standing up, it's not going to be the same as when I'm lying down. I should have planned for that. Stupid mistake.

The smell of the wood takes me back to the forests of Bistrița-Năsăud, my home which, in all likelihood, I'll never see again—never *care* to see again. I think about how many things must have changed over the past century. They probably have internet now. Facebook. Netflix. I wouldn't be surprised if they watch *The Real Housewives of Beverly Hills* or something equally disturbing. It's better to never set foot there again than to discover they keep up with the Kardashians along with the rest of the world.

Anyway, the last time I was there was a disaster.

"Mister *Doe*." Mrs. Dilliberato's voice lifts on the second word. Almost flirtatiously. A new tack, perhaps? "I'm tired of waiting. Tomorrow, I'm filing the papers to give you official notice."

Hah! Even I know that from the date of filing those papers to the date the sheriff comes to put a lock on my door, I have a good two, maybe even three, years. And if we're going to get contentious about it, I might just stop paying rent altogether. Fortunately, I live in a city that favors tenants' rights over landlords' rights. I'm not trying to take advantage, it's just that current circumstances dictate.

At first, the idea of a coffin in my apartment felt a little silly, but I don't regret it now—it's part of my heritage, no matter how trite some customs might seem in the modern age. I find it reassuring. Comforting. Although I admit the pressure against my left shoulder is enough to drive a person mad after twelve straight hours. The padded silk lining eases my pain, though—a nice touch if I do say so myself. And the clever way it converts to a work/study desk with just the touch of a button. It's a masterpiece of creative design, and I'm not just saying that because I designed it. I only wish I could share it with the world.

"You can't hide from me, Mr. Doe!"

But the coffin, well, that's also pure camp. Why *not* have a little fun if I have to spend half my day inside my apartment? Awake with nothing but my thoughts to keep me company.

> **MYTH: Vampires sleep in coffins. Nonsense! That's just for the movies. And also, back in the day, if you lived in a sleepy little hamlet in the Transylvanian mountains where everyone was into everyone else's business, there weren't a lot of places you could hang out before sunset without people wondering why you religiously avoided the sun. SPF and skin cancer weren't things we worried about back**

then. A coffin was purely for the sake of convenience, a place where people wouldn't go looking for you when the sun was shining. Encouraging you to come out and enjoy the beautiful day. Expecting you to help with the harvest or sowing of crops.

Let's just call my coffin a reminder of days gone by. A nostalgic tribute to my roots. A way to avoid feeling so alone.

Mrs. Dilliberato jangles her key chain one more time. Her footsteps fall away as she moves down the hall towards the staircase.

CHAPTER TWO

My alarm jangles like a bad reminder of Mrs. Dilliberato's keys. The sun has officially set so it's safe to rise and shine, as they say. Rise, yes. Shine, maybe not so much. Since sleep is not a thing I can do, I prefer to think of my days as a time of meditation and reflection. As a longtime practitioner of transcendental meditation, I try to fit it into my twelve hours and feel out of sorts if I don't.

I rise from my coffin, rub my tender left shoulder (making a mental note to add a bit more padding to that area), and elongate my limbs until I hear the snap that ensures they're correctly in place and will remain that way until I retract them.

My day starts with night. I have two hours to make myself look and feel like your basic 17-year-old kid for my job at the 24-hour diner down the street—the Gobble-Down-Suck-Up, a name that references both the chocolate shakes for which we're famous and the burgers people turn out for in droves. I can't stand the sight of dark pink meat-juice oozing out from between our patrons' lips and sliding down their chins. The young. The old. The smooth-skinned cheeks. The grizzled jaws. They all come, and they can't seem to get enough. Barbaric, really.

Someone has pushed my mail under the door—probably dear Miss Henrietta Devine who constantly worries about mail being stolen from the cubbies in the lobby of our building. Lobby is really too kind a word… transition area is more like it. In any case, she worries (and rightfully so) about our mail and many other things. About me.

About the other tenants of this ruined structure which passes for an apartment building. About the homeless souls who fight every day to exist on the streets. About those who would prey upon them.

I don't think she worries about Mrs. Dilliberato. Nobody worries about Mrs. Dilliberato except, perhaps, Mr. Dilliberato, and I'm not even sure about that.

It occurs to me that worry is the purest and most honest display of love that exists. During my brief time of "living" I only knew love once. I didn't worry about her. About Nadia. But I was young and completely ignorant of the ways of the world and how things can go very wrong very quickly. I wonder... if worry equals love, what does it mean when one worries about oneself? I nip this thought-spiral in the bud by transferring my attention to the mail sprawled across the threshold.

Bills.

Campaign literature from candidates in the upcoming election (I always read these very carefully, although I'm ineligible to vote since I technically don't exist).

More bills.

Overdue notices for past bills.

Notice from the utility company that my power has been shut off due to non-payment (I'd noticed).

A letter from a literary agent (I recognize the stamped, self-addressed envelope from an agent I queried years ago).

Dear Mr. Doe:

Thank you for your query! We appreciate the opportunity to review your work, but unfortunately, it's not a good fit for our list at this time and we just didn't connect with the characters the way we hoped we would. Please don't be discouraged, though. Publishing is a marathon, not a sprint, and you only need one person to make your dream come true.

Best.

Sue Smiley Literary Agency

"We make your dreams come true."

PS: Just a personal note about THE LAST VAMPIRE. Vampires aren't selling these days so you may have difficulty finding an agent. A bit of advice: Consider shelving your manuscript for a few years while you work on something new. Perhaps after some time passes, vampires will make a comeback.

They won't. Make a comeback, that is. Who could know this better than me, the *real* last vampire?

Perhaps I should have queried my manuscript as the memoir it truly is—not as a made-up fantasy designed to titillate or frighten people with otherwise boring lives. But I don't want the scrutiny that would come from outing myself. I've read about Ishi of the Yahi, the last member of the Yana Native American people indigenous to Northern California in the central Sierra Nevada. The poor chap was housed in a museum, put on display for the amusement of the finer members of society who cared nothing for the real man. For the real Ishi. And when they were done with him, all interest lost, the money stopped coming in. And Ishi continued to live out a life of painful loneliness until he died ignobly of a white man's disease.

Of course, for me, the end will never come. Generations from now, I'd still be relegated to an existence as an object of curiosity to be poked, prodded, and studied like a lab rat.

So, no. Vampires won't make a comeback. Vamps are so yesteryear, and there you have it. It's a hard truth to accept. I try to have a little fun with it, especially on Halloween. But to say that my very existence is no longer relevant—that hurts.

Very carefully, so as not to topple it, I add this rejection letter to the pile that reminds me every day of who I am and what I should and shouldn't expect.

I sprinkle a few flakes into Clementine's fishbowl. She rises to meet them, mouth agape with eager anticipation, eyes wide with wonder at the flakes which arrive every day, seemingly manna from Heaven. Her gleaming orange body shivers and shimmers in delight.

I check her bowl once... twice—worried I've dropped in too little or too many flakes, either way jeopardizing Clementine's health. I know I'll check on her a few more times before I leave and worry about her for the rest of the night. I cautiously add a few more flakes and then second-guess myself by scooping them out before Clementine can get to them.

Is it my imagination or is she looking at me disdainfully? Another thing I'm bound to worry about. I log it into my "worry journal" where all concerns go in my attempt to diffuse their power over me.

CHAPTER THREE

FACT: If you want to hide, the best way is to hide in plain sight. People will accept almost any truth you present to the outside world.

Picture Marilyn Manson. If you can't picture him, Google him. Now imagine him thirty years younger. You're imagining me.

Now picture him twenty pounds heavier, a ruddy complexion, and auburn hair. That was me 300 years ago before I was taken (or "turned" as some people like to call it). The proper term is *infected*.

Over the centuries, people have told me that I look like many of the more famous bad boys of history: Lord Byron, Billy the Kid, Elvis Presley, James Dean, Marilyn Manson, and yes... even Timothée Chalamet. But the truth is that I look like none of them, with the exception of Marilyn Manson. People see something dark in me they either need to tame (or flee from), by identifying it with something familiar. None of this is truly relevant but physical appearances seem to be what people focus on, and mine is easy enough to describe.

My age... equally nebulous. I look like a 17-year-old high school dropout. Actually, I'm 317 years old. But who's counting centuries? And I do have a few degrees beyond high school—thirty-seven, in fact—including advanced degrees in Animal Husbandry, Creative Writing, Phlebotomy, Philosophy, Hematology, Music Theory, Witchcraft, Romanian Studies, Infectious Diseases, and Hungarian Studies, to name a few.

To prepare myself for work, I apply a generous dollop of pomade to my hair and comb it through, fixing my unmanageable locks into helmet-like obedience. My hair is jet-black, artificially so. It suits my more modern look better than the natural reddish hue. Next comes the pancake makeup, tinted slightly for a beach-tan glow. I've become quite good at applying makeup over the years and, if anyone notices, they don't comment. As long as no one touches me (which no one ever does), they can't feel the unyielding leathery texture of my skin which otherwise appears quite normal to the eye.

Today is a good hair and makeup day, and I find myself breaking into a rare smile as I gaze at my image—which is smiling back at me.

> **MYTH: A vampire doesn't know what they look like except as described by an eyewitness or sketched in a portrait. More nonsense. It's true I can't see myself in a mirror, but I have no trouble seeing myself in the selfie mode of my smartphone camera (thank goodness for technology) although I don't appear in the actual photo. Why? Who knows? I would refer you to someone at the Apple Genius Bar.**

Before modern technology, I forced myself to stand in front of a mirror as though I could actually see myself and practice smiling mirthfully with, of course, limited success. Paying a dentist to file down my eye teeth helped. They turned a mirthful smile into a cause for alarm in most people I encountered. Now, I file my own teeth which grow back persistently, if not rapidly.

But even centuries ago, I was able to see a vague rendition of myself in a pool of clear water. So, yes, just another unhelpful myth—one of many.

Today I'm excited and (dare I say it) happy. Tonight, I begin a class in criminology, a field I've never studied. My first night class begins at exactly 9:00 p.m., allowing me to put in a few hours of work beforehand—not enough to keep up with all my expenses, hence the rent problem with Mrs. Dilliberato, but enough to keep me in blood money.

So to speak.

I'm nervous but excited. After all, what could be more enthralling than studying the dark side of humanity? The real mystery is how it's taken me this long to consider a career in law enforcement, especially when it's become difficult for me to pinpoint a subject matter I haven't already mastered. With my fluency in most languages—at least the romance languages—I could be a valuable asset. A detective able to seamlessly integrate into many communities and one with an innate understanding of evil.

I can hardly wait.

I knock the back of my skull with my knuckles before I leave my apartment—exactly five times. If any knock is muddled (they have to be clear knocks) I must start over again. It's a ritual I use to protect me from worry—sometimes it works and sometimes it doesn't.

Today I feel good, so I just let it go at the five knocks. Other days, I use back-up rituals—heel-tapping or a complex system of blinking: three fast, three slow, three fast. My backup rituals come in handy when my skull-knocking might be too obvious in public—although, I can make the movements precise and pass it off as head-scratching.

But honestly, who would ever hire me as a detective? This class is most likely just another waste of time and money. Another pipe dream for achieving anything beyond mediocrity and barely scraping by in spite of eternal life.

I tap my right heel, followed by the left. I get the expected response within thirty seconds—a loud thump on my floor. The neighbor in the apartment below keeps a broomstick at the ready to thump his ceiling whenever my heel tapping gets too loud. Now I have to repeat the process to make sure I got it right. Another broomstick thump is the final nail in the coffin of my optimistic mood.

I think eternal life holds me back. Perhaps knowing your years are limited is what drives one to achieve their dreams.

Keeping myself in a right state of mind is a full-time job. It's exhausting.

CHAPTER FOUR

Someone is following me. I can sense it. Behind me and rapidly closing the gap.

I turn my head to stare into the darkness once… twice. My nerves jangle like Mrs. Dilliberato's keychain (lately it seems everything jangles like Mrs. Dilliberato's keychain).

My pursuer is close, so close I'm prepared to assume the "attack" pose.

"John Doe!"

"John Doe!"

My muscles release.

It's Fernando and Peter, known as the Wheelie Boys, because they drive electric stand-up scooters with handlebars. They move about town so quickly they're often gone before I even realize they're there. Tonight, on my way to work, they circle like vultures. Probably hungry.

"Can you get us some fries, John Doe?" Peter. Or was it Fernando?

"And a chocolate shake?" says Fernando on their second rotation around me.

Sometimes I do. Sometimes I don't. The fries, that is. Never the shakes, that's a bridge too far. The appetites of these boys are insatiable.

"John Doe, did you hear?" *Zoom*

"Another murder." *Zip*

"Last night." *Zap*

I've often thought that Fernando and Peter would make excellent vampires, with their stealth and speed.

They often seem to know things before anyone else mainly because they cover so much ground in a day. They're natural information-gatherers, much in the same way a dry mop collects dust bunnies on its journey from one end of a room to the other. Where they find time to fit in school and other boyhood activities that 12-year-olds engage in, I'll never know.

"Meet me at the back door," I say, and they circle one more time before falling into a line and trailing about twenty feet behind me. "What murder?" I ask, but they're talking to each other and don't hear my question. "And shouldn't you boys be wearing helmets?"

A near miss. Thank goodness I didn't assume the attack pose. Imagine Peter and Fernando's shock and horror—anyone who's seen it will tell you it's truly a fearsome thing to see a vampire in attack position. It's gone beyond just a pose only a handful of times in my life. Mostly we assume it in order to frighten off those who might do us harm because, after all, if we can avoid violence just by threatening it, who would choose otherwise?

My fangs have recently been filed down and, even if they hadn't, they wouldn't be visible to the human eye except at close range. But I don't need my fangs to look fearsome. My natural demeanor is terrifying although, more often than not, I'm the one who's terrified.

Still, I'm grateful it didn't come to that tonight. Peter and Fernando are good boys and they'd never dream of doing me harm.

***

The Gobble-Down-Suck-Up is hopping, the patrons jostling each other, brimming with excitement while they wait in line on this very cold, very damp evening. As usual for dinner time, we're filled to capacity, and the wait is an hour long. I enter through the back door where I slip on my hair net and white kitchen-worker tunic top and drawstring trousers.

"Glove up, John," Dimitri passes me a pair of disposable latex gloves all kitchen workers are required to wear. He instinctively avoids touching me as he drops them into my open hand. Everyone avoids touching me. I doubt they're even aware of it—like a horse that shies away from a hidden snake—it's an act as unconscious as breathing.

FACT: What seems most obvious is least obvious. It's why I took the name John Doe. If something seems too strange to be true, people will accept it on face value.

"Doe! Get the sides on these plates," Calvin calls out to me. He's the owner/cook and no one dares to disobey Calvin.

"And stop wearing that blue nail polish, would ya," Calvin says. "You can dress up however you want at home but at work I want you lookin' professional."

I clear my throat meaningfully. "Umm... discrimination?"

"He's right," Dimitri chimes in. "I mean, technically as long as he's gloved up and performing his duties adequately... he has the right."

And everyone knows I perform my duties more than adequately. I'm the best and most efficient employee they have, some of which can be attributed to my ability to move about quickly without drawing attention to myself. That in combination with over a hundred years' experience working in diners (taverns or inns as they used to be called). I'm good and I know it.

Sure, I could paint over the natural blue color of my nail beds. I could transform them to a realistic pink but why bother? It's just one more thing I'd have to keep up with, and the fact that everyone thinks I'm purposely painting my nails blue gives me a certain cachet. It adds to the mystique of the personae I've carefully crafted: John Doe, counter-culture rebel, bad boy extraordinaire.

Everything about me is carefully crafted. I'm a creation of myself for the outside world to view. Honed to perfection over centuries. Nothing is left to chance which is why I take two hours to prepare for work. Chance could lead to discovery and discovery would be catastrophic. Nothing about me could be described as a careless afterthought.

My appearance.

My discernible personality.

My character traits.

My ability to blend into the background.

My non-confrontational tactics.

My...

And then she walks into the kitchen through the swinging door. Rust-brown hair grazing the tops of her shoulders. Eyes the color of grey alder tree bark. A dewy complexion... shining from her natural oils... smooth... inviting. Her legs are thick and her torso is thin, like a ballerina. The straps of her apron cinch her narrow waist, emphasizing her generous hips.

I'm transported. Speechless. Although I have practically no need for oxygen, my withered lungs struggle to make use of the little which is required.

"Doe! Close your mouth before a moth flies in," Calvin says. "Molly's the new waitress, taking over for Doris. Molly meet Doe. Now both of you get to work."

"John," I manage to croak so feebly she can't possibly hear me.

Molly? But surely this is Nadia. For a moment I have no concept of time which ebbs and flows around me in a swirl—I'm caught in its vortex.

My putrefied heart attempts to animate. The walls of the kitchen rush about me like a merry-go-round. Molly has moved on without giving me more than a second's glance and a weak smile, but my feet are rooted to the sticky floor smeared with meat juices and sugary syrup.

I am a carefully crafted creation of myself.

Nothing about me has been left to chance.

Nothing about my external presentation is a careless afterthought.

But inside my head, chaos and doubt reign supreme.

Self-love is nothing more than self-worry.

Time is liquid, constantly reshaping itself, and too much of it can be too much to bear.

FACT: Your heart will never recover from your first true love.

CHAPTER FIVE

The Last Vampire

By John Doe

Chapter Five

Although Zoltan had his complaints about his father, Bela wasn't a bad man, at least not in the carefree, early days of Zoltan's childhood. Bela tended the sheep, the pig, and the land, and expected his wife and son to do their part as well, whether that meant weeding, hoeing, caring for the chickens and collecting their eggs, carrying water from the well, cutting grass for the animals, and pickling the produce which would sustain them through the winter. Food continued to be satisfying, if not exactly plentiful, so Zoltan never went hungry. But all of that was about to change.

When neighboring Moldavia abolished serfdom in the eighteenth century, a mass migration of immigrants from Transylvania began to flood the area. Bela was tempted to join them, holding out the dream of becoming a landowner one day—his own boss, a serf no longer. And with only his wife and one good-natured son to care for, he was relatively free to risk the journey and whatever awaited him in the new lands. Opportunity. Whether it led to failure or success, the allure was all-consuming.

Then one day, a traveler from town stopped by asking for water, and although he complained of feeling feverish, they fed him at their table and gave him water from their well. When the traveler departed on his small horse-drawn cart,

Zoltan was concerned the traveler was faring so poorly, he'd topple over and fall to the ground. Zoltan watched the cart as it rolled away from their home, down the dirt road, finally disappearing into the inky night.

A week later Zoltan became terribly ill. A week after that, his mother fell sick as well. Although the pustules that covered their bodies eventually scabbed over and the scabs eventually fell away, Zoltan was left permanently scarred across much of his face and body, and his mother was left without her sight. Now instead of two healthy helping hands, Bela had a wife who needed looking after and a son still weak from a devastating illness. Bela's dreams of freedom from serfdom were crushed and he was forced to beg for help from the landlord of the estate, a stern nobleman who rarely interacted with the serfs who worked his land. Any help came at a cost and the costs only continued to mount.

But when one is poor, if life does not play out perfectly (which it rarely does) any unfortunate illness or other happenstance can turn an already perilous existence into a tragedy. For Bela and his family, tragedy was breathing down their necks.

First the pig was sold. Then the sheep. Then the chickens. After that, their sole source of sustenance was the tiny vegetable garden. Rain did not arrive when the ground was too dry. Sun did not appear when the crops begged for its life force. The dog, a mangy cur who had stolen Zoltan's heart, no longer ate scraps from the table but instead had to fend for itself—field mice or whatever part of a carcass had been abandoned by scavengers.

The worst things were, the meaner Bela became. When his father kicked the dog, Zoltan got between them, and when his father slapped Zoltan, his mother threw herself in front of her son. One day, Bela's mother decided to give up on her dreary life. The small amount of energy reserves she still possessed slowly trickled away as she refused any food or drink. Within two weeks, she was dead.

After that day, Zoltan never conversed with Bela, following his orders without hesitation but never making even the slightest eye contact. Their meager meals were eaten together in silence. Days went by when Zoltan was on his own due to the increased frequency of Bela's visits to the nobleman-landlord as their needs grew along with their continuing bad fortune.

The dog had long since run away and met with whatever fate, Zoltan didn't know. It was just the two of them—Bela and Zoltan—eking out an existence so dismal, so gloomy, that no one ever again referred to Zoltan as a good-natured lad. And although Zoltan's red hair still glowed naturally in the sunlight, it was the only thing about him that shone. Zoltan was sure that his chance at happiness had come and gone forever. He didn't see any way out of his damnable well of misery.

Until one day.

Being dead has done wonders for my skin, flattening out the pox scars so they're literally undetectable after 317 years.

I see the melodrama in my life story. Perhaps I can rework it in a way that would cause an agent to sit up and take notice, ignoring the fact that vampires aren't currently trending. The part about Moldavia, I admit, is a little dry if you have no familiarity with the area or the era.

"...eking out an existence so dismal, so gloomy..." It's a little much, I admit, although true. Perhaps I could dispense with "so gloomy" and just leave it at "so dismal"?

And "damnable well of misery"? Too old-fashioned. Maybe "hopeless existence"?

There's definitely room for improvement.

I pause to remember my mother who's been gone so long that sometimes I forget the sound of her voice, and even her appearance is just a vague memory. She wasn't the kind of loving mother that people expect or crave these days. She was a hard woman with an instinct for protecting her progeny, which is what I took for love back then. In fact, this was my only example of the idea of love until I met Nadia and discovered what the word could truly mean. Not just in terms of the pleasures of flesh, but rather the unselfish giving of oneself to another, with no other reason than a difficult to describe warming of the heart. Fuzziness of the mind. It's been such a long time since I've felt that, I no longer think it's possible.

Although, I've felt fondness since then. Yes, fondness is the closest I've come.

"What's that?" Molly nods at the sheets of paper which collectively make up Chapter Five of my manuscript. "You working on something? Homework?"

I've drawn up a chair to the table in the back of the kitchen where the workers sit when we take our breaks. I have five minutes before I have to leave if I'm going to be on time for my first criminology class. In reality, I have thirty minutes if I want to take the easy way—the vampire way—because it's no myth that we're able to move so quickly our movement can't be perceived by the human eye.

But I prefer to walk the normal way. The slow way. I prefer to observe my surroundings and take my time. What's the point of saving time if you have an unlimited supply?

I prefer to waste my time.

"No, no. It's just... just something," I say.

"A love letter?" She waggles her eyebrows.

"No. Heavens no."

She settles down in the chair next to me. Her voice is high-pitched. Slightly nasal. Nothing like Nadia's voice, which was like a song. I could stay the extra fifteen minutes and talk to Molly. Get to know her, but her voice is nothing like Nadia's. She is nothing like Nadia.

"I have to go," I say, pushing my chair away from the table. "I can't be late for my first day of class."

MYTH: If you live long enough, you'll eventually come across the reincarnation of someone you once knew.

FACT: If you live long enough, you'll eventually come across a random distribution of genetic material that will physically present in a way eerily similar to someone you once knew.

CHAPTER SIX

Here's the real reason why I want to walk to class tonight. It's the thing most people want to hear about for their own prurient or perverse interests. The thing I'm least inclined to talk about and the thing that's most likely to land me in trouble.

I'm hungry, gosh darn it.

Everyone knows what that means. Or think they know.

But I'm not like everyone and the idea of consuming blood directly from its source is so distasteful to me that I can't even begin to contemplate it. So I get it indirectly from my own source—the most reliable source I've had since I was infected. I call him Mr. X. He's the reason I'll never move away from this city, at least not as long as he's still alive and working.

Mr. X works in a lab at a major hospital, and he's able to siphon off enough... blood (oh, ugh, I hate that word, but it is what it is)... to keep me healthy and alive to the extent I am. And right at this moment, I'm feeling a little peckish. In fact, I'm just on the verge of being hangry, as the young people say these days. It's been a week since I've sustained myself, so I've arranged for a rendezvous with Mr. X at our usual meeting place. Rent can wait. Gas and electric bills can wait. Water bills can wait. But Mr. X must be paid and must be paid on time.

It's true that I could provide for myself—and do it on the cheap—but that won't happen ever again. I've done that many, many times, I'm not proud to say, but my experience was always the same. The first time, I was convinced I'd given my "supplier" a bacterial infection. She was a kind woman, mother of three small children, who had let me a room in her home to help make ends meet. The next morning, I moved out with no explanation, but I returned multiple times without her knowledge to check on her well-being. I knew I hadn't suckled long enough to infect her. Just like the deer tick which must remain attached for hours before transmitting Lyme disease to its host, a vampire must also remain attached for many hours in order to transmit the virus. Since many vampires enjoyed the sensation, they remained attached for the requisite time.

But not me. I was in and out fast. I was one of the enlightened who didn't care to drag another soul down into my personal hell. Many of my vampire friends were decent in the same way. We sought out the company of like-minded vampires—the moral ones, we liked to think of ourselves.

It should be noted: I always use the past tense when it comes to vampires. More on that later.

Oh, the virus, yes, another thing that's little understood. Vampires infected their hosts by transmitting a virus—*vampirovirus*—which has yet to be discovered by traditional scientists and now, likely, never will be.

So, I worried myself sick over the health of my former landlady until I was finally convinced she was perfectly fine. Each time, I had the same worries and the worrying itself caused me great distress. I began to worry about my own health, about the possible diseases a host might unknowingly transmit to me.

There have been many times I had no other choice. Eat or die. But I always tried to be considerate. And clean.

FACT: Vampires don't get sick and CANNOT die again since we're already dead. Well, almost a fact but more on that later.

> **FACT: Being confronted with facts doesn't always alleviate worry. If one is scared to fly in an airplane, it doesn't help to know the chance of being killed in a plane crash is infinitesimal. Fears are seldom logical.**

Mr. X assures me that he tests each vial of blood I buy from him for the complete spectrum of viruses known to man. Perhaps he does or perhaps he doesn't, but I don't allow myself to consider the latter. And perhaps occasionally I do allow myself to wonder about the viruses that aren't yet known to man. Like vampirovirus, for instance. But I can't allow it... *won't* let myself go there.

A fellow's got to eat, after all.

***

The freaks are out in force tonight, and they think *I'm* strange. There are the usual hustlers peddling everything from illicit drugs to illicit sex. Not even their kind will approach me, though. They're not so depraved they can't sense a depravity far more powerful than their own. A large metal door covered in explicit graffiti opens and belches out a thumping, ear-popping bass. The smell of stale beer and sweaty bodies follows a millisecond later. The door closes, swallowing both the noise and scent of debauchery. Neon lights adorn nearly every entry along the grimy sidewalk in colors so multi-hued they meld into one toxic purple glare that glistens off the wetness pooled around the base of the gutters.

I think about Clementine and wonder how she's feeling. I fear I may have underfed her tonight and she may be experiencing the sharp pangs of hunger I'm experiencing right at this moment.

"Doe." The whisper is so soft I've almost walked past it. "*Doe.*" It comes again, this time more insistent.

I stop and swivel on my left foot. The alley, my meeting place with Mr. X... I nearly passed it, being so lost in my thoughts.

"What the hell is wrong with you, man?" he says, holding out the paper bag once I've slipped out of the light into the darkness of anonymity this alley provides.

"Sorry," I say, rattled by my inattention. I can't afford to make mistakes and inattention is always the precursor to mistakes. "The usual?" I ask, passing him five twenty-dollar bills. This will last me for two weeks.

Mr. X disappears into the alley. Once I'm sure he's gone, I open the bag and remove one of the vials, gulping down its contents. It's not enough so I open a second vial—which seems to do the trick for now. The taste is disgusting, salty and slightly metallic, but the feeling I get is priceless. The one saving grace is the slight hint of garlic which, contrary to popular opinion, is not something vampires fear. Why should we, it's delicious.

I feel renewed. Reinvigorated. Ready to meet any challenge. I pull a Kleenex from my pocket and dab at my lips to remove any trace of the red stuff. Then I carefully place the remaining two vials (still wrapped in the brown bag) in my backpack with my partial manuscript, my phone, and tonight's class syllabus along with a notebook and pen.

Then back onto the street where I look for a place to dispose of the used Kleenex, littering being unthinkable to me. But there aren't too many waste depositories in this neighborhood, so it's another few blocks before I come upon one. On the utility pole where the trash basket hangs, someone has stapled a flyer, surrounded by hundreds of others—rooms for rent, cheap massage services, movers wanted (references not necessary), and many more. But this particular one stands out. I've seen it before.

ARE YOU FEELING SAD?
ANXIOUS?
LONELY?
NEED SOMEONE TO TALK TO?

A phone number is provided with an invitation to call between the hours of 9:00 p.m. and midnight. The graphics are a cut above the other flyers, but that's not what first drew my attention to this particular notice drowning in a sea of colored paper and staples. The simple truth is that I answered *yes* to every one of the questions.

Then I do something I haven't had the courage to do since the first time I saw the flyer. I snap a photo with my phone before I continue walking towards my class.

***

Shall we talk about viruses, the perfect engines of destruction which only become imperfect when they kill off every possible host, thereby committing virtual virus-suicide?

Viruses have been on this planet long before humans, and they'll be here long after humans have self-obliterated. Always adapting. Mutating and adapting.

You could say my entire life has been determined by viruses. The smallpox virus. The vampirovirus. And the final one, which has been worst of all.

CHAPTER SEVEN

THE TYPE OF BUILDING is common in this part of the city where I live and work. From where I'm standing, it looks one step away from abandonment. A sign on the outside reads:

SPACES FOR RENT

The walls inside are pale green, a shade that only seems to be popular for industrial buildings and hospital corridors. The dim lighting reveals a crude cement façade underneath the peeling paint. Seeing no elevator, I take the stairs. On the wall of the stairwell, someone has taped a hand-written sign reading:

CRIMNOLGY CLASS THIS WAY

A crude arrow drawn on the sign points up.

Another sign with a different misspelling and another "up" arrow is on the landing of the second floor, so I keep climbing. When I see the same sign on the third-floor landing, I'm glad I had that second vial of blood. By the time I arrive on the fourth floor, I'm running a bit late. But I don't rush as I follow the signs to the only lit room in this building.

"Ah, you must be John Doe," says a portly man who's obviously the instructor since he's standing at the front of the classroom. He's wearing jeans, athletic shoes which reveal big toes on the cusp of busting out, a t-shirt emblazoned with the logo of our local football team, and a corduroy jacket (complete with leather elbow patches) which has seen much better days. A collection of ragtag desks of different sizes, shapes, and colors are arranged facing him, each with a white plastic lawn chair tucked underneath. "Take a seat," he says.

I choose a table that seems to be the sturdiest of all the remaining options, despite the fact that it's about a foot higher (or the chair is a foot lower) than is ideal for writing purposes.

"I was just telling the others that, with this small number of en...roll...ees, if anyone drops out I'll probably have to cancel the course. Just not worth my time, to be honest."

The five other students all turn and stare accusingly at me as though I might be the one dropout who would ruin it for the rest of them. I try to smile reassuringly—although I've only practiced mirthful smiles, which I hope is close enough to reassuring. It seems to do the trick since everyone turns their attention back to Mister...uh...*Detective* Onslot (which is what he has written on a white board propped up on the wall behind him).

I check my phone for the photo of the original class flyer, scrolling back through about a month's worth of pictures until I come across it:

LERN TO BE A DETECTIVE IN 2 MONTHS

HI-QUALITY INSTRUCTION

Perhaps the quality of the flyer should have given me a hint as to the quality of the instructor, but the price was reasonable, and I'm not made of money these days.

"So, maybe you'd like to know a little more about me," Detective Onslot says. "And I'll be straight-up with you because I expect the same honesty from you all." He looks each one of us in the eye as though seeking confirmation. Everyone remains expressionless, except for me. I look down at my table when his eyes connect to mine, but that's because of my natural shyness.

"Okay," he continues. "Straight-up." He breathes heavily and his face is perhaps pinker than it should be. "I was... let go from the police department due to an error on their part combined with some damned political correctness." His bald head is shiny with perspiration and I can see a drop of it trailing down the side of his neck. He impatiently swipes it away with the back of his hand. "Anyone have a problem with that?" he asks as though he's prepared to fight anyone who does. The other members of this small group seem to have mastered their poker-face. I glance down at my desk again, his stare having overpowered me like a junkyard dog staring down a chihuahua.

"Doe," he says. "You got a problem with that because if you do, you can just get yourself up out of that chair and leave right now and I'll cancel this entire GD class, pardon my French."

Five faces swivel to look accusingly at me again and, not wishing to be the cause of their class being canceled, I simply shake my head and do my best again to smile reassuringly.

"After fifteen years..." he mutters, shaking his shiny round head. "You'd think there'd be some loyalty after fifteen years." He picks up a sheet of paper and stares at it for a minute. "Okay, now that we got that out of the way, let's go over the syllabus (only he pronounces it slli-bus)." He stares at the paper for a few more seconds before crumpling it in his hand and tossing it into a nearby garbage can. "Forget about the sllibus," he says. "We're going to do things a little different in this class. This is a *real* world class where you'll learn *real* world things, not like those other fake-ass classes. Any questions?"

But nobody has any questions, and I can tell he only asked that to give him some time to think of what to say next. It's obvious to me he's completely unprepared to teach a class. He probably never expected his flyer would attract actual students.

"Okay, if there's no questions then we'll move on," Onslot says. "This first class we're going to get to know each other, okay?"

With such a guarded group I find it hard to believe anyone's going to get to know anyone in this class. I certainly don't want anyone to get to know *me*. And it does seem like a waste of time when we're supposed to be qualified detectives at the end of two months.

"Rule number one," he says. "Your partner is everything. *Everything*, do you understand? You count on them 200% and they need to do the same with you. 200%. You understand?"

We all nod. Although, I know it's impossible to count on someone more than 100% and even then, it's very rare.

"So, get that through your head right here and right now before you even *think* of becoming a detective. You got to know your partner better than yourself. What their next move is going to be before they even know it themselves. And you have their back. *Always!* Got it?"

A few drops of spit fly from his mouth and I wonder if anyone else noticed. My vision, being particularly acute, can be as much a curse as a blessing. In this case... *curse*.

We all nod. Apparently, we understand the concept of having our partners' backs.

"And let's just hope you never have a partner who... *betrays* you. Who..." he trails off and swipes away the gathering perspiration from his brow. "Never mind about that." The flickering fluorescent light above Onslot makes him look positively demonic.

All kinds of alarm bells are ringing in my head, but I don't want to disrupt the hopes and dreams of my five classmates, nor do I wish to draw attention to myself.

"So, I'm pairing you up, okay? Whoever I pair you up with is your partner for the rest of this course. You got each other's backs, okay? And today you're going to spend the rest of the class getting comfortable with each other."

The alarm bells ringing in my head level up to five-alarm-fire. But what can I do except remain motionless, wish for invisibility, and wait for the inevitable pairing off?

I have grossly overestimated the wisdom of taking a night class in criminology.

CHAPTER EIGHT

"HAS ANYONE EVER TOLD you that you look like Johnny Cash?" Angela asks me.

Angela Ruiz is my partner for the duration of this course. Onslot, in his infinite wisdom thought we'd make a good team—or perhaps just paired us because we are both dressed all in black.

"Once. In 1954." The words come out before I can stop myself. Another skill I possess which can be either curse or blessing is my total recall. In this case, combined with my insecurity and reckless willingness to go to any lengths to gain acceptance from my peers… *curse*.

I force a laugh which must sound unnatural to her ears, and then I attempt a pivot. "Has anyone ever told you that *you* look like Johnny Cash?" I ask.

Admittedly, not the best pivot.

"You mean Vivian Liberto, right? Johnny Cash's first wife. Plenty of people have told me that."

So, she's a fan. Oh, how I could regale her with my stories if only she knew and if only I could. It was Vivian Liberto who told me in 1954 that I looked like Johnny, her husband. I was living in Memphis back then and had an excellent supplier for the red stuff, though not as reliable as Mr. X. I met them all—Elvis, Johnny, Vivian. They weren't really famous back then, not like they would come to be. I met Vivian at the diner where I was working—everyone dropped in there at one time or another. It was in 1954 when I first started dying my hair jet-black and shaping it with pomade—a fashionable style at the time.

Now that I take a second look, it's true there's a distinct resemblance between Angela Ruiz and Vivian Liberto Cash. The sensuous mouth, prominent eyebrows, and luscious skin tone. All wasted on me, of course, beauty being something I can only appreciate in the abstract.

Only Nadia's memory can stir emotions within me. Only with Nadia did I love as a human—alive and brimming with the juices of young lust. After I was infected, the concept of love became as alien to me as building a nest on an ocean wave would be to a sparrow.

But I can still appreciate a pretty face or even a handsome face. It's all the same to me because, without any desire to follow through, the symmetry (or asymmetry) of what makes a face (or body) appealing to others is simply like reading a good book.

The thin chain around her neck catches the light and my attention. A tiny silver cross, so thin it's a marvel of workmanship, rests on the soft layer of flesh that covers her sternum. The black V-neck of her sweater creates a frame to isolate and highlight the beauty of this simple, yet stunning, piece of jewelry.

> **MYTH: Vampires hate crosses and silver. Why would I hate crosses? My mother was a devout woman and I loved my mother dearly, at least for a time. As for silver, it's my favorite precious metal, being highly overlooked (in my opinion) in favor of the gaudiness of gold.**

I'm a trained silversmith, a trade I learned in Augsburg in the late nineteenth century. In fact, a pair of silver candlesticks I'd forged are still on display to the public (I won't say where) due to their exceptional craftsmanship. None of this is to brag, only to say that I know a fine piece when I see one. The last time I saw a piece similar to Angela's necklace was around the neck of my one true love, Nadia.

"There's just one thing I want to get straight if we're going to be partners spending a lot of time together," Angela says. "I'm not into you, and I never will be. I'm a lesbian. Into girls. Okay?"

Apparently, she's misunderstood my fascination with the tiny silver cross that rests upon her chest.

"Oh, me neither. Not into you. Totally. Never could be."

She sighs deeply, her eyes boring into mine. "You don't have to be juvenile about it," she says, her voice as calm and patient as a mother explaining to a young child the need to wash his hands. "What I said has everything to do with my orientation and nothing to do with you personally. Just want everything out in the open, like Onslot said. Total honesty."

"Likewise," I say. "Total honesty. You're just... not my type."

Another sigh—less patient, as though with each sigh, her reserve of patience is being depleted. "See, that's what I mean," she says. "I'm trying to be mature about this and it seems like you're being vindictive by attacking me personally. I'm not sure I can work with you if that's the way you deal with things."

"Not vindictive," I say. "Just..."

"Are you gay?" she asks.

"No. Not gay." The more pressure I'm under, the shorter my sentences get.

"Asexual?"

"Yes! Totally. Asexual."

I'm not asexual but Angela has backed me into a corner.

"So just say that, then. Instead of a personal attack about me not being your type which just feels to me like... nah, nah, you're not invited to my birthday party."

I'm completely unprepared to move forward with this conversation. I'm drowning, barely able to keep my head above water, and about to sink below the surface for the third and perhaps final time. All the other students have stopped speaking to each other and are now focused on us. Even Onslot, who's been checking the clock on the wall every few minutes, is staring. Maybe my voice got a little too loud or maybe it's just our body language.

FACT: [...]

Okay, maybe the matter is too complex for a factoid. I'm old-fashioned by definition and when I came of age in the eighteenth century, sex wasn't openly discussed and still makes me blush. But the simple truth is that the vampirovirus spares only the essential parts of our anatomy necessary to carry on in vampire form. Since vampires don't reproduce, at least not in the way humans do, hormones and even the genitalia are superfluous. To put it delicately, my *down-there* is barely visible, and testosterone—well, I no longer remember what it feels like to be controlled by that substance. I prefer to think of myself as a... romantic.

Angela doesn't seem to notice any of that though. She continues, her voice still steady. Still patient. "I just want to work out any issues before we get into some kind of life and death situation and our lives depend on trusting the other one completely, you know. And we fail the other just because our egos... or lack of trust got in the way."

I nod and lower my volume to just above whisper. "You do know this class isn't accredited and won't be accepted by any police academy, right?"

"Of course, I know."

"So, what brings you here?" I ask, feigning indifference, which seems to be enough to take the attention off of us. "To this class. For me, it's insufficient funds to attend a real college."

"*CSI*," Angela says. "Plus, I work full-time and I'm saving money to go to college hopefully in a year or two."

I should have guessed. The *CSI* show is probably the reason why most of us are here.

"So, you want to..."

"Sharpen my skills," she interrupts. "And hopefully make a name for myself in the process."

"A name?"

"You know. Solve a crime… something no one's been able to figure out. We'd be doing it together so that's why it's so important for us to click. To have good chemistry."

"Do you think we do? Click?"

"Maybe not now," she says. "But I think we could be a good team if we set aside our egos and work at it. But total honesty going forward, okay? Onslot seems like a dick but he does have real world experience, and I agree with him about the partner thing."

"I agree," I say. "He does seem like a dick."

Angela couldn't have been blessed with a partner with less of an ego than me. Honesty? Now that's another thing entirely.

"So more about me," she says. "I'm eighteen and graduated high school when I was sixteen. I live with my mom and work at an antique weapons store. Maybe you've heard of it… Up In Arms? How about you?"

I've heard of Up In Arms but never been there. I long to ask if they carry a Wogdon dueling pistol such as the type used in the Alexander Hamilton/Aaron Burr duel. I own one of a limited set (bequeathed to me by a former employer I won't name) and have been looking for its mate for over 200 years. But I decide now would not be the time to ask.

"I'm seventeen. Never graduated high school. I live by myself and work part-time at the Gobble-Down-Suck-Up."

I wonder why it never occurred to me to get a job at Up In Arms, not that I'm an expert by any means but it sounds far more interesting than being the veggie chopper at a diner. But then again, it's doubtful they're open at night.

"I go there a lot for lunch… love that place. Surprised I never saw you there."

No surprise.

"I work evenings."

"Should we... are there any questions you want to ask me about myself? I feel like I'm driving this discussion and that's not what I want either."

But there aren't any questions I want to ask. I'm more afraid of Angela than comfortable with her. Her blunt manner. Her unapologetic ambition. Her easy self-confidence. Coming up with enough phony background information about my life in order to appease her will take some quick thinking.

In this case, not being caught in a lie caused by spinning a web of deceit, my total recall... *blessing*.

I worry about the temperature of my apartment. With my electricity shut off for three days now, I'm concerned Clementine may be too cold and not survive another night. I can't bear the thought of arriving home to find... I mustn't think about it, lest I cause it to happen. I logged it into my worry journal but that doesn't mean it couldn't happen. I've logged other worries that later came true. Tonight, I'll hand deliver enough cash to pay my utilities for another month, although I'd been hoping this would be an expense I could cut. There's an after-hours depository.

Angela is looking at me expectantly. I'd almost forgotten she was there.

"I'm an only child," I begin truthfully. "My parents emigrated from Romania where they were into money-laundering. I was just a kid, so I don't remember much, but I know phony passports and visas were somehow involved. Dad eventually went to prison for counterfeiting currency and a few years later he died in a jailhouse ambush. Mom fled to South America and left me with a neighbor when I was ten. Never heard from *her* again. After that, the neighbor got busted for drug-dealing and, since I was already living under the radar, I fended for myself through odd-jobs and couch-surfing. Studied for the GED in my spare time and eventually passed. So, I guess you could say out of all of that came my desire to pursue a career in law enforcement and here I am trying to be a better person. Escape my legacy of crime... that sort of thing."

Angela's jaw drops, and I know she's impressed. I could have made it a little less theatrical, but the made-up drama is minimal compared to my real-life drama.

> **FACT: If something seems too strange to be true, people will accept it on face value.**

***

On my way home, I get the feeling again that someone's following me. At first, it's just a feeling that makes the hair on the back of my neck stand up like a mad dog's. I begin to whistle the minor second from Bartók's *Bluebeard's Castle*, a tune which normally comforts me although many find it troubling. After a few minutes of whistling for comfort's sake, I switch to ultrasonic whistling, inaudible to the human ear. When a few nearby dogs begin to bark and howl, I raise the pitch to an even higher frequency.

Now I know it's more than a feeling. Someone *is* following me. Is there ever an instance when being followed is a good thing? I don't think so. Following someone invariably leads to negative consequences for the person being followed. So why? And who? Has someone caught on to me? Does someone know my true identity? Will I be forced to flee once again, leaving behind the only true friend I've had in decades—dear Miss Henrietta Devine? Leaving a home where I'm relatively comfortable. A job where I feel secure and have gained a modicum of self-esteem and respect from my peers... from my co-workers, that is, since I have no peers. Leaving behind the most reliable supplier of the red stuff I've had since... since... I don't want to think about Florida right now... too painful.

Just then the Wheelie Boys zip past me and, if I didn't feel the rush of air left behind in their wake, I might not have noticed them at all.

"John Doe!"

"John Doe!"

They seem to outrun their disembodied voices in the same way a bolt of thunder trails behind a flash of lightning.

"Be careful."

"The Six o' Clock Slasher's back at it."

So, it's the Six o' Clock Slasher, is it? At it again after laying low for the past few months. Some people speculated he was dead or had moved onto so-called greener (or in his case, redder) pastures.

I don't have anything to fear from the Six o' Clock Slasher or any other murderer for that matter. After all, a man can only be murdered once. But the night air feels clammy and cold against the back of my neck, and something akin to an electric pulse runs up and down my spine. Whoever catches the Six o' Clock Slasher would be a hero to everyone in this town. I pull my hoodie up over my head and take the fast way home.

The vampire way.

FACT: Vampires utilize echolocation, our own personal radar system. We can determine where rapidly moving living things are when sounds we make (a high-pitched whistle inaudible to the human ear) bounces back to the receptor cells of our inner ears in the form of an echo.

Try to imagine the following: You're walking down a lonesome stretch of highway and hear a speeding car coming up behind you. You have a pretty good idea where it is and how quickly it's approaching. If the car suddenly veers off-road and runs parallel to you or comes straight at you, you'd know it through your sense of hearing even if your eyes are closed. Echolocation is similar to hearing but far more effective in that it can locate an approaching person or beast in total darkness or when background noise makes it impossible to hear. A vampire's echolocation is attuned to rapid movements of a living thing. Because our ears are extraordinarily sensitive (perhaps the most sensitive part of us) echolocation can be painful.

So, there you have it. There's very little good that comes from being a vampire, but echolocation can be a gift, albeit a painful and occasionally terrifying one.

FACT: Echolocation is a vampire's sixth sense.

FACT: Humans don't have a sixth sense.

CHAPTER NINE

The Last Vampire

By John Doe

Chapter Nine

If he had previously viewed the world through a cracked, yellowed lens, after Nadia's arrival the world became a wonderful place where magic was not only possible but happened every hour of every day. The cracked, yellowed lens was soon transformed into a rose-tinted crystal. Zoltan was in love.

Multi-hued wildflowers dotting the emerald fields of his valley were tiny flags declaring his newfound joy. Whereas, previously, Zoltan had trudged through his daily chores with a sense of mounting despair, now he ran towards his duties as though they were saviors from his personal misery, the keys to his blossoming happiness. Work in the fields with Nadia by his side was not work. It was freedom. With her help, the acreage prospered once again. Provided for them. Crops grew in abundance. The grass grew tall enough to support farm animals. Although Zoltan worked harder with Nadia by his side, it never seemed like work while they warmed their young muscles, taut with exertion, under the giving sun.

With Nadia always on his mind, Zoltan pushed Bela from his thoughts, even when they were dining directly across the table from each other or sleeping in such close proximity the foul breath of Bela's snores would awaken Zoltan from a deep sleep, causing him to turn away in disgust and face the wall.

Nadia now occupied Zoltan's old room, and at night she waited for the sounds of Bela's heavy slumber before tiptoeing outside where silver moonbeams and Zoltan awaited her. Hand in hand they walked to the edge of the beech forest and spread a blanket, laying in each other's arms for hours, exchanging kisses, tender caresses, vows, and declarations of love. It was during these moonlight interludes that they first began to make plans for the day they would escape to begin a life of their own, far from the darkness of Bela's legacy.

In the meantime, their lives continued to improve. One day, Bela brought home two chickens. A week later, it was two lambs. Not long after that, he brought home a sow that soon gave birth to ten piglets, as well as a donkey and cart that Zoltan used to carry their produce to the village market. In order to save up for the time when he and Nadia could escape, on market days Zoltan always put aside a coin or two in a secret pocket Nadia sewed into his trousers.

He never gave thought to the debts which Bela had accumulated during their darkest days—money borrowed (with steep interest) from the nobleman-landlord. The debts were his father's business, and Zoltan assumed they must have been paid off as evidenced by the bounty all around them. He didn't even question Nadia's fortuitous and unexpected arrival into their lives, having been told she was just a young girl whose family was down on their luck, sent by the nobleman-landlord to whom her family was indebted, in order to assist Bela and Zoltan who had proven themselves capable of digging out of a hole, who only needed the small boost that an extra pair of strong hands could provide.

The palm of my hand is practically itching from the weight of my phone. I've glanced at the photo of the flyer at least a dozen times.

ARE YOU FEELING SAD?
ANXIOUS?
LONELY?
NEED SOMEONE TO TALK TO?

Perhaps a switch from third person point-of-view to first person will make my manuscript seem more modern. And perhaps even a switch to present tense from past tense. This would be an overwhelming amount of work but, as it stands, it's not generating any interest—and what have I got, if not time?

Clementine is fine. My bill has been paid so I can expect power back on tomorrow. The class went as well as could be expected, and I think I'm actually going to enjoy it. I see a way forward with my manuscript. I do feel a small abdominal cramp that hasn't gone away since my last meal, but I've felt that in the past and it's always led to nothing. So why do I still feel unsettled? Where do I go to find peace?

My phone says it isn't quite midnight yet—five minutes to go.

I dial the number on the flyer, slowly poking out the individual digits one by one, leaving myself the option to change my mind before I punch in the final 9.

"Hello?" A girl's voice on the other end, sounding impossibly young.

My finger automatically goes to the red hang-up circle to disconnect the call.

Now I can never again call this number because she'll know that I called once before and hung up. If I call back immediately, I can pass it off as a slip-up of some sort. If I wait more than a second or two, I've made my permanent decision.

My phone rings. It's the number I've just called, and I'm terrified to answer but terrified not to.

"Hello?" I say, hearing the fear in my voice while doing my best to suppress it.

"I just got a call from this number," she says.

"Oh, yes."

My pause is way too long.

"Did you mean to call me or was it a mistake?" she asks.

"I saw your flyer," I say, and it feels as if I'm literally coughing up the words like pebbles caught in my gullet.

"Cool," she says. "I wasn't sure if anyone would actually see it."

"I've seen your flyers around town," I say, more relaxed now that the conversation has shifted away from me to focus on her flyers. "The graphics are pretty eye-catching, and you've got prominent positioning on the utility pole at the corner of 5th and R Streets. It's hard to miss when you're waiting for the light to change."

"Do you want to schedule an appointment?" she asks. "Sorry, I don't mean to interrupt but my office hours are over, and I need to get going."

"Good idea. Great idea," I say stupidly. "Sorry. Didn't mean... to hold you up."

"How's tomorrow at nine?" she asks.

"At night?"

"Yes. My office hours are from 9:00 p.m. to midnight just like it says on my flyer."

It seems like a strange time to hold office hours but who am I to question? After all, it was partially the nighttime hours that first attracted my attention. There's no class tomorrow, although we've already been given a homework assignment—as an afterthought, in my opinion, in order for Onslot to justify his fee. With daylight savings time over, it's already dark by 5:00 so I've switched my hours at the Gobble-Down-Suck-Up to be free in time for my class. And anyway, tomorrow's not even a workday so I was planning on dropping in on Miss Devine or having her over for tea. It's either that or stay home and work on the manuscript.

"Tomorrow at nine is fine, then," I say. "Where's your office?"

She rattles off a surprisingly upscale address. I don't know what I expected but I suppose something in my neighborhood for someone who advertises by flyers stapled to utility poles. The distance is greater than I'm used to traveling, so I'll have to go the easy way.

The vampire way.

CHAPTER TEN

My phone startles me awake well before I'm ready to rise from my coffin. I use the word "awake" loosely, as I've technically been awake all along but in a deeply soothing meditative state with very few thoughts in my head. It's maddening to be disturbed this way, but I only have myself to blame for not muting the phone before going to bed.

I push open the lid of my coffin and sit up, still somewhat groggy as a result of the rude interruption. In no hurry to answer the phone, I perform a few shoulder rolls and discover, to my delight, that the extra padding has done away with my shoulder tenderness. I rise from my coffin and stretch my limbs, snapping them into position. Then I turn an admiring glance towards my coffin-creation before pressing the button that rotates it 180 degrees, transforming it into a workstation which can be adjusted to any level from sitting to standing.

I think I'll stand while I write today.

The phone has stopped ringing, but I don't bother to check to see who called.

Both good news and bad news await me this day.

The good news: The electricity is back on. The refrigerator I never use is humming away. The one light I own, a floor lamp, glows in the corner of my room. And the place is warm again, which doesn't matter to me one bit, but Clementine seems happy judging from the energetic laps she's taking around her fishbowl.

MYTH: Vampires can't handle any light. Untrue. Remember, there wasn't any such thing as electrical lighting back in the day. Artificial light is well tolerated to a point, but I keep it to a minimum. I keep a large supply of the old-fashioned incandescent yellow light bulbs which are harder and harder to find these days, the LEDs having too much blue and red light for my peace of mind. Normally, I light candles when I'm home.

FACT: Sunlight is deadly, so I've hung the best blackout shades money can buy in the one window of my tiny apartment.

Oh, the bad news. Someone slid an envelope under my door while I was sleeping… uh… resting. Mail is never a good thing, but this particular envelope is hand-addressed to me. I recognize Mrs. Dilliberato's handwriting.

NOTICE TO PAY RENT OR QUIT
THIS NOTICE TO PAY RENT IS GIVEN PURSUANT…

…blah, blah, blah

HEREBY REQUIRED TO PAY…

…blah, blah, blah

IF YOU FAIL TO PAY…

…blah, blah, blah

So many capital letters! It wasn't a good idea to overuse uppercase letters, which are meant to convey the serious nature of this notice but after the first sentence or two, lose their impact. I crumple the paper into a ball and score a basket into the trash can I've nailed high up on the wall.

So... not good but not terrible either. I knew it was coming and, somehow, I'll bring my account current before eviction occurs. I always do. It's just the negativity that bothers me... never a good way to start one's day. I'll try to replace the negativity with something positive. Oh yes, Miss Henrietta Devine. I'll go knock on her door right this minute and invite her over for a cup of tea since I'm awake so early. Only 5:30 p.m. It's dark, therefore safe to leave my apartment.

But then I remember the phone call and decide to check.

It was Angela Ruiz.

I could phone her back but what on earth does she want from me on a non-school day? The homework assignment doesn't call for working with my partner, being merely a simple questionnaire about my personal experience in criminology—whether as a victim of crime or a victim of the law itself. Naturally, I'll tailor an answer that will reveal nothing about my real life.

Angela is becoming an annoyance. A thorn in my side. First, all her prying and lecturing me about not being forthcoming and acting in a childish manner. Now, disturbing me during a time of repose. I may need to have a word with her about boundaries, but she would most likely interpret that in a way that would turn *me* into the bad guy, the less than stellar partner. And if Angela rejects me as her partner, more than likely no one else in the class would want to switch with her, leaving me no option but to drop the class which would lead to Detective Onslot canceling the entire course, ruining the dreams of all and placing the blame squarely upon my shoulders.

I don't need to return her call now. Perhaps I'll revisit the idea later.

The peephole of Miss Henrietta Devine's door darkens so I know she's on the other side, checking before she unlocks the four deadbolts I've installed for her. Each year, she asks for a new deadbolt and I'm always happy to oblige. I know Mrs. Dilliberato won't do it.

"Oh, it's you, Johnny," she says, ushering me in with an urgent wave of her hand, gnarled by years of painful arthritis. She's wearing a fluffy blue bathrobe with matching slippers. Her silver hair is closely cropped, the tight curls combed backwards into submission. Her eyes are luminescent.

"I've just come to invite you for tea," I say. "If you're free."

"Me free?" Her laugh is so rich and comforting, she could probably bottle it and sell it for a fortune. "When am I ever *not* free to have tea with a handsome young man? Mind if I come as-is?"

The lilt of her Texan roots is almost imperceptible, but I have an ear for accents, and many years of traveling the world. I can identify anyone's geographic origins after only a minute in their presence. Miss Devine was astounded the first time I did so with her. I passed it off as having spent some time in west Texas, which of course I have—long before she was born.

"Absolutely," I say. "Friends never stand on ceremony."

The truth is Henrietta Devine and I frequently visit back and forth in our casual wear.

"Johnny, you have the funniest way of talking for a kid your age," she says. "You're truly an old soul."

Ah, Henrietta, I think, although I'd never dare address her so informally. *If only you knew what an old soul I really am.*

She reaches for the key which hangs on a hook by the door and follows me for the ten paces down the hall to my apartment, padding softly in her fluffy slippers. I've prepared a nice layout, using my two best (and only) antique porcelain teacups and matching teapot with cream and sugar containers. The pattern consists of varying shades of pink roses encircled by spiky green leaves—a 3-D design on the teapot but replicated in a painted motif on the other pieces. Everything trimmed in gold, of course. Some people might question my flamboyant taste but, personally, I'm crazy about the tea set. It delivers a thrill every time I lay out the entire set. If Miss Devine knew how old it is—much older than her—she'd probably be too afraid to use it. But what are *things* for, if not to be used?

Although I do still have some tea from my travels through China in the early part of the twentieth century, I save that for myself, not knowing if it's toxic to a living being. I quite enjoy the flavor—pungent, teasing. This might be a good place to point out that, aside from the red stuff, I need tea in order to live. At least in the fullest sense of the word—*live*—which is to say, more than just exist. I grew quite fond of tea at one point in my life and somehow the fondness grew into an essential. It's the only other substance I ingest, much to Miss Devine's hurt feelings after numerous invitations to cook dinner for me. I've used multiple food allergies as my excuse, and eventually she stopped asking.

"There you are, Miss Clementine," she says, Clementine being a favorite of hers.

She often fish-sits when I'm out for an extended period of time. "Just so she doesn't get lonely," Miss Devine would say. Miss Devine has her own goldfish, Cleopatra. When Clementine goes for a visit, Henrietta places the two bowls side by side "so the girls can have a good ol' chat and catch up with each other."

Miss Devine picks a few flakes out of the jar of fish food next to Clementine's bowl. "She looks hungry, Johnny. When she's swimming fast like that and coming up to the surface, she's trying to let you know."

Of course, Clementine always behaves in precisely that manner because she doesn't know what's good for her the way I do. I fear I'm going to spend the rest of the night worrying that she's been overfed which is actually more dangerous than being underfed. When Miss Devine turns her back, I lightly touch the surface of the water to retrieve a flake Clementine hasn't already ingested.

"Did you see the notice I slipped under your door, honey?" Miss Devine asks, and then without waiting for an answer, "Of course you did. I'm sorry Johnny because I'm really not snooping but I know that handwriting and I've seen an envelope like that before. It's an eviction notice, isn't it?"

"Nothing I can't handle," I say, while I pour a stream of hot brown liquid into her cup. Because I know she likes two cubes of sugar, I pick those up with the sugar tweezers and drop them from a low enough height to avoid even a minor splash.

"Johnny. Please don't take this the wrong way but do you need money? I have money, you know. More than I could possibly use, and I'd be happy to… loan it to you. I'd be happier if you just took it as a gift."

"No, no, no," I say, doing my best to sound grateful rather than indignant. I know the woman has a heart of gold and would make the same offer to anyone she thought was in need but there are plenty more worthy than me. I always manage to come up with funds when I'm up against a deadline. I just don't mind making Mrs. Dilliberato work for it. After all, what else does she have to do?

"Fortunately, the wheels of justice turn mercifully slow at times, and don't I always land on my feet?" I ask.

"No doubt," she says, slowly shaking her head as though there is indeed doubt. "No doubt. But don't you ever weary of leaving your fate up to fate?"

FACT: Miss Devine is a master of the rhetorical question.

"I saw those boys, by the way," she says, pivoting to another subject since we both know there's no good answer to her question. "Those wheelin' boys."

"The Wheelie Boys?"

"Peter and Fernando," she pulls her chair up to my coffin-table and lifts the teacup to her lips. I detect only the slightest tremor which I consider remarkable for a woman her age, well into her nineties. "They told me the killer's back. The Six o' Clock Slasher everyone calls him."

"I heard the same," I say, pulling up my own chair directly opposite to hers. "But I haven't seen it in the papers or heard anything on the news."

"Those boys always know everything first," she says. "So, you jus' be careful. Keep your door locked and don't answer for anyone without checking first."

"The same goes for you, Miss Devine," I say.

"Now, you know I'm always careful. You don't have to worry about me." She furrows her brow, without which it would be impossible to find a line on her smooth brown forehead. Even with my rather advanced makeup skills, I can't replicate that unlined look. "It's the helpless I worry about," she says. "The folks who don't have doors and walls to protect them."

"I understand and share your concern," I say. "But if I remember correctly, the Six o' Clock Slasher only strikes inside people's homes."

"And just where did they come up with that crazy name?" she asks, *tsk-tsking* the prelude to her own answer. "I don't know why they have to dignify these savages with a clever name. Why not just call them a number? Murderer #1. Murderer #2."

"Probably because at this point the number would be so big no one would be able to remember it," I say, leaning over the table to refill her cup. "He usually strikes at dinner time… around six o'clock."

Another *tsk-tsk* and then my phone rings. I glance at the screen and see it's Angela Ruiz calling again.

"Aren't you going to get that?" Miss Devine asks after the third ring. "Don't mind me, I can wait."

"*It* can wait," I say, beaming my most mirthful smile at Miss Devine whom, I know from past experience, won't recoil from it. "Right now, I'm busy entertaining a lovely lady."

She beams a smile back at me and hers is truly mirthful. Radiant. I latch onto the image of Miss Devine's smile so I can practice it later.

CHAPTER ELEVEN

The building I've arrived at is a sleek, modern design in the pricey part of town. The doors to the lobby slide open but, once inside, I have to call the office because, at this time of night, the elevators only work with a security code. The youthful voice answers and says she'll come down to meet me in the lobby. When the elevator door finally opens, I'm amazed to see the youthful voice matches a youthful appearance. She couldn't be a day older than me (minus the three centuries) and perhaps even younger. She ushers me inside the elevator, swipes a plastic card, and presses the button for the 30th floor. Those penthouse offices must have an amazing view of the city lights this time of night and must also be extraordinarily expensive. I'd better inquire about the fee before I waste any more of her time or mine.

From the lobby to the 8th floor, we both engage in the "elevator stare"—eyes directed straight ahead, occasionally glancing at one's shoes, and once or twice raising one's gaze to the ceiling, anywhere but at the person standing next to you. Between the 8th and 9th floor, there's a temporary thaw and the girl speaks, while still keeping her gaze focused on the elevator door.

"Cold night," she says.

This gives me the permission I need to examine her more closely. Her hair is brown and straight and cropped evenly at chin-length, almost as if she'd done it herself in front of the mirror with a pair of ordinary scissors. She wears no make-up, perhaps a little lip gloss, faded jeans, fuzzy boots, and a plain navy-blue cardigan. Nothing beyond her age is remarkable.

"It is indeed," I say.

The elevator moves surprisingly slowly for a high-rise building, or maybe the awkwardness of being trapped in this box with this strange girl just makes it seem that way.

"Did you have trouble finding us?" she asks between the 17th and 18th floors.

"Not at all," I answer. We return to the elevator stare.

I decide it's my turn now.

"It's unusual to find a doctor who holds night-time office hours," I say between the 22nd and 23rd floors. "It must be very expensive... to see... the doctor."

"Not at all," she says, stealing my previous answer. "We use a sliding scale."

I exhale the tension I'd been holding inside. A sliding scale? You couldn't slide much further down the scale than I have. I can't believe my luck in finding a top-notch therapist—a fancy one at that, probably treating celebrities and corporate CEOs—who would charge me only what I can afford, which is basically nothing.

The elevator sighs to a stop and the doors whisper open. I follow the girl into just the kind of office lobby I imagined from 300 feet below—white wool carpets, glass tables, and cushy leather seats that smell like the real thing and look to be softer than my own skin. The girl walks behind the receptionist's desk and pulls out a patient information sheet.

"Name?" she asks without looking up.

"John Doe," I say. "D-O-E."

She glances up and eyes me suspiciously, or is it my imagination?

"It's okay," she says, "you don't need to use an alias. We're very discreet and never share any information about our patients. HIPAA, you know?"

I clear my throat. "That's my real name."

"Age?" She returns to looking at the paperwork.

"Seventeen."

Again, she glances up. Is she looking at me skeptically this time? She looks back down.

"How much can you afford to pay?" she asks.

"Very little," I answer, and then elaborate further. "Practically nothing."

"Oookay." She's jots something down on the paper. "We'll just say *nothing* in that case. Follow me, please."

She walks out from behind the receptionist's desk and I follow her down a hallway to a door which opens up to a cozy, yet luxurious, space with a divan, and two snazzy armchairs with reclining capabilities. There's a beautiful piece of art hanging on one wall, and a few impressive-looking diplomas hanging on another. The lighting is subtle and gives off a faint pinkish glow. I've been treated by the best, including the great Sigmund Freud (who turned out to be *not* so great), and I can safely say this is the nicest therapy space I've seen.

"Choose your seat," she motions. "You can lie down if you like or sit in a chair. Whatever makes you more comfortable."

I choose one of the chairs and she chooses the other, pressing a button on the side to slightly elevate her feet. "Make yourself comfortable," she says. "Feel free to help yourself to the water on the table next to you."

"Thank you. I'm not thirsty," I say, wondering when the doctor will come in.

"Do you smoke?" she asks. "Feel free, although this is a smoke-free office. But go ahead if you like."

"No, I don't smoke," I say, wondering why she would invite me to smoke in a smoke-free office. This girl is unusual, and her gaze (now that we're out of the elevator) is direct and slightly unnerving. Whereas before I thought there was nothing remarkable about her, now I can see that her eyes are extraordinary. I see intelligence behind them. Curiosity. Confidence. I see more than one should expect to see in the eyes of such a young person.

"Shall we begin, then?" she asks.

I shift in my seat which causes my hip bones to crack much more loudly than I'd prefer. I gently stretch my right leg to make sure everything's still in place. "Will the doctor be joining us tonight?"

"That would be me," she says with no defensiveness in her voice. Her gaze continues to penetrate. "Are you not comfortable with a female therapist?"

What? Her? This girl?

"Of course I'm comfortable with a female therapist," I say. "It's just that... it's just that..."

"It's just that?" She raises her eyebrows as though inviting me to continue. She has a small notepad and pen in her lap, although she has not yet used them.

"It's just that… no offense or anything but you look like you're about sixteen."

"No offense taken," she says. "I am *exactly* sixteen. And four months. And..." She laces the fingers of her hands together, her gaze unfocused, drifting upwards as though in prayer. Her lips move, almost imperceptibly, though no sound escapes them. "And twenty-three days," she says finally. "Does that bother you?"

"*Bother* me!" I sputter. "Bother *me*?"

"Bother you," she says evenly. "Does that bother you?"

"Only... in all the time I've been alive, which has been a considerable amount of time, I've never heard of a therapist who manages to get all the degrees necessary for that vocation by the time they're sixteen years old. And... and... however many extra months and days you just mentioned."

She jots something down on the notepad.

"What did you just write?" I ask.

"I find it interesting that you consider your lifetime to be *considerable*. Considering, that you're only seventeen years old."

"What does that have to do with anything?" My fingers clutch the armrests of my chair so tightly I'm glad I filed down my nails before coming here, lest I shred through this plushy material, exposing the generous stuffing beneath.

"I'm not sure," she says. I have to hand it to her that she hasn't betrayed a hint of emotion throughout our entire exchange thus far. She is nothing if not even-keeled. "But it might have some relevance and I don't want to forget that you said it. It's just a clue, one of many. Everything we say reveals clues about ourselves."

I take as deep a breath as my withered lungs will allow and then let it out with a rasping wheeze.

"Are you or are you not Dr…" I peer at the diploma on the wall. "Thottfel?"

"I am not," she says.

"Then who *are* you?"

"I'm Bibi Thottfel, Dr. Thottfel's second child and only daughter," she replies. "Dr. Thottfel is my mother."

This is just too much to bear. All the trouble to get here… well, really no trouble at all except for talking myself into it. Convincing myself of the necessity. Swallowing my anxiety in the hours leading up to it. For *this*? For *her*?

"You brought me here under false pretenses!" I sputter indignantly. If I had any blood inside me, it would be boiling right now.

"No, I didn't," she says. "My flyer was very clear. It simply asked if you were sad, anxious, lonely, and—"

"Yes, I know! And needed someone to talk to."

"And were you? Did you?"

"Yes and yes. But this…this is *malpractice*!" A drop of spit flies from my mouth, which in and of itself is something of a marvel since my mouth is generally bone dry. The girl notices it and maybe jots something down on that pad of paper again, but I can't be certain since I'm almost literally seeing red.

"How can it be malpractice when I'm not even in practice?" she asks.

"I can report you, you know," I say. "To the authorities." Of course, I can't report anything to anyone without drawing unwanted attention to myself—me, John Doe, who exists only in the shadows.

Her lower lip quivers so slightly it might have gone unnoticed were it not for my superior vision. Suddenly, she seems vulnerable, her confidence like a car windshield struck by a pebble at high speed, cracks beginning to spider away from the point of impact.

"Which authorities? My mom?" she asks, and I can hear the quaver in her voice as clearly as if it were a church bell tolling on Sunday morning.

The entire windshield collapses as she reveals herself to be nothing more than a child in fear of a parent. I know what it's like to be afraid of a parent, although I'd be willing to bet her mother is nothing like the monster who was my father. Bibi's worst parental nightmare is probably a tongue-lashing, not being bartered away and left to die.

"No," I say. "I'm not going to report you to your mom. Or to anyone else." I slump down in my chair until my head is only inches above the seat cushion.

"You mentioned that you have no financial resources," she says. "Do you have medical insurance?"

"Of course not," I say. Medical insurance is something else well beyond my realm of possibilities. It requires things like social security numbers. Money.

"Do you still need someone to talk to?" she asks, and I can hear the hopefulness in her voice. "I'm a really good listener."

"Yes," I say. "I suppose that much hasn't changed."

"Would you prefer..." She motions to the divan and it does seem like a more inviting alternative. I trudge over to the divan and lie down, one leg sprawled in front of me, one leg carefully placed on the floor in case I find it necessary to perform a heel-tapping ritual. My left arm dangles over the side, my fingertips grazing the plush carpet.

"Let's begin," she says, somewhat too cheerfully for my taste.

CHAPTER TWELVE

The Last Vampire

[REVISED: FIRST PERSON, PRESENT TENSE]

By John Doe

Chapter Twelve

"Wake up, son." My father is shaking me soon after I've fallen asleep. I know it must be hours before dawn. Nadia's kiss still clings to my lips.

The full moon spills in through the thick pane of glass, lighting our room up like a torch.

"Quiet, so you don't wake Nadia," he warns. "She needs her sleep."

"And I don't?" I mutter under my breath.

"What did you say?" He brings his hand up, poised to slap me but I'm not willing to take a beating right now.

"What do you want?" I ask instead. Bela can't mistake the hostility in my voice, but he lets it go.

"You need to leave right now and go see Istvan. He'll explain what he needs when you get there."

What our nobleman-landlord could possibly want at this hour of the night is beyond me. My mind still thick with the cobwebs of sleep, I try to make sense of it.

"Is he ill?" I ask. "Should I stop in town to collect the doctor?"

In the dark, my father looks a hundred years old. A hundred years evil. Under the moonlight, his grizzled beard resembles the mold that grows under the lip of our well.

"If I needed you to get the doctor, I would have told you to get the doctor," he says in a voice not his own but a whiny imitation of the way he hears mine. "Now get going before I help you to get going by kicking your stinking behind out the door." He sits down hard on his side of the bed, his breath heavy and menacing. "Lazy, good-for-nothing," he adds for good measure.

Lazy? Good-for-nothing? Only my efforts combined with Nadia's have kept my father out of the poorhouse. I work every day from dawn until dusk with only a few minutes to gobble down lunch. Let's not even get started about who has the stinkier behind. But I know how much money I've been able to secretly stash away on market days. Nadia and I will be leaving soon and then my father can see what it's like to cope without his good-for-nothing son. In the meantime, I'm biding my time, biting my tongue, and counting down the days.

Without a word, I pull on my outer shirt, pants, and boots, and trudge out the door. After harnessing the donkey, I glance at the window of Nadia's room, a bit concerned to be leaving her home alone with my father. But Bela has never made any improper advances and I've never even caught him stealing a glance at her. My father is too filled with bitterness and hatred to think of anyone other than himself, and he knows I'd kill him if he laid a hand on Nadia.

I begin the long journey through the hills to the castle, a journey that lasts nearly an hour. The night is infused with life by the dazzling glow of a moon so full I can make out its mountains and valleys. But the gentle rocking of the cart and the late hour of the night combine to make me so tired that only my rolling head continues to keep me from sleep. Were it not for my steadfast donkey and its ability to forge a path without my guidance, I surely would never make it to my destination.

Around a bend, over a small bridge, the castle looms dark and forbidding before me. Istvan emerges from the woods which surround his estate, apparently having just returned from a moonlight walk. His face glows like a second moon. His topcoat rustles when he walks. He feels for the ground in front of him with a polished wood cane adorned by an ornate ivory handle. I've never been behind the walls of this castle before and I wish I could keep it that way, but my weariness soon overcomes the strong sense of anxiety I feel in his presence.

"Zoltan," he says. "So good, you've made it."

I believe it's the first time I've ever seen him smile, but what a wretched smile it is. Tight-lipped and grim, almost like an unrepentant murderer being led to the gallows—one who's determined to have the last word even in the moments before death. "You will rest, of course," he says. "Then we'll begin."

I'm so desperate for sleep, I don't even bother to ask what it is that we're going to begin. I've had an especially trying day bundling bales of hay for the animals and carrying them on my back to the shed. It's back-wrenching work and the bulk of it falls on me. I know it will begin again at dawn, providing I can dispense with whatever it is Istvan needs and then get home before Nadia and my father awaken. Just ten minutes of sleep is all I need.

Only ten minutes.

"You've slept for four days and nights." Istvan is standing at the foot of my bed staring at me. The long thin fingers of his pale hands link together in front of him. My head throbs, my muscles twitch uncontrollably, and my bones ache from the inside out. My sheets are drenched with sweat although it's cool outside and the window is wide open.

"Am I sick?" I ask. "Have I...been ill?"

How could this have happened that I've slept four days and nights? Nadia must be out of her mind with worry. My father must be furious with me.

"You've been ill," Istvan says. "I've sent word to your father so no reason to be concerned. You're well enough to go home now,"

But I don't feel well enough to go home. I don't even feel well enough to get out of bed. Istvan yanks me from between the sheets and throws my clothes on the bed. Once I've managed to dress myself, he half-drags me to the donkey cart and, as an afterthought, tosses a small blanket over my lap. He slaps the donkey on its haunch and the donkey cart lurches down the rocky path, each bump sending spears of agony throughout my besieged body which, unbeknownst to me, is becoming a corpse.

Wait. First person, present tense—I wouldn't yet know my body is becoming a corpse.

He slaps the donkey on its haunch and the donkey cart lurches down the rocky path, each bump sending spears of agony throughout my besieged body. What was soothing only four days ago has now become a torture which I can barely endure. Again, I send thanks to my donkey who picks its way carefully among the potholes to find the smoothest path, as if sensing my suffering.

By the time I reach our cottage, I've lost all consciousness but, somehow, I hear Nadia's scream and that revives me sufficiently to help her help me out of the cart and into my bed. If my father is nearby, I don't see him or hear him.

I am at least grateful for that.

This is the part of my book that always makes me cry, though sometimes it seems more like a piece of fiction than something that really happened to me. It makes me cry to recollect the last truly spontaneous human emotion I would ever experience. Nadia's scream that day is something I'll never forget even if I live to be a thousand. What I must have looked like to her, falling from the donkey cart into her arms. The love we still had for each other at that moment was the only thing that willed me to walk the final twenty paces to my bed where I would lie for the next few weeks. I didn't know it then—I only *felt* like I was dying. But Nadia must have known. She must have known I was already dead.

For weeks, I lay in that room which took on a smell so

odious that, on several occasions, Nadia retched into the bucket by the side of my bed. I didn't understand what was happening to me—the transformation that takes place when one is infected by the vampirovirus. The body literally going through the process of burying itself, mummifying my corpse as efficiently as if an ancient Egyptian were preparing me for the tomb. Organs shriveling—the lungs, the kidney, the liver, the stomach and digestive tract.

The heart.

I had no idea what had happened—how could I? The only trace of anything out of the ordinary were two small spider bites on my neck, which Nadia had initially taken for flea bites and feared the plague. How could I have connected this to what Istvan did to me? That he had leisurely supped on me that first night when I was still a young man living life to its fullest.

> **MYTH: Vampires leave two puncture holes as evidence, making a vampire bite a simple thing to diagnose. False! If our incisors were large enough to leave such a... calling card, they would bust right through the artery, creating a bloody mess and certainly rousing the victim to fight back. Instead, the tips of our incisors are needle-sharp, needle-width, and almost fully retractable. Make that a baby needle! Because we release an anticoagulant when we bite (much like a mosquito) the human body's immune response to the bite creates itching and swelling (again, much like a mosquito). The anticoagulant is nature's gift to vampires, necessary for obvious purposes—a vampire would otherwise be forced to contend with blood clots during the act of feeding. And from our own saliva comes the vampire's final gift to its victim—the gift of sleeping through one's death, for our saliva**

> **contains a chemical which mimics the effects of narcolepsy in the receiver.**
>
> **Cells die off and new ones grow—parasitic cells that function only in the most basic sense of the word for a new form of survival which requires almost no cell turnover compared to those in a living being. This slow turnover is what gives vampires eternal life, though I suspect there is some outer limit to how long we can survive. The juices so essential to humans—spit, blood, semen—all become useless to our new cells' survival and are therefore absorbed by the primal tissue that remains. Going forward, we must seek the most nutrient-rich fluid from external sources (and we all know which one that is) in order to produce the most meager of fluids ourselves. Sweat. Tears. Liquid gold to a vampire.**

During this process, the old corpus rots away and is replaced by the new. It was this foul, rotting smell that drove my Nadia further and further away from me although she bravely continued to attend to my needs—a washrag on my forehead, a loving word in my ear. My father never once entered my room that I know of, but I heard his boots clomping on the other side of the bedroom wall.

Then one day after what felt like going to hell and back, I realized that I felt fully alive again—not in the same way as before, in a way even more so than before. I could see more clearly than ever, as if a fog had been lifted from my vision that I never knew existed. I could hear a doe bleating for her fawn far off in the forest. Although I was still regurgitating any food that Nadia tried to spoon into my mouth, I could smell, and what I smelled was delicious. The foul odor had dissipated by then (mummification now complete) so Nadia spent more time at my bedside, singing to me and telling me stories. Urging me to drink the soup that I constantly pushed away.

That day, I took her hand in mine and caressed the smooth skin, up and down the delicate underside of her arm until I saw goosebumps erupt along the trail of my fingertips. And it was then that I finally understood exactly what I had been smelling and craving. Slowly, almost erotically, I brought her arm to my mouth as if to kiss it, my lips drawing back to reveal incisors that had been growing while the rest of my body had been shrinking. I was only a gnat's breath away from the bite that would have changed Nadia's life (and my life) forever when a self-loathing overcame me, an emotion so powerful I never could have imagined it possible. I dropped Nadia's arm just as she instinctively recoiled from me, upsetting, with a clatter, the stool where she'd been sitting. As she stood and stared at me in horror, I looked up to see my father standing in the doorway. I hadn't seen him since the night I'd gone to the castle.

"It's time for you to leave," he said as calmly as if he'd been waiting for this day all along.

And because I couldn't bear the way Nadia was looking at me, I rose from my bed and left my home without a word.

CHAPTER THIRTEEN

"SOMEONE'S OUT THERE ASKING for you," Molly says to my back as I'm bent over a mess of glass shards and spilled red wine, a rag in one hand, a dustpan in the other. I'm slowly becoming accustomed to her uncanny resemblance to Nadia. It's disturbing, but I continue to find ways they're more different than alike. For instance, the mole behind her left ear. It's not there. And only now with Molly's hair pulled back in a ponytail am I able to determine that.

"Doe. Molly. Enough with the chit-chat. Let's get back to work," Calvin scolds.

I wonder how he manages to keep track of everyone's activities while maintaining his intense focus on the grill in front of him where hamburger patties are churned out at assembly-line speed, each one with just the right amount of pink in the middle.

"Uh, beg pardon?" I say. "I was not chit-chatting."

Calvin knows he'll never find another worker as good as me, but he still rides me hard. I know it's just a song he sings to maintain the military melody of the kitchen. None of us are exempt from his slings and arrows and none of us takes it personally. Well maybe Dimitri does but I certainly don't.

"Forty-five seconds, Doe," he says. "You've got forty-five seconds to take care of that mess and then I want all the tomatoes sliced for the salad. *All* the tomatoes, okay? Not just half the tomatoes, *all* the tomatoes. And make that diced, not sliced. And get to work on the potatoes too... we're running low."

We're probably the only restaurant that hand slices our potatoes for French fries. Each one comes out with a unique shape, so people automatically know these aren't going to be ordinary fries.

Back to the mess (not of my making) which awaits me. Only because Calvin spotted it when my foot happened to be near it, did it become my responsibility.

"In fairness," Dimitri, who carries the crucible of fairness everywhere he goes, calling out its absence wherever he encounters it, says, "John didn't knock that carafe to the ground."

"Oh yeah?" Calvin says. "And who would that be who knocked over the carafe?" Five raw patties sputter and hiss like angry serpents on the grill. Calvin flips one after another with Zen-like efficiency.

"And if he doesn't pick up all the glass shards, someone could step on one and hurt themselves." Dimitri continues to make the case on my behalf, which I haven't invited, nor do I welcome. But Dimitri is... well, he's Dimitri.

Molly pushes her way through the swinging doors, two plates perfectly balanced on each arm. A minute later she's back empty-handed. "They're still out there asking for you," she tells me just as I'm sweeping up the last of the broken glass.

"Who did you say knocked over that carafe, Meat Tree?" Dimitri is too long a name for Calvin to be bothered with.

"Who's *they*?" I ask Molly. "What do they look like?"

I'm expecting the Wheelie Boys for sure.

"Why *you* did, sir," Dimitri says. He seems surprised at the question, and I'm surprised Dimitri doesn't realize he's being set up.

Molly pours two chocolate shakes from the blender (something Dimitri is supposed to have done) and spritzes a generous helping of whipped cream into each one. She wipes a spill from the side of one glass and then disappears back into the diner with a shake in each hand.

"Oh yeah, it *was* me," Calvin says, pressing down on the patties with the back of his heavy metal spatula. "I almost forgot. I'll tell you what, Meat Tree, why don't you get over to the cutting board and start slicing those tomatoes for Doe so he can take the rest of the night off to inspect the floor. Maybe there's a shard he hasn't discovered yet. And *dice* them, don't slice them!"

Dimitri looks dumbfounded. "But I'm the fountain boy," he protests.

"Get to work, fountain boy." Calvin slides a patty onto an open bun and reaches for the next one.

"It's okay, Dimitri. I got this," I whisper.

Dimitri isn't good around knives, knows very little about slicing versus dicing, and before you know it, we'd have a thumb or a finger in tonight's salad. The fluorescent bulbs above my workstation were removed when I told Calvin they triggered migraines. The fact is that prolonged exposure to blue light is bad for my health, causing painful skin lesions. Calvin bought my story and allowed it but, unfortunately, the darkness of my workstation makes it difficult for someone with normal vision to see what they're chopping. And Dimitri is clumsy enough as it is. I can chop the entire basket of tomatoes in the time it would take Dimitri to chop one, and slicing potatoes is even harder than chopping tomatoes. I know this. Calvin knows this. And Calvin knows I'll step in for Dimitri, so he pretends not to notice.

Still, I can't resist a last swipe at Calvin—good-natured, of course.

"What d'ya think?" I wave my fingertips in Calvin's face as I walk by and he jumps back like he's just seen a vampire. "Do you like my new color?"

I've painted over my natural blue nails in a sparkly pink.

Calvin grimaces like he's just witnessed someone

wallowing in dog excrement. "What the hell, Doe!" His usual unflappable composure is being seriously tested.

"You *said* no more blue." I waggle my nails at him one more time. I'm enjoying this, I really am.

Actually, I *really* am. Henrietta Devine helped me out this afternoon—the Disco Pink color was already in her collection, a shade she saves for special occasions. Who knew that painting one's nails could be so much fun? I could get used to it. And that smell of ethyl acetate? Divine!

"I need burgers." Molly's in the kitchen again. "Many burgers. The animals are restless."

"Doe, I should dock your salary for that," Calvin grumbles. "Now get those fixings on the buns for Molly. Pronto!"

"Already done, boss." It isn't but, by the time anyone looks over to see if it is, it will be.

Molly marches over to me, hands on hips, and lets out a deep sigh. "They're still there, John. Still asking for you. And I'm kind of getting tired of them."

"Ah, they're just little kids," I say. "Give 'em a serving of fries to share and deduct it from my dinner tonight."

Although I don't eat, I always take a doggy bag home for Henrietta's midnight snack. That little lady has an appetite that belies her size.

"Um... not little kids. Not want fries," she says. "C'mon, John, deal with it. I'm busy." She turns and walks away.

By then the entire basket of tomatoes has been sliced and diced. And there's a tall mound of freshly sliced potatoes just waiting for their hot oil bath. If people in the kitchen weren't as busy as they were, they might actually be astounded by the speed of my hands. But nobody notices. Everyone's too focused on their own jobs.

FACT: Assuming that people notice the good or bad about you is a form of vanity. People only truly notice the good or bad about themselves.

"You heard her, Doe," Calvin says. "Deal with it. Go take care of your friends out there and make sure to deduct the time from your break. Starting now." He holds up his watch and presses the side knob to start the timer.

"I wish you wouldn't let him talk to you that way," Dimitri whispers as I walk past him.

"I wish *you* wouldn't let him talk to *you* that way," I reply.

For all my insecurities, Calvin's barbs are like water off a duck's back to me—they're nothing. But to Dimitri it's entirely different, although I know he could walk across the street and get a better job at higher pay.

I remove my work tunic and hang it on the wall hook beneath my name. I'm irritated that Peter and Fernando are taking up my break, a time when I should be working on my manuscript. I push through the swinging door and scan the room. A hand rises above the masses of patrons squeezed into every nook and cranny of the diner and waves at me.

Angela Ruiz.

And someone else. A girl I don't recognize.

CHAPTER FOURTEEN

"***You haven't been answering*** my calls," Angela says, stating the obvious. "Why not?"

"What are you doing here?"

The best defense being a good offense.

"Looking for *you*. Remember? You told me you worked nights here."

I hate being on this side of the kitchen door and usually do everything I can to avoid it. The air is oppressive for someone like me who needs maximum oxygen for his puny, shrunken lungs. The people who surround me make noises I don't like—belches, farts, sneezes, coughs. All those human noises I long ago said goodbye to and now find to be simply tedious, if not downright depressing.

The other girl at the table hasn't said a word but she's following our conversation intently, looking first to Angela and then to me.

"If we're going to be partners, we need to make ourselves available to each other," Angela says. "Otherwise, what's the point?"

"The point? I didn't realize our partnership extended beyond the classroom."

The young man sitting behind me abruptly stands and, with a careless shove, sends the back of his chair crashing into mine, without so much as a backward glance, let alone an apology. People don't realize how fragile the bones of a vampire are—porous really, like a bird… or a bat. It allows us to move about quickly but also makes us more susceptible to hairline fractures and their accompanying excruciating pain. Strong muscles, weak bones. Doesn't make sense, I know, but that's how it is.

I probably wince because the girl at our table (whom I have yet to be introduced to) smiles sympathetically. Angela doesn't seem to notice.

"Listen, Doe. Are we partners or not? Because the last few days it doesn't seem like we are and my *real* partner here," she motions to the girl, "Lilibeth, well, she's been more of a partner to me than you've been. I mean, she literally *is* my partner, but she's been more of my partner in crime than you have. Anyway, you know what I'm saying."

Why-oh-why did I think a criminology class would be a good idea? Next time, crocheting. Beauty school. Basket-weaving. Anything!

Angela reaches down to her waistband where a leather strap anchors a small holster at her side. For one brief panicked moment, I fear she's going to pull out a gun. Instead, she pulls out a bottle of Tabasco sauce. She carefully removes the top bun from her hamburger and liberally douses the meat with the spicy red sauce. Then she hands it to Lilibeth, who does the same thing to the burger in front of her, after which she passes the bottle back to Angela who re-holsters it.

"We do provide Tabasco sauce, you know?" I say, pointing to a bottle sitting right there on the table in front of her.

"Sure, you do. But not everyone does and who knows when you might need it." Angela turns to her friend and they smirk their agreement about the apparent necessity of carrying a personal stash of Tabasco sauce in its own special holster.

"It looks like you're carrying a gun," I say.

"But I'm not."

"But it looks like you are."

Angela looks over at Lilibeth and rolls her eyes. "Back to business," she says. "Aren't you curious about why I've been texting and calling?"

I *am* slightly curious, but I'll never admit it to her. Just then Molly appears at our table with a large salad. "Here you go, hon." She sets it down in front of Lilibeth who looks up at her, smiles warmly, and nods her approval. "Let me know if you need anything else." I recognize the tomatoes I diced just minutes earlier.

It's only then I allow myself to fully take in Lilibeth's appearance: her bushelful of curls which are either prematurely silver or dyed to look that way; her wide, cat-like eyes which she casts like a net, drawing every detail back to her attention; a small mouth with lips that pull back to reveal an angelically disarming smile and tiny pearl-like teeth crowding together in the bottom front as though they were trying to give each other a big hug. I wonder why she doesn't speak.

Standing behind Angela and Lilibeth, Molly holds up her arm and taps her watch, which I take to be a warning about me not going over my break time. Calvin's probably in the kitchen making threats about what he's going to do to me if that happens: dock my pay, make me wash dishes, make me scrub out the dumpster, make me clean the toilets, fire me, etc. Molly doesn't yet know Calvin like I do.

"Okay, I'll bite," I say, chuckling to myself at the double entendre of that expression (if Angela only knew, she might chuckle with me... or she might run screaming from the restaurant). "Why have you been relentlessly calling and texting."

"Aha!" Angela says, turning to Lilibeth with a thumbs-up. "Lilibeth thought you were ignoring me, but I just figured maybe you had bad cell reception. So, you admit you saw all the missed calls and texts and were purposely ignoring me."

"I admit," I say. "Go on."

Angela doesn't seem to derive any real pleasure from Lilibeth being correct, but she gamely proceeds.

"You do know we need to pick a class project—a case study we follow from beginning to end," she says. "Where we apply all the stuff we learn in Onslot's class. And that our project is going to be like ninety-seven percent of our final grade beyond the pop quizzes and homework which only make up three percent?"

"I did not," I say.

"Didn't you read the syllabus?"

"Nope."

"When were you planning on doing that?"

"Sometime before our next class, but now you've saved me the trouble."

Lilibeth is gingerly picking out the tomatoes and olives from the salad and setting them to the side of her plate.

"Don't you like those?" I ask. "I chopped them myself."

"She saves them for last," Angela says. "Don't get all butthurt about it. She'll eat them."

I swivel to face Angela. "First off, I'm not butthurt, as you so crudely put it. I'm just concerned the salad isn't up to her standards and I want to know why. It's called customer service... have you heard of it or do you just smite your dissatisfied customers at Up In Arms with an antique battle axe? Second, I'm sure Lilibeth can speak for herself, if you don't mind."

Nothing like a crude comment to raise my dander. Honestly, the obsession for vulgarities these days is borderline pathological. Even in my bloodiest and most desperate days, I tried to maintain some civility by keeping my language tea-time clean. But sometimes I think maybe I should pepper just a few expletives throughout my manuscript to make it a little more relatable. A little more modern. Just a few here and there, and nothing terribly obscene. Butthurt, indeed. Although, I suppose it does get the point across effectively.

Angela has put the plate containing Lilibeth's hamburger on top of her own (now empty) plate. She picks up Lilibeth's hamburger and dives into it.

"And now you're eating Lilibeth's hamburger," I say to

no one in particular.

Angela's cheeks puff out from the enormous mouthful of beef and bun she's bitten off. It's going to take more than a few chews before she can commence swallowing. Meat juice streams down her chin and she brings her napkin to her mouth to dam the flow. I look down at my lap until I'm sure she's cleaned herself up—bad memories and all. I hate the customer side of the Gobble-Down-Suck-Up. Why did I agree to come out here?

"It's actually mine," she says, her speech still clogged with food. "Lilibeth's a vegan. And, no, she can't speak. Or she can, but not to you." Angela leans over her plate so the morsels of food that fall from her mouth while she's talking don't make it to her lap.

"Meaning?"

Angela's taken another large bite, so I have to sit and wait while she finishes the revolting process of masticating, swallowing, masticating, swallowing, and periodically dabbing at her face with a mangled paper napkin.

"Meaning that Lilibeth is Deaf. She does speak ASL, but since I'm still learning and not very good at it yet, she's been kind enough to lip-read tonight, although that's not her preferred method of listening."

"Why didn't you say so?" I turn to Lilibeth. "I'm sorry, had I known, I would have been speaking directly to you," I sign. My ASL is perfect. Like I said, I've had plenty of time to become fluent in many different languages.

Lilibeth seems delighted and we continue the conversation about the salad, whether it's to her satisfaction (very much so); how long have she and Angela been together (four months); is she in school (she's an artist and attends a high school specializing in fine arts); is Angela always this annoying (Lilibeth finds Angela's direct manner to be more charming than annoying). To each her own.

Angela raises her eyebrows, surprised but not displeased. She continues to eat her second hamburger and only when she finishes does she interject herself back into the conversation.

"I'm still learning ASL," she repeats. "So, if you don't mind indulging me so I can be part of the group too."

"I'm just surprised," I say, unable to resist the dig, "why you chose a class in criminology instead of ASL so you could get up to speed more quickly."

She glares at me, making her eyebrows look more like furious caterpillars than brow-sweat barriers. "I do both, Doe. I can walk and chew gum at the same time, you know."

"Mm-hmm. So, what were you going to say about the case study, and why you're here to see me? I should be getting back to work."

Angela sets her glass on the table with a dramatic flourish, making me want to inspect it for cracks. "You probably don't know this, Doe," Angela says. "But the Six o' Clock Slasher's back."

"I actually *do* happen to know that," I say, and I think my calm manner is pretty impressive.

Angela raises her considerable eyebrows. "And *how* do you know?" she asks.

"I have my contacts," I say. "And how do *you* know?"

"Really?" she says. "We're going to play games like children, are we?" Her face contorts into a pained expression, as if she's watching a favorite nephew in the throes of a temper tantrum. "I'm not going to hold back from you, Doe, and I'd appreciate if you extend me the same courtesy, so listen up. Lilibeth's uncle lives right across the street from the last victim. Right. Across. The street. The police are trying to keep the whole thing hush-hush, probably so people don't panic and wonder why it's taken them two years and they still haven't caught him."

"Or her," I say.

"Statistically speaking, it's bound to be a him," Angela says.

I've known many "her" killers in my time. Too many.

But I'm not interested in arguing with Angela since she's probably right.

"I'm sorry, Lilibeth," I sign. "That must be awful for your uncle."

Lilibeth nods gravely.

"And furthermore," Angela says. "I knew one of the last victims before the Slasher disappeared three months ago. He was one of the best customers of Up In Arms where I work. Super nice guy."

"An unfortunate coincidence," I say, shaking my head. "For you and Lilibeth to have this terrible six degrees of separation."

"Or is it?" The corners of Angela's luscious lips creep up into a sly and knowing smile. "Is it unfortunate or is this our big moment, Doe? Our chance to put ourselves on the map. Our way to make a name for ourselves now and forever among history's greatest detectives."

"Are you suggesting us?" I speak and sign simultaneously, and both Lilibeth and Angela smile and nod at the same time. "You can't be serious. We're going to solve the case of a serial murderer who's eluded the entire police force for two years. Just because Lilibeth's uncle knows one victim and you knew another? You're both crazy!"

"The way we see it," Angela glances at Lilibeth, "maybe we were brought together for this reason. You know, fate. People will talk to us, say things they might not tell the police. We're approachable. And you too, Doe—well, you're not approachable but we'll absolutely give you equal credit when we bust the case wide open. Because we're partners! And also because you're Onslot's student and Lilibeth isn't and doesn't want to be."

"Kind of you," I say, not meaning a word of it.

"You're welcome." Angela, the girl with no sense of irony and no apparent sense of humor. "So, we're going to get to class thirty minutes early tomorrow, okay? We want to be the first ones to claim this project for our ourselves before someone else beats us to it."

She pushes her chair back and Lilibeth does the same. "We're all good now? Don't want to keep you from work any longer." She holds out a twenty-dollar bill as if to pay me for the meal. "You can keep the change for your tip," she says.

"Pay at the cashier, please," I say. "And be sure to leave a tip on the table for your server, who is Molly."

"See you tomorrow, Doe." Angela reaches into her pocket and drops a few ones on the table. "Remember, thirty minutes early, so don't be late. And for God's sake, answer your texts from now on. You never know when a break in the case might come."

I'm signing goodbye to Lilibeth and expressing how nice it was to meet her when Angela intrudes with a final thought.

"Prepare to share your contacts," she tells me. "Partners can't hold stuff back from each other and you said you have contacts. I want in on them, Doe, seeing as how I'm sharing mine with you. This is a two-way street, so don't forget it."

Lilibeth and Angela clasp hands and thread their way through the jungle of tables and chairs towards the door.

The Wheelie Boys? I don't think so.

Somehow, I have the feeling I've been played or used, or am in the process of being played or used. But I know it's my natural inclination to be suspicious of people, and I remind myself that Angela doesn't seem to have a deceptive personality.

Still, I think I'd rather be slicing and dicing in the kitchen than hot on the trail of the Six o' Clock Slasher.

Later on during my shift, I spy Molly thumbing through a celebrity magazine. I know she likes fashion and also loves movies. I have a big question to ask her, though I'm a little nervous about it. Since I've finished cleaning the counters and chopping the onions there's very little to do during a brief lull. I slide over to where Molly's sitting, screwing up my nerve along the way. I've been thinking my look needs an upgrade, but I have no idea where to start since I haven't done a major upgrade in more than fifty years.

"Can I sit down?" I ask, even while realizing how foolish that sounds. Of course, I can sit down. It's the employees' break area.

She looks up at me and smiles... no, glows. Molly glows. "Of course," she says. Her voice which I initially found to be a bit nasally, I now find to be endearing. Playful. Without guile. She smiles again and her eyes crinkle and twinkle. Smize. That's what Molly does—she smizes, as they say these days. "What's up?"

I glance over at the burger grill and see Calvin's not there—a bathroom break, most likely, which he rarely takes, only when there's a lull.

"I've been thinking," I say. "About maybe changing my hairstyle. Maybe my entire look, you know, even my clothes. I'm not good at that and I was wondering—"

"I'd love to help," she says. "Is that what you're asking?"

I nod.

"Okay, let me think about it though. I don't want to jump at the first thing that comes to mind. Let me look at you for a sec."

Molly's eyes settle on top of my head and fall away to my shoes, lingering here and there along the way. It does make me feel a bit funny, but nothing like lust. It's as though a soft electric blanket has been draped over me, turned to a slightly warm setting, and then rigged to deliver a mild electric shock... but only for a minute, you understand. There's nothing like lust left in me after vampirovirus ravaged my sex hormones and organs, and 300 years of disillusionment finished up the job.

"I'll give it some thought," she says.

CHAPTER FIFTEEN

Clementine is dying.

I've tried every way I know to save her, but I fear it's too late. I should be home with her instead of sitting in a roomful of strangers, listening to meaningless drivel that has nothing to do with my life. So why don't I go home?

I'm afraid to.

I'm afraid to witness Clementine's last moments on Earth... in her bowl... taking in her last lungful of water. I can't bear to see her dying convulsions. I know I should have left her in Henrietta's care for her final hours, but I'm so ashamed of my complicity in her death. Even worse, I'm ashamed of my inability to be there when she needs me most.

Clementine is one in a million, a no ordinary *Carassius auratus*—or common goldfish as they're known (a misnomer if I ever heard one considering that Clementine's color has more in common with a tangerine peel). But Clementine has a heart of gold so, for her, the name is entirely appropriate—perfect, in fact. She's one of the best, a true friend and companion.

"...I aimed my gun at the door handle, fired off two shots, and then identified myself loudly before going inside—"

"Detective Onslot?"

"Yes, Angela."

"Shouldn't you have knocked first and identified yourself as police before shooting the door handle?"

Onslot is remarkably tolerant of Angela. She has

clearly become the leader of this classroom and Onslot knows it. The other students have taken to wearing Tabasco sauce holsters, imitation being the sincerest form of flattery. Only Onslot and I remain Tabasco-holsterless.

"And wouldn't it have been safer to kick down the door to avoid accidentally shooting someone on the inside?"

Because of Angela's superior status in the classroom, I've been elevated amongst my classmates by virtue of being her partner. The same isn't true for Detective Onslot, who now views me as a threat he isn't scared to take on any chance he gets. Maybe he feels that, by diminishing me, he can diminish Angela and win the power struggle everyone knows is going on. Everyone except Angela, that is. She doesn't seem to be aware of it and actually appears to be fond of Onslot on some level.

"Also, aren't two shots unnecessary? It seems like one shot would have been enough to shatter the lock. What d'ya think, John?" She turns to look at me, and I know she's just trying to share a little of her magic by bringing me into the discussion. The protective coating of her own charismatic sheen.

"Yes, what *do* you think, Doe?" Onslot asks, his eyes narrowing at me. I know he doesn't want an answer. He's trying to intimidate me as a way of reining in Angela. He needn't worry, I have no intention of being a vocal participant in the classroom discussion. Having perused the syllabus, I know class participation is given zero weight in the final grade and that suits me just fine.

"Whatever Angela just said. That's what I think."

We'd won the Six o' Clock Slasher case, if "won" is even the proper term. Angela arrived thirty minutes early and waited for Onslot a block away before anyone else could get to him. I arrived five minutes late, having been consumed with Clementine.

Here is my crime.

Having cleaned Clementine's bowl upon awakening

today, I neglected to add a conditioner to neutralize the chlorine and chloramine in her water, thereby exposing her to toxic chemicals. I thought I had added it, was *sure* of it but, apparently, I hadn't because an hour later Clementine was listless, keeping close to the porcelain mermaid on the bottom of her bowl. When I tapped the side of her bowl, which never fails to get her attention, she didn't move from that spot. I immediately performed a second water change, checking multiple times to ensure I'd added the conditioner, but Clementine's condition continued to deteriorate—at least there was no improvement. When I could stand it no longer, I fled from my apartment—a coward, completely undeserving of the privilege of Clementine's companionship. And now, I don't know how I can face going home.

How can I ever forgive myself?

Loneliness. Let's talk about it. It pierces the soul with an arrow that can't be removed, rendering a wound that will never heal without the antidote—a true companion. Some prefer solitude, as I do, although I wasn't always that way. But solitude and loneliness are two different things. Solitude is a choice. Loneliness is thrust upon you.

"I'm So Lonesome I Could Cry," a classic song by country singer Hank Williams (Google the lyrics), perfectly describes the emotions I've grappled with ever since the Spanish flu pandemic of 1918—which killed up to five percent of Earth's human population, and one hundred percent of its vampire population. One hundred percent minus one. Me.

How do I express that in percentiles? I have no idea because that would require an accurate count of the world's vampire population in 1918, a statistic no one knows for certain.

Why was I spared? I also have no idea, although I have a solid theory.

MYTH: Vampires don't enjoy the company of other vampires. Sigh. This is the silliest myth

of all. Just as living humans migrate to some and avoid others, vampires do the same. It depends on the vampire since no two are cut from the same cloth. I've had close relationships with vampires with whom I had much in common, and I've taken great pains to avoid the pathological, psychopathic sort. The soul-suckers, as I used to call them. Bitter, mean creatures who refer to humans as meat blobs or blood bags, as if they were never ones themselves. As if they wouldn't have given anything to be one again. But you can always find that sort, even among the living.

I have no choice as to which vampires I'm drawn to and which I instinctively avoid because there are no others. The companionship and understanding among peers that most people take for granted—that's been stolen from me. Even the pathological sort of vampire would be better than nothing. Nothing in this world is as lonely or as sad as being the last of your kind.

"Now we're each going to take a minute to share our case studies with the other members of this class. Who wants to start?" Onslot moves to a corner of the room and pulls out his phone where he proceeds to bury his attention, not even trying to disguise his disinterest. He reaches for a cigarette from his shirt pocket but then, perhaps realizing where he is, puts it away.

"I'll start," Angela volunteers to no one's surprise. "John Doe and I picked the Six o' Clock Slasher." Classroom murmurs follow.

I've heard that serial killers feel a certain affinity for each other, sometimes going so far as to study each other's methods. Although they never meet, they still know that others *like* them are out there. I wonder if the Six o' Clock Slasher takes comfort in that knowledge and it sickens me to put myself in his mindset, likening it to my own. I'm a wretched, shameful being who doesn't deserve the space I'm taking up on this planet. I'm a poor excuse for a friend...a coward who walks away from his dying companion. I'm the loneliest living thing on Earth, if one could call me living. If I'm even good enough to be called a *thing*. Even the Six o' Clock Slasher is better off than me.

"Do you have anything to add, Doe?" Onslot asks, without looking up from his phone. I hadn't realized that Angela was done talking.

"Perhaps," Angela says, "I could have a minute to finish what I was getting at."

"Go ahead," Onslot sighs.

I rap the back of my head five times with the knuckles of my right hand. Angela's voice is white noise in the background. She said she was going to get at something, but for the life of me I can't tell what she's getting at. I tap my right heel against the floor five times and then repeat the process with my left heel.

The classroom feels unbearably hot, but I know there's no heat in the building because no one ever takes their jackets off in class. Tonight, one girl has brought a blanket with her and it's wrapped snugly around her shoulders.

"And then I got the idea..." Angela is saying. Onslot stares at me as though a giant sloth had made its home on top of my head.

My neck and shoulders cramp from tension and seem to be in danger of spasming.

It feels like a giant sloth has made its home on top of my head.

Are rivulets of perspiration cascading down the slope of my forehead? I reach my hand up to check but pull away when I think of the possible consequences. I use theatrical makeup which generally stays put no matter what, but I don't have total confidence in it at the moment. And I certainly don't have perspiration to spare.

"So that's why I think it's important to..."

What is she saying and why won't she stop talking?

Why is Onslot staring at me?

I blink three times fast. Three times slow. Three times fast again.

Onslot can't seem to take his eyes off of me.

"Mr. Doe," he says, but Mr. Doe seems a million miles away from me being me.

My breath comes faster and faster as if I'm running a race.

"I have to... I have to go." I stand abruptly, knocking my chair over in the process. All eyes swivel towards me. My chest heaves, my lungs fight for air. The faces of the other students are a blur of indistinguishable features. Indistinguishable and yet somehow hostile. The walls begin to turn in a slow spin. Someone else says my name. Angela? The buzzing in my ears is too loud. Too loud. My rituals have failed me and in fight or flight, I choose flight. I stumble on my fallen chair. Someone... Angela... steadies my arm and moves the chair out of my way.

"Bathroom... I have to go to the bathroom," I say, and my voice sounds like someone else's voice. Coming from someone else's mouth.

Does Onslot say "down the hall"? I'm not sure because I'm already walking out the door, preparing to take the quick way home—the vampire way.

But then I notice Angela's behind me. Calling out to me. Scurrying down the stairs right on my heels.

"Wait up!" she says. "Doe! What's the matter? Doe!"

"Go back," I say. "Finish our presentation... what you were saying. I have to go."

"Doe." She catches up to me and takes hold of my arm which is nearly as devastating as what I fear might be waiting for me at home.

No one touches me. People are instinctively repelled by me and naturally keep at least a few feet distance. Being touched is... well, it's perilous. My skin doesn't yield to the touch like normal human skin. And the feel of a human's touch—let's just say it's not a good thing for either party involved. But Angela has done it and I have survived it, albeit with my innards churning like lava. Fortunately, my thick sweatshirt prevents her from touching my actual flesh.

"Doe," she repeats, more quietly and calmly. She drops her hand from my arm, perhaps sensing my acute discomfort. "Are you having a panic attack?"

I am. I'm having a panic attack, a terrible one, but I can't admit it to her.

"I just have to get home," I repeat. "Something... someone very close to me is feeling poorly."

"Then I'll walk with you," she says gently. "That's what partners are for."

I don't want her to walk with me now that I'm determined to get home as quickly as possible to face whatever it is I have to face.

"What about class?" I ask. "What about explaining our project?"

"Never mind about that. This is more important."

I'm taking the stairs down two at a time and, to her credit, Angela keeps up with me without getting winded, nor does she ask me to slow down. We leave the building and melt into the night. Although I'm itching to take the vampire way—I can barely contain myself—I force myself to slow down, maintain a human pace, albeit a fast one.

I repeat the mantra I was first given by the Maharishi in 1968. With every step. With every breath. The mantra wasn't intended to become just another one of my rituals, but I turn to it on occasions when all else fails. After a few minutes, it begins to have the desired effect. My steps slow. My breath slows. My mantra slows.

We walk in silence until finally Angela speaks. "You know, John. It's okay... to talk to someone... to me... or anyone. I've experienced panic attacks before, and I thought I recognized the signs. I saw something in your eyes."

How could she?

"Anyway," she says. "Just want you to know that I'm

here for you. Anytime."

After that, we move through the dark streets, past flickering rainbows of neon lights, ducking through alleys lined with rusting dumpsters. Barking dogs behind chain-link fences. Neither of us speak but the effect that Angela's presence has on my quivering, shrunken heart is close to serenity. My breathing, although never normal, has returned to normal by vampire standards. I'm prepared to face what I must face. I'm prepared to deal with whatever must be dealt with.

I feel an enormous sense of gratitude.

"John Doe."

"John Doe."

Peter and Fernando glide through the shadow that hugs the backside of the buildings in this alleyway. Before we see them, they've circled around and slowed their speed to match our pace.

"Word is you're after the Slasher."

"Is it true?"

Angela looks up at me, a huge question mark stamped onto her face. She shrugs her shoulders to which I shake my head.

"I'm not after anyone," I say.

How they know what they know when they know it will always be a mystery to me. And I prefer to leave it that way.

"See you at work tomorrow, John Doe," says Peter.

"Is that okay, John Doe?" asks Fernando, but before I have time to answer they're already out of sight.

It's the time when footsteps echo and the rotten smells of city life recede, leaving behind at least a semblance of fresh air. A few hours from now it will begin again. The sun will welcome back its harsh shadows. The throbbing wave of humanity will wash away everything in its path that isn't garishly obvious. The beauty that flowers only at night won't even be a memory except for those of us who live on the dark side of the planet.

Angela Ruiz and I walk the final steps to my apartment in silence. An old lady is curled up in the alcove that fronts my building. She's sleeping soundly, one thin arm cradling her spotted dog for warmth. The two are wrapped in an army surplus blanket that looks like it's been through several world wars. Her hair is iron gray and feathered from the evening mist. Her countenance, in sleep, is peaceful, and I wonder if she's dreaming of happier days and a softer place to lay her head.

I turn to Angela. "It's them."

"Them?"

"Those boys. Peter and Fernando. They're my contacts, and I'm sharing because... well, because we're partners."

She smiles a truly heart-warming smile which says a lot because my heart is so very cold. "Thanks, Doe," Angela says. "Want me to come up with you?"

"No, I'm okay now." I shove my hands deep into my pockets, wanting to say more but not knowing what to say. "Thanks."

"No problem," Angela says. "You'd have done it for me."

I look from side to side but seeing no one, I leave her with a warning. "Be careful walking home. You know... the Slasher."

"He only strikes at dinner time," Angela says. "And only in—"

"—people's homes. Be careful just the same."

"See you soon, Doe," she says.

I kneel down to stretch the blanket over the sleeping lady and her spotted dog. I pull off my sweatshirt, roll it into a semblance of a cushion, and gently raise her head while I slide it underneath. She stirs but doesn't wake. I step over her carefully, then fumble through my pockets to find my keys. Once inside, I move quickly up the stairs, vampire style. But when I'm standing in front of the door to my apartment, I turn the key as slowly as possible—human style—to allow myself time to prepare.

On the table, in her crystal palace, Clementine darts joyously back and forth, thrilled to see me and apparently famished.

I remove the phone from my pocket and text Bibi's number to schedule my next appointment.

CHAPTER SIXTEEN

The Last Vampire

[REVISED: FIRST PERSON, PAST TENSE, ADULT VERSION]

By John Doe

Chapter Sixteen

After all these decades, does anyone really understand what led to the first World War? An archduke assassinated by a young man acting on orders from a terrorist group called The Black Hand. There are historians who can make sense of it in hindsight, but back then most of them couldn't keep up with the rapidly changing events that took the world to the brink of destruction, a terrible war no one ever could have predicted. The only thing about which most of us were certain was that a lot of people—good people—were dying. And it wasn't just the living who cared—those of us infected by vampirovirus, the decent and moral among us...we hated the war as well, some going so far as to fight alongside the living, not fearing for their own lives but brave nonetheless.

Naturally, I was exempt from military service having been officially dead for over two centuries, most of which time I'd spent trying to come to terms with what had been done to me by the son-of-a-bitch who was my father. How did it feel to be sold into eternal damnation in order to pay off my father's debts and buy him a young bride who was my one true love? In four words: pretty damn freaking terrible. I was more than just butthurt.

This isn't working. I'm sacrificing my voice for the sake of relevancy. The first person is okay for now, but the adult language is unacceptable if being modern means lowering my standards.

The Last Vampire

[REVISED: FIRST PERSON, PAST TENSE]

By John Doe

Chapter Sixteen

I never stopped dreaming of a way to reverse my condition, returning me to the realm of the living, even though the world I'd known and the woman I'd loved were long gone. When Dmitry Ivanovsky isolated the first virus in 1892, I began to wonder if viruses might be responsible for many of the sicknesses of men. I further wondered if there was a way to isolate the "soldiers" within our bodies that naturally rally to fight off disease. If I could somehow administer to myself high doses of these "soldier cells" I might have a chance at reversing the infection I'd been doomed to carry into eternity. I might become human again.

This is not to brag that I was responsible for medical advances for which I was never credited—although I was. This is simply to lay the groundwork for what would come next. Perhaps a blessing. Perhaps a curse, depending on where one stands, and I can only relate it from the point of view of where I stand now.

Around this time, I formed a close friendship with a renowned physician, Dr. Freidrich Ostentaysius. Had life played out in a different way, Dr. Ostentaysius would have changed the course of modern medicine, however he, like me, was infected by the vampirovirus—in his case, resulting from the charms of a beautiful French actress who had her way with him one night, and was never seen again. When the doctor and I first met in Northern France, we found we had many things in common, including a curious mind, a love for traveling to far-off places, and a deep distaste for drinking blood directly from its source. We soon became fast friends.

With my theories and Dr. Ostentaysius' tireless work in a laboratory (to which he gained access at night) we explored the concept of reversing our disease—and I say "disease" because by then, Dr. Ostentaysius had managed to isolate the vampirovirus which is where we were focusing our attention for obvious reasons. I agreed to be the guinea pig and he the overseer. We set to work.

During WWI, our work slowed to a crawl because the laboratory's resources were being directed at ways to prevent or slow death in wounded Allied soldiers. But I continued to take the injections of what we now call gamma globulins—again, I don't say this to brag but it was my theories and Dr. Ostentaysius' brilliant work in the laboratory that isolated this serum for which we had great hopes. Sadly, I saw no improvement in my condition after two years of injections. That is to say, the vampirovirus remained robust within me.

Which brings us to 1918.

As bad luck would have it, we were living near one of the epicenters for the outbreak of the Spanish flu. The military hospital (whose laboratory we were "borrowing" at night) began to see multiple cases of a flu so virulent, soldiers fell like flies. One of the first to die was my dear and brilliant friend, Dr. Ostentaysius. It was a stunning loss not only to me, but to history and all of humanity. Sadly, his death would never be seen for the tragedy it was because, to most, he had already died decades ago after a night of debauchery. No one would notice the passing of a man who lived in the shadows, traveled only at night, and avoided the company of the living. But the most shocking aspect of my friend's death was the realization that vampires were not immortal—they could succumb to disease, at least this one...the Spanish flu.

Frightened and feeling very much alone, I continued the injections of gamma globulins, knowing that Dr. Ostentaysius would want me to do just that. When my supply ran out a few years later, the pandemic was over, and I was still alive. Alive but dead.

A century has come and gone, and I've circumnavigated the globe many times. I've made enquiries in locations where vampirism once thrived. I've stalked the likely gathering places in cities and towns, throughout the tropics and into the arctic circle. I returned to my beloved forests of Bistrița-Năsăud where I would have been thrilled to encounter even Istvan, the nobleman monster who desecrated my life. But alas, I was unsuccessful at every turn.

After that, there was no other conclusion. I was the last vampire on Earth, having survived the Spanish flu only because I'd self-administered gamma globulin injections for four straight years. To this day, I continue to scour the internet and track down any leads, but they only lead me to deranged impostors.

I am the Ishi of vampires.

I am the last of my kind.

MYTH: Vampires have eternal life. That's what we used to think until the Spanish Flu debunked that myth. I have yet to encounter another virus able to kill or even sicken a vampire, and I've never so much as caught the common cold. Was it a medical fluke, that we immortal beings were susceptible to this one perfect viral match for which we had no chance of survival? Or is something still lurking somewhere, waiting to strike? In a pigsty. In a chicken coop. Waiting for the opportunity to jump the species barrier from animal to human, from human to vampire.

If it happened once, it could happen again. One day a virus will reassert itself and find its final vampire victim in me.

CHAPTER SEVENTEEN

"HAVE A SEAT." BIBI motions towards the available seating options. "Or lie down again. Whatever makes you comfortable."

I head for the divan and unwind into a semblance of serious contemplative posture. Bibi plops down in the same chair as last time.

"Has something happened since we last talked?" she asks. "I mean... why did you call? Don't get me wrong, I'm glad you did." She reaches over to the table beside her, picks up the notepad, then flips through the pages until she apparently comes to where we left off.

"Nobody sees that, right?" I elongate a finger with a crackle and aim it at the notepad.

"Please," she says, and I'm worried I've offended her. But it's a fair question. She's not a licensed therapist and therefore not bound by patient/doctor confidentiality. I'm counting on the fact that she's learned about professional ethics from her mother who actually *is* a real therapist. But Bibi's mature for her age. Remarkably serene. I have to go with my gut and believe she'll do the right thing by guarding my private information. And what other choice do I have?

None at the moment.

"Do you have any new patients?" I ask, trying to keep the possessiveness out of my voice and secretly hoping she doesn't. "Besides me?" I want to be the sole focus of Bibi's attention—like discovering a new restaurant and having it all to yourself until it goes viral and you become relegated to waiting in line for a table, instead of being fussed over and treated like a king. I say this only from observing the arc of the Gobble-Down-Suck-Up, of course, having not been interested in restaurants for quite some time.

"Not yet," she says. "But I just put up a lot of flyers in some new places, so here's hoping I will soon."

Here's hoping you won't.

"Let's dive in," she says. "What's up?"

What's up?

What *is* exactly up? My panic attacks. My constant obsessing about Clementine which at least means, for now, I'm not obsessing as much about myself.

"I've been struggling with a few things," I say. "My writing, for instance."

"Your writing?"

"Yes. A... novel I've written."

Gadzooks! Why did I say that? No one can resist posing insensitive questions to an author. Have I heard of you? What have you written? Can I find you in my local library?

"Wait. You're an author?"

I don't like how surprised Bibi seems at this revelation. On the other hand, am I? I've never referred to myself as an author before, but I *have* written a book. Does that make me an author, or must I be published to call myself one?

"Well, it depends on one's definition," I say. "Technically, yes, because I've written a... novel. But practically speaking, no, because I can't seem to interest a publisher. Or even an agent."

"So, that's what's bothering you?"

That and the existential struggle I grapple with each and every day. My bleak future that stretches out for an eternity with no happy ending in sight. My overwhelming loneliness that sometimes feels heavier than a mountain of rocks, darker than a bottomless pit, more difficult to escape than a black hole. My pointless, constant worrying that's about as useful as a fur coat in the summer, and often leaves me feeling spent and... defeated.

"Well, yes. At the moment. That and... other things."

"Let's go with the writing before we get into the other things. Why do you think it bothers you so much?" Bibi mercifully doesn't make eye contact for the most part, allowing me the illusion of talking to myself which causes the words to flow a bit easier.

"Well, for obvious reasons. It feels like a rejection."

She shifts in her chair. Taps her pen against the notebook in a rhythmic beat, which I recognize as "Twinkle, Twinkle, Little Star," and brings said pen to her mouth where she taps it against her bottom teeth three, four, five times. "What's the book about?" she finally asks.

I pounce on my answer because I'm prepared for it.

"I'd rather not say at the moment."

It comes out a little too triumphantly, as though the act of keeping my manuscript a secret is a great victory of some sort. As though thousands have been clamoring for the key to the lockbox where I safeguard this story that I've been peddling to any and every agent I can locate who's expressed even the most remote interest in acquiring new clients.

"Porn?" she asks as casually as if she's just asked for my billing address.

This is really too much. Who exactly does she think I am? I swing my legs around so I can sit up and make direct eye contact with her because sometimes direct eye contact is necessary to punctuate one's outrage. "Heavens no!" I exclaim.

But the outrage doesn't fuel me for long. My indignation fades as quickly as the time it takes me to collapse onto the divan again. My legs, too long for its short length, dangle over the end.

Bibi chuckles.

"What's so funny?"

"Nothing," she says. "It's just that my grandma says that sometimes, 'heavens no.'"

I have to be careful about my idioms when speaking to a younger person—even Henrietta, as old as she is, chides me on occasion about my dated language.

A document search! I need to do a document search as soon as I get home to make sure I've removed anything remotely dated from my manuscript, except when called for by the historical era.

"No, it's not porn," I say. "More like fantastical historical fiction."

Out of the side of my eye I see Bibi jotting something in her notebook.

"What are you writing?"

She bites her lower lip in concentration.

"Fantastical historical fiction. I want to look it up when I get home," she says.

"I don't think you'll find it. Anyway, that's probably not correct. Honestly, I'm not sure that's an actual genre."

"Well, there's a start," Bibi says. "If you don't even know what genre your book is, how're you going to sell the idea to someone else?"

She has a point. She allows me a moment to let it sink in.

"Let's get back to why writing makes you feel bad."

"I didn't say writing made me feel bad," I say, but did I? Did I actually say that to her? I rack my brain. Does it?

"You kind of did."

Writing makes me feel bad? But it's not writing that makes me feel bad, it's...

"I said that not being able to attract the interest of agents or publishers makes me feel bad."

Completely different.

"Isn't that part of writing?"

I asked for this. I volunteered for therapy. But I didn't expect this demand for introspection from a girl of only sixteen. I expected... emotional support. Pats on the back.

Someone to tell me everything will be alright if I can only just talk all the prickliness out of my brain. That the agents and publishers are the ones at fault for rejecting me, adding to the intensity of my natural anxiety.

"Well… yes, I suppose it is."

"So, let's talk about that."

I close my eyes and think about all the hours I put pen to paper (yes, actual pen to paper is how I write). Then the hours where I transcribed my words to a document I could print out and mail (wherever a mailing address is available, which is rarer every day) or email (whenever a physical address isn't available). Having come of age during a time when trees seemed like a natural resource that could never be depleted, it's been hard for me to transform along with the rest of the world into a paperless society, although I do my part by only reading eBooks. I think about the pile of rejection letters in my home, on the brink of teetering over, having grown to such a great height. Yes, even the email rejections get printed out and added to the stack. It's a form of self-flagellation, I suppose.

"It feels like a personal rejection," I say. "Like nobody wants me. Like I'm irrelevant."

"Aren't rejecting your manuscript and rejecting you two different things?

For this question, I have to not only close my eyes but squint hard to force the blood that still circulates (via my nourishment) into my brain, although my brain functions quite well when it comes to most things outside of myself.

"Yes and no."

"How so, no?"

It takes me minutes of reflection to come up with each answer, but it seems as if Bibi already has the next question hovering at the tip of her tongue. As though she's already anticipated my answers. Which makes me wonder if she's brilliantly insightful… or if I'm just not as complex as I imagine myself to be.

"Because I've poured my heart and soul into it."

"But it isn't *you*, is it?"

Only an author knows the answer to that question.

"Yes, in a sense it is."

"So, is it true what they say about authors? That the characters in the book are really based on you or people you know?"

Everyone asks this. Everyone wants to end up as a character in your book or at least recognize someone they know.

"Some more than others," I say. "Some authors have the ability to create characters seemingly out of thin air, although they'd need to have a little experience with the personality traits in order to write them convincingly."

"And you? Is it true with you?"

"Perhaps more than others."

"So, this book... is really about *you*?"

How we got from there to here in such a remarkably short period of time is emotional whiplash. It's not something I was prepared to address, and if I had been prepared, I certainly would have been prepared to deny it.

"Yes."

"Then it's not really..." she glances at her notepad, "fantastical historical fiction. It's a memoir?"

Although I've been marketing my book as historical fantasy, I came up with the more complex-sounding genre to impress, or perhaps to confuse, Bibi. Either way, I feel a burning shame and, if I were capable, I would be blushing at the moment.

"Perhaps."

"Can I read it?"

God, no! A million times no. In no reality would that ever be a yes. Were worms to eat me from the inside out, it would still be a no.

"No."

"Honestly, it would make my job so much easier."

"Still, no."

She takes a deep breath and lets it out slowly. Not in an exasperated way. Just in the way of someone preparing to do something difficult.

"You've let all these other people read it," she says. "People who don't know you or care about you."

Precisely.

The tight line of my lips probably informs her that no answer will be forthcoming.

"Okay, then we'll do it the slow way," she says. "It's all the same to me since you're my only patient. But I'd have thought you'd want to save yourself some time and money."

"But you're not charging me anything," I say. What I don't say is that I have all the time in the world. Time to spare. Time to waste.

"Fair enough. Okay, let's get back to it. The personal rejection thing, that makes total sense to me now that I know it's a memoir."

"So, you agree with me that it's a personal rejection?"

"Nah. I think maybe your book is just boring and you have to spice it up or something. But I have no way of being able to verify that since you won't let me read it."

"That's exactly what I've been thinking." I swing my legs back around to sit up again. "I've been trying to figure out a way of presenting my prose in a more... *compelling* fashion."

"Mr. Doe? May I call you John now?"

"Yes, by all means." I recline once again and bring the back of my hand to my forehead in a motion I realize must look overly dramatic. I move my hand from my forehead to cross over the other hand resting on my chest. This still feels too dramatic, almost coffin-like. In fact, this is exactly how I sleep in my coffin at home. I sit up abruptly.

"What's wrong?" Bibi has been observing all my fidgeting. She writes something in her notebook.

"It's just... this divan is very uncomfortable."

"Sit in the chair, then." She points with her pen to the

white leather chair next to the divan. "It's a recliner."

I move from the divan to the chair which is as plush as a rain cloud. A button on the side reclines me silently into a comfortable position which accommodates the length of my legs. Now, where to put my hands? I place one on each armrest which seems to work for the time being.

Bibi looks up from her notes. "Do you think that maybe... just maybe... you're too young to have had an interesting life. I mean, no offense but you're only seventeen and there can't be a lot to write about at this point. I'm sixteen and I probably have a more interesting life than most people my age, but I don't think it's interesting enough for a memoir yet."

"Negative," I say.

She chews on the end of her pen, taps her bottom teeth again, looks down at her written notes.

"That isn't helpful. You're going to have to give me more than just one-word answers." She rises from her chair and places the notepad on the table beside her. "By the way, do you want a water? I have sparkling."

"No thanks."

"Well, I do," she says. "BRB."

"BRB?"

"Be right back." She looks at me curiously.

I take the time to digest what Bibi's said. I could get the whole thing over with and just give her the manuscript. That way I could get both a critical assessment of my writing and an objective take on my life—the good, the bad, and the demons that inhabit my psyche. But undoubtedly, she would laugh at me. Why should she believe a word of it? And if she did believe it, what would she think of me?

I turn over in my mind what she's said about whether I'm depressed about the rejection of my writing or the rejection of myself. And, honestly, I'm not exactly clear if it's possible to separate the two. If writing provokes such anxiety, why do I continue with it? She's right, selling my work is part of writing. Would I write for the sake of writing—like a private journal or diary—or do I need to be validated by a publishing professional? I decide it's the latter. So, does that mean I don't really love writing and I just want to be validated for something other than working in a diner and having the ability to quickly chop tomatoes and slice potatoes? Probably.

"Okay, I'm back." Bibi plops down in her chair and takes a long draw from her bottled water—sparkling. She recaps it, sets it down on the table, and belches. "Sorry. The bubbles always get to me."

"No problem," I say. It would take a lot more than one burp to repulse me.

"So, I was thinking," she says. "My mom's best friend is a publisher. Maybe I could ask her to take a look at your manuscript."

But I don't want that. I want to be accepted on my own merits.

"I wouldn't want that," I say. "I need to know I can make it on my own."

"Yeah, probably not the best idea anyway. Mixing business and friendship. Besides, I think they only publish coffee table books."

She eyes me carefully as though she sees something—a fly on my forehead, a stain on my shirt.

"What?"

"Has anyone ever told you that you look like Edgar Allen Poe?"

Only a few thousand times.

"No. Never."

"That could be a good thing," she says. "You could be the next Edgar Allen Poe—modern-day version."

"If only," I sigh. "But I don't know if the world is ready for the modern-day version of Poe." My finger finds the side button on the chair and I silently raise myself to an upright sitting position. "You've actually helped me a lot tonight," I say, although I'm not at all sure that's true. She may have actually hurt me which I'll know a few hours from now in the solitude of my apartment, with only Clementine, who is never judgmental. "You've given me some things to think about."

But are they the right things to think about or will they just lead to another rabbit hole? More thoughts to snag my existing thoughts and drag me down further.

"That's what I'm here for," Bibi says cheerfully. She glances at her watch. "At the beginning of our session you said 'other things' were bothering you too. Do you mind my asking what those other things are?"

"Nothing really. Just... on occasion... frequently... I tend to obsess about things like... my health, for instance. And accidentally killing my goldfish. Things like that." The pages and pages I've filled over the years in my worry journal would floor Bibi if she ever read them.

She glances at her watch again. "I've gotta get home before my curfew. You wanna come back and talk about it? Shall we schedule our next appointment right now?"

"Better if I call you when I have my calendar," I say, although my calendar (which consists of very little) is in my head.

I've taken a giant step by admitting what I just admitted and the only reason I was able to is because I was on my way out the door. But now they're out in the open, the "other things" feel slightly diminished as though I've just allowed a weak ray of sunlight to shine on the mildew of my mind. As if I've just released a wild boar from its trap and allowed it to run free—run away and leave me be.

But if the ray doesn't choose to linger...

I hope I have the courage to make that call. Schedule that next appointment.

CHAPTER EIGHTEEN

Angela Ruiz texted me requesting that I attend a meeting with her at Lilibeth's uncle's house—the one who lives directly across the street from the most recent victim of the Six o' Clock Slasher. Since, for obvious reasons, I can't do it during daytime hours, I arrange to meet her at 6:00 p.m. (appropriate given the circumstances). It means I'll have to call into work and let them know I can't be there until later. Calvin won't like it one bit, but he'll never fire me. He'd have to pay ten employees to do what I do on one salary.

I tell Angela I'm busy weekend days (her time off from work) because I have to help Miss Devine make her rounds. This is partially true because I do make rounds with Miss Devine when she scours the city, block by block, looking for people who need help the most and figuring out ways to get it to them. She goes mostly at night when we can find the regulars hunkered down in their regular spots. Naturally, I can't let Henrietta be out on the streets alone, especially after dark.

All this finagling and lying about why I can't be anywhere when the sun is shining makes for a rigid schedule and limited hours to work. Unfortunately, Mrs. Dilliberato has been coming around more and more frequently, disrupting the hours I need to edit my manuscript and the time I need to reflect and rejuvenate.

I opened the door for her the other day. She peered over my shoulder, probably looking for some sign of misbehavior or neglect of the premises that would further invalidate my lease, as if non-payment of rent wasn't enough.

"You think you're pretty clever, don't ya?" she said. "You think you know just enough about the law to keep one step ahead of me. Well, I've got news for you, Mister. John. Doe. I know the law too and I probably know it a lot better than you."

This is far from the truth because I have the equivalent of a law degree, although it's from a different state and about fifty years old. But the law doesn't change *that* much.

"Mrs. Dilliberato, I don't know what you're talking about," I said. "I've been making payments on good faith. It's everything I can afford right now, and I'll pay more whenever I'm able. I'm doing my best."

Why do I dislike this woman so much? She's somebody's daughter and wife and sister and friend. She's got to be *somebody's* friend. And yet...

And yet, I sense that Mrs. Dilliberato senses something in me that instinctively repels her. Perhaps her senses are keener than most. Keener than Henrietta's for example who doesn't see any of the darkness within me.

I *will* pay and have every intention of doing so. It's just that there are only so many hours in the night and of those hours there are only so many I can devote to work. Perhaps I'll ask Calvin to extend my shifts from midnight to 4:00 a.m., although there isn't as much demand for kitchen workers during those lean hours.

But the law being the law, every time Mrs. Dilliberato accepts any payment from me (no matter how small) it proves that she's extending my lease by accepting my good faith efforts to pay. And I don't know this because I think I'm pretty clever, or even that I am cleverer than Mrs. Dilliberato. I know this because I bothered to read the fine print in my lease.

***

Before I leave to meet Angela, I have to install the new mermaid I purchased online for Clementine's bowl. Her mysterious illness hasn't recurred, but I suspect that heavy metal poisoning might have been the cause, lead being the most likely culprit. Why she recovered, I can't be sure but, not wanting to take any chances, I purchased a new mermaid from a seller that claims their products contain no elements toxic to fish.

It might be simpler to have no mermaid at all, just to be on the safe side, but Clementine is attached to her mermaid and quality of life is something I can't overlook. This particular mermaid is more ornate than I'd like but I hope Clementine won't notice. The figurine is perched on a coral bed with shells and various sea creatures at her feet, as though she's a princess holding court. Her thick, muscular tail (a sparkling shade of sapphire) matches the brassiere that covers her small breasts. Her long brown hair with auburn tints swirls around her slender neck and narrow shoulders. Her tiny grey eyes gaze into the beyond. She looks like Nadia.

But she is not Nadia who, after all, was not a fish but a country girl very much of the earth. I wash the tiny figurine in the sink to make sure it's perfectly clean before placing it on top of the bed of clean crushed coral I've laid down on the bottom of Clementine's sparkling clean bowl. She swims eagerly back and forth in the glass jar, waiting to be returned to her bowl. I add the water conditioner to the water I've poured into the bowl, wait the requisite amount of time (approximately thirty minutes). Tap the back of my head five times with my knuckles. Then, just as I'm about to gently scoop Clementine out of the old water to put her back into the bowl, I experience a crisis of confidence.

Did I add the conditioner? Certainly, I did; my memory is excellent. But did I? I'm not at all sure. I know I held the bottle in my hand and shook out the required number of drops... but was that this time or am I recalling a past cleaning? After some back and forth, I decide it's just not worth the risk to Clementine's health if I'm wrong, let alone the hours of worrying that're bound to follow.

I empty the water from the bowl and begin again, this time setting my phone to self-record so I can film myself adding the conditioner to the fresh bowl of water. I won't be visible on the recorded video, but the conditioner bottle will be, as will the drops coming out of it. It's not the first time I've done this, and I don't like to give in to it since I change Clementine's water daily. On the other hand, if it gives me peace of mind, where's the harm?

Now I must wait for another thirty minutes. And Angela is waiting for me.

I'm often late for things because of my rituals and self-doubt. I'll need to travel quickly when I'm done.

The vampire way.

***

I choose to walk the last few blocks to Lilibeth's uncle's house, not wishing to startle anyone by literally popping up out of nowhere. The weather has finally shifted from autumn to winter and I felt the subtle change the exact day it happened. The exact moment. The dampness of the cold. The power of the night. A vague sense of something coming to its natural conclusion with none of the playfulness of spring, complacency of summer, or flux of fall. I welcome winter, the season when I feel closest to being alive. Tonight, it's drizzling as though a giant cloud has crumpled into a heap over the city and turned itself inside out.

"John Doe."

"John Doe."

I hadn't noticed Fernando and Peter. Using their large-wheeled scooters to gain a height advantage, one holds a flyer above his head, positioned directly on top of a utility pole, while the other staples it into place. Placed just those extra twelve or so inches higher, their flyers stand out from the myriad of others.

"What are you boys up to?" I stop to ask.

"Working," says Peter.

"We have a job," says Fernando.

I peer at the poster which provides a website address where people can sign up to advocate on behalf of rescue animals. A smart move to hire these two who can probably plaster an entire city with promotional material faster than the employer could print out flyers.

"Good for you," I say. "Making some decent money?"

"We're saving up," says Fernando.

"Hey, John Doe? You can still get us deals, right? Because we're saving up," says Peter.

A deal, I know, means free fries with an occasional burger for them to split. It's not really a deal—deal implying something that's discounted from some amount to another (lesser) amount that is greater than zero. But I let it go. Growing boys are endlessly hungry. I remember what it was like to be a small boy with a huge appetite.

"Sure thing. Well, I guess I'd better get going." I don't want to keep Angela waiting a minute longer.

"Wait John Doe," says Peter. "We'll go with you to the next pole."

"Why are you here in this neighborhood, John Doe?" asks Fernando. "Still hot on the trail of the Slasher?"

"Why would you ask that?"

It slightly annoys me that the Wheelie Boys always know what I'm doing without my ever having told them.

"That's the house right up there," says Peter.

"Where the last murder happened," says Fernando.

"Just half a block up and on the left side," says Peter.

"The white clapboard siding," says Fernando.

I keep walking with my hands shoved deep inside my pockets, my beanie pulled down so low that my eyebrows are completely covered, my wool neck-scarf wound so high it covers my chin. It's not that I'm cold—I'm cold-blooded, after all, so cold is my normal state. It's just the way I prefer to move about town—anonymously. In the winter, I can do that without attracting attention.

"I'm not going there," I say. "I'm actually going to visit someone in the house right across the street."

We've arrived at the next utility pole and Peter performs a sharp U-turn, coming to a sudden stop while Fernando glides to a slow halt, digging around inside his shoulder bag for the staple gun.

"Your girlfriend's house?" Peter asks.

"I don't have a girlfriend," I keep walking and now their voices trail behind me.

"See, I told you she wasn't his girlfriend," I hear Fernando saying, and for some reason it bothers me that he didn't at least consider that possibility.

"Bye, John Doe."

"Bye, John Doe."

I raise my arm in the air without turning and flick my hand back and forth in a farewell motion.

CHAPTER NINETEEN

Uncle Ramon opens the door. His hair is steel gray, his eyes dark brown, his skin light brown, his face spidered with wrinkles although most of them don't show up until he smiles.

Which he does.

"Come in, you must be Angela's friend."

With my hands firmly rooted in my pockets, I hope he doesn't extend his hand—he doesn't. It almost always works, although I'm sure some people find it rude. But, hey! I'm a teenager and teenagers can be that way if their parents didn't raise them right. If all else fails, I perform a slight bow which catches most people off-guard in a positive way.

Uncle Ramon probably makes a mental note: *Worse than a limp handshake, this kid has no handshake at all.*

And I make a mental note: *Be extra courteous to make Uncle Ramon forget about the handshake that never happened.*

"Yes, sir. My name's John Doe." I walk past him and enter the house.

> **FACT: When interacting with people at least twenty years older than you, using the terms "sir" or "ma'am" will normally score you points. Less than twenty years, the person will be insulted.**

I judge Uncle Ramon to be a good thirty years older than my supposed seventeen years. It works.

FACT: As corny as it sounds, yes, a vampire must be invited into a home or else they can't enter. It's a bother and a constant source of irritation. I've arrived at parties as part of a large group (many, many years ago before my panic attacks started) where everyone who wasn't vampire passed easily through the the open door without a second thought, while those of us who were vampire, stammered and shuffled our feet until the host (door-opener) would finally say something along the lines of, "Hurry up and come in. You're letting in the cold air," not realizing who it was they'd just invited into their home. If things got out of hand at a party and the host yelled, "Everyone out, party's over," one could always pick out the vampires. We were the first ones to leave. As for restaurants, movie theaters, or any other public location, these rules don't apply.

Inside the house, I hear female voices coming from the back.

"This way," Uncle Ramon says. "The girls are in the kitchen."

In the cozy, bright yellow kitchen, Angela, Lilibeth, and an older woman who I assume must be Lilibeth's aunt, are gathered around the kitchen table admiring a lifelike sketch of Angela, and sipping hot chocolate topped with marshmallows.

The older woman gets up from her chair, "Can I get you a cocoa?" she asks. "I'm Lilibeth's Aunt Elsa. She starts to extend her hand but then quickly withdraws it, probably noticing how lost in my pockets my own hands are.

"Nice to meet you, ma'am. I'm John Doe. Can I call you Aunt Elsa?"

Works like a charm.

Elsa has an extreme Nordic look—hair so blonde as to

be white, steel blue eyes, porcelain white skin colored only by high rosy spots on her sculpted cheeks. I politely decline the cocoa and remain standing, taking my lead from Uncle Ramon.

"That's... you." I point from the sketch to Angela.

"Lilibeth drew it," Angela says, the pride in her voice impossible to miss.

"Amazing," I sign. "I wish I had a talent like that." Lilibeth's natural luminosity seems to increase tenfold, gently tinted by a blush.

"The girls were just filling me in," Elsa says. "On what you all are up to, and I just hope you're being careful." She shakes her head slowly and her eyes take on a faraway look. "Such a shame about what happened to poor Myrna," she says. "What horrible monster would... well, I just hope you'll all be careful not to get in over your heads."

Oh, Aunt Elsa, if you only knew how far over my head I already am.

Lilibeth places her hand over Aunt Elsa's and signs to her. "I'm so sorry," Lilibeth says. "It must be terrible to lose a friend like that." Elsa nods her agreement.

"I can't even imagine," Angela speaks. "I really *really* appreciate you doing this for us. I know how painful it must be for you to talk about it."

"Talk about it or not," Elsa concurrently speaks aloud and signs, "what happened happened and we can't undo it through our silence, although I wish we could. So maybe what you young people are doing will help in some way... maybe you can come up with a clue for the police if you all put your heads together."

I'm not sure what Lilibeth is thinking but I'm pretty sure Angela and I are on the same page. We're not going to put any effort into thinking up clues to be passed on to the police—the same police who have botched this case for the past two years and, from what the reporters say, haven't come up with a single clue as to the killer's identity during that time. It wasn't my idea to track this killer but, once I commit to something (or someone), I try my best to follow through. I don't share Angela's dreams of glory or even hopes for success, but I do know a thing or two about the darkness that lurks in the heart of men. And for that and that alone, I can be helpful to Angela the way she was helpful to me during my most recent most vulnerable moment.

"Is everyone ready?" Uncle Ramon asks. "I can take you over there now." He holds a cluster of keys in his closed fist.

"I'm not going," Lilibeth says. Her hands move as lightly and swiftly as a swallow in flight. "This is Angela and John's thing." She shakes her head emphatically. "I can't handle this stuff."

"I'm not going either," says Aunt Elsa. "Lilibeth and I will stay here and have a good chat. It's been too long."

"Ramon and Elsa were Myrna's best friends," Angela explains. "She gave them a key to her place and, now that the police have finished their investigation, we're allowed to go in."

"We need to finish cleaning up and getting the place ready to sell," Elsa says. "We've been donating most of her things to charities. She didn't have any close family that we know of, so we inherited her cat which we don't mind at all. Beanie's such a love bug."

As if on cue, Beanie appears out of nowhere and rubs against Elsa's bare leg. Elsa reaches down to stroke the coal-black fur of his back. His yellow eyes lock onto mine from underneath the table and for a second I have to fight the urge to flee.

> **MYTH: Cats and vampires are somehow in cahoots. How exactly depends on who you listen to, but some go so far as to suggest that vampires can take the form of cats, which I can attest is far from the truth. Life would be a lot easier if I had the ability to shapeshift into a cat whenever the mood (or necessity)**

> **dictated. Still, I've never been comfortable in the presence of cats, unable to escape the feeling that somehow they're able to see right through my carefully constructed exterior to what lies beneath.**

"Well then, Angela. John. Shall we get this over with?" Ramon asks.

***

Exsanguination.

Shall we talk about it? The word itself sounds so clinical. Bloodless. If one had to imagine its meaning based solely on the sound of the word, one would most likely succeed.

Having your body drained of its blood is not a painful thing, per se, if there's no underlying traumatic cause. I can vouch for that. In my case, I went to sleep and woke up with none of my blood... or very little of it, just enough to survive in my new lifeform as a vampire. Had I been completely drained I wouldn't have survived at all, and there are days when I think that would have been for the best. Most days, however, I feel the primal urge to survive in any form, even the miserable one I now inhabit. What was left of the blood in my body after that night was a paltry mix of serum with more vampirovirus proteins than actual red blood cells.

Standing in Myrna's kitchen and listening to Uncle Ramon's narrative, I learn that Myrna wasn't so lucky, if luck is a word that could ever be associated with me.

"I found her sitting in that chair." Ramon points to one of four kitchen chairs tucked under the table. "Elsa sent me over to check on her when we hadn't seen her for a few days. She wasn't answering her phone... or the door, so I used the key she'd given us and let myself in. It was... it was..." His emotional distress prompts his facial muscles to contort horribly, as though he's on the brink of a scream that won't come. Ramon seems like a proud man. Old school. He wouldn't want two teenagers he barely knows to see him crying.

"It's okay." Angela puts a hand on his shoulder. "You don't have to stay with us if this is too hard. We can take a look around and lock up once we're done."

"No, no, no," Ramon says. "I'm okay. It's just hard thinking back on it. At first, when I saw her slumped over the table, with her head resting sideways looking opposite from me, I thought maybe she'd had a heart attack or something. I rushed over and sort of picked her up like..." Ramon mimes lifting the upper half of Myrna's body with his encircled arms. "But when her head flopped to the side, I saw it. Her neck was slashed from ear to ear. You don't forget something like that anytime soon."

Angela's shoulders squeeze together while lifting upwards. "I don't imagine you would," she says. "Pretty bloody, huh?"

Ramon closes his eyes with a half-shake of his head. "That's the thing... practically no blood at all, just a few drops on the table. Cops said the guy cleaned up after himself since there was bleach residue on the floor and table. They said he most likely killed her here in the kitchen and then carried her to the sofa over there in that room. Then, when he was ready to leave, he brought her back to the kitchen and positioned her in the chair."

"Blood on the sofa?" Angela asks.

"Again, just a drop or two."

"Any blood spatter patterns?" Angela asks, and I wonder if this is something she learned from watching *CSI*.

"I wouldn't know," Ramon says. "They didn't tell us shit other than what I just told you. Maybe you shouldn't touch anything," he adds. "Just in case they want to come back and dust for fingerprints again. They have Elsa's and mine because we've been eliminated as suspects."

I don't have fingerprints. Just like the scars resulting from smallpox filled in with dead skin cells over the years, so have my fingerprints. A useful feature if I were a criminal, which of course I'm not.

A drop or two of blood is all it takes to prick my senses, even blood that was spilled many days earlier, since cleaned up and invisible to the eye. I could extend my finger and point to the exact spot on the table where it dripped from the gaping smile on her throat before landing on the surface of the Formica table. As we make our way from room to room of the small home, the scent comes and goes—first on the sofa; then on the bed (still visible to my eye on a dark maroon bedspread which the police didn't see fit to take in for testing); another few drops in the hallway connecting the bedroom to the bathroom, cleaned with bleach but still obvious to me. This killer—the Six o' Clock Slasher—was wandering around with Myrna's body, looking for a place to sit with her in comfort. Since I can't share that knowledge with Angela, for obvious reasons, I make a mental note of my observations should they prove useful at some later date.

The only thing that doesn't make sense is the elephant in the room. Bleach or not, only a few drops of blood resulted from Myrna's death. There was never any great splash of the gallon or so one would have expected. I know this. I assume the police must know it too.

So why?

But that tangy, delicious scent of the few drops I do detect—full-bodied like a fine wine, rusty like a hickory-smoked side of beef—it makes me half-mad from hunger. I realize it's been days since I've eaten. I force my gaze away from the smooth juncture where Angela's throat intersects with her jaw, her carotid artery pulsing a beat every bit as alluring as a concerto played on a Stradivarius violin.

I'll contact Mr. X the minute I get home.

In the meantime, there's nothing else about Myrna's life as evidenced by the simple possessions she's left behind... nothing that points an arrow, directs us towards the person who robbed her of the rightful time she should have had left on Earth, just as I'd once been robbed long ago. Angela and I move slowly through the rooms the way someone would walk through a holy place and, when we're done, we exit through the front door where Ramon is waiting to lock up after us.

CHAPTER TWENTY

Angela and Lilibeth are staying overnight so I'm out in the cold, alone with my thoughts. I could travel quickly and be home in no time, but even with Clementine's company I'd still be alone with my thoughts. I decide to walk in hopes of clearing my head. What I've seen tonight has my every nerve on edge.

The receptor cells in my ear canals begin to tingle, at first pleasantly but then painfully. I'm being followed as clear as day—although day hasn't been clear to me for 300 years. I press my hands against my ears, willing the throbbing to go away but, when I remove my hands, it's still there. Throb. Danger. Throb. Danger.

Is it too much to ask for a few minutes of peace? Don't I at least deserve that?

I look around for the Wheelie Boys but they aren't anywhere in sight. Their prying and pleading for food favors would be a welcome distraction just now. Friendly faces are what I crave and there are so few. So very few.

I stop walking. Look to my left. Look to my right.

Does every day have to be a battle? Every minute of every day. Come out from the shadows, you coward! Whoever you are, what do you want from me? If you know my secret, let's get it over with. Anything is better than this... this constant threat hovering over me.

The throbbing stops.

Maybe it *was* the Wheelie Boys and they've turned onto a different street. Maybe just a random person jogging with their dog at night, someone who happened to be going in the same direction as me and has now reached their home where they're comfortably hunkered down for the night. Warm. Safe.

Myrna lived in a gentler neighborhood than mine, but it didn't save her in the end. Regardless of one's neighborhood, none of us are safe from the darkness in men's hearts which burrows into every nook and cranny of every city around the world. I've seen it. Felt it. Tasted it. It's timeless.

My city, like most, is one of contrasts. In Ramon's neighborhood, the houses are snug. Homey. Maintained. Outlined by rectangles of bright green grass. In the spring, multi-hued tulips, geraniums, and pansies line pathways connecting streets to front doors. In my neighborhood, neon signs provide the color, bleeding onto sidewalks, dark and slick with rain. My city is every city—I've been around long enough to know.

Myrna was a woman in her sixties. Shoved aside. No longer considered relevant by society. She was an unmarried, childless woman who had already reached the age of invisibility to most except to Ramon. Elsa. Beanie. Perhaps there were others. For sure there were others because a woman like Myrna would never open her door to a stranger and there was no sign of a forced entry. So, yes, it's certain there were others, but who?

People will say they care about Myrna's death by the hands of the Slasher, but they won't. Invisible people give others a coveted false sense of security.

It could never happen to me, they tell themselves. *I have people who care. I matter. I could never disappear from the face of the Earth leaving only a ripple behind.*

I understand this about the invisible. We are the sacrificial lambs. The exceptions to prove the rule. The ones who allow others to sleep at night, confident in the sanctuary of their dreams. But this, like most things, is a lie based on flawed assumptions. None of us is safe. Not even my darling Clementine.

When you've lived for 317 years, you know what it's like to be five years old. Ten years old. Twenty. Thirty. Fifty. A hundred. You know what it's like to watch children be born. Grow up. Grow old and die. You know what it's like to love someone with every fiber of your being, and then have them toss you aside like a peanut shell. Although I'm 317, I'm also 53. I'm also 250. But eternally, I'm seventeen years old with the excruciating weight of the centuries on my shoulders.

I don't fear the Slasher. No man can kill me again.

I fear what men do to each other for power or gain. I fear how people treat others for their own amusement or because of intolerance or sometimes for no reason at all.

I fear evil.

CHAPTER TWENTY-ONE

The Last Vampire

[REVISED: FIRST PERSON, PRESENT TENSE]

By John Doe

Chapter Twenty-One

Fifty-five years is a very long time but it's the time that I needed to gather my courage. Much has happened in fifty-five years and many lessons have been learned. I've learned what I will and will not do under any circumstances. I've learned how to "stay alive" and do it my way. I've learned something about the world, having traveled throughout most of the European continent. I've learned about music—Beethoven, Mozart, Vivaldi. I've read the complete works of William Shakespeare in his native language. I've studied art. Dance. Fencing. In short, I've become a cultured man.

I've also learned to love the night and fear the day. And I've learned how to be invisible in plain sight. I've certainly learned to hate but I haven't yet learned how to stop loving. Now, I hope to learn more about the supposed most powerful force on Earth...the power of love.

My face has hardened into a mask that serves me well. The pox marks of my youth have flattened, filling with decades of dead skin cells which deposit like cement in a pothole. I no longer slough off skin cells at the rate of a million a day. Nothing about me happens quickly anymore except the speed at which I can move. Even my heart rarely beats, although I know it's capable of feeling. I know this because I haven't stopped thinking about Nadia. Not even for one hour of one day.

Now I'm ready to be reunited with her.

I don't kid myself. We can never have what we once had, mainly because I'm no longer capable of the pleasures of the flesh. Not even a kiss can pass through my lips, lest I endanger my beloved in any way. But it's not the earthly pleasures I crave from Nadia. It's the connection of our souls that we once had...that I still have. I want that more than I want anything. I need it. I hope that Nadia still feels the same way, but I don't doubt she does. I have faith that Nadia's initial shock when she discovered my "infection" will have waned over the decades. She will no longer fear me. She won't look at me in that horrible way she did the last time I laid eyes on her.

In my favor, I'm still a handsome lad. Although, I'm now seventy-two years old, I look as if I'm seventeen. If one doesn't get too close. If my face powder doesn't get damp from the evening mist. If she doesn't touch my arm or my chest, trailing her fingertips along the ridges of my muscles (which no longer exist) the way she once did. I've been told I bear a striking resemblance to Ladislaus Hunyadi, a dashing Hungarian nobleman famously beheaded in the fifteenth century. Of course, my resemblance dates back to the time when he was full of life and still in possession of his head.

I have no illusions when it comes to Nadia's youth and beauty. At seventy-two, I know time will have taken its toll. After all, Nadia is not a vampire—not that I'm aware of—and physical beauty is fleeting and inconsequential. I'm prepared for her new appearance and, in fact, have plotted it in my mind. Drawn it on paper. I will remain unphased by the changes that time has wrought.

As for my father, I can only hope he's dead. He would be well into his nineties by now so the chance of his survival is almost nil. I can't allow myself to think that of Nadia. I would have known if she'd died. Would have felt it in the chambers of my puckered heart.

For fifty-five years, I've made myself a better man—a

man any woman (Nadia) should be proud to call her husband. I've worked hard, mostly at taverns serving the inebriated and the weary, robbers and gentlemen alike. Working every hour of every night until the last patron lays his head upon a splintered table sticky with stale brew. I've saved every coin I ever earned, taking my meals from barmaids once they retired to their quarters at night—never supping long enough to transmit the vampirovirus, leaving them only with two annoying itchy bumps which they would take for a midnight spider come to feast when they were sleeping.

For months I've been preparing. I had waistcoat and breeches made to my exact measurements. Silk stockings and leather shoes with buckles too. I've even purchased a cocked hat and, although I couldn't see my reflection in the mirror, the tailor assured me that I cut a very fine figure.

Only a horse was missing for my transportation, and with the last of my five decades of savings, I bought the finest horse (although somewhat advanced in years) that I could afford. Although he's old, the dazzling whiteness of his hide shows off my clothing to its best advantage. I'm certain to make a grand impression on Nadia. I can feel it in the tiny cavities of my porous bones.

***

When I ride into the village, it's as though nothing has changed. Fifty-five years melts away and it seems only yesterday I fled this hamlet of my youth. Memories of my poor mother come flooding back—she did her best with me and how was she to know that her best wouldn't be good enough for either of us. I glance at the crest of the mountain looming over the forest. The palace is visible through the low-hanging clouds and I sense Istvan's presence just as though his sour breath has filled my nostrils.

Zoltan is back!

I want to shout it out so loud that everyone in the village will look through their windows, open their doors and step outside to identify the man behind the booming voice.

Zoltan is back and he will prevail!

I pause to review my edited manuscript, lingering on the following sentence:

The pox marks of my youth have flattened, filling with decades of dead skin cells which deposit like cement in a pothole.

My memory is excellent, in fact I have total recall, so it distresses me to realize I can't be sure if I ever saw actual cement before the early nineteenth century. I'll have to check on that... what with agents looking for the slightest excuse to reject my "novel." And should I ever be so lucky as to get a publishing deal and it should slip past the sharp eye of an editor, an observant reader is bound to discover the inaccuracy and rate my book down for this one seemingly innocuous detail.

But I make no such announcement as my confidence wanes during my ride through the narrow dirt streets of the village. I suddenly wish I could lose my expensive clothing and blend in with the villagers who have all come out to gawk at me as my horse plods along towards the modest cottage where I lived as a boy. The horse would have been enough. I shouldn't have splurged on the clothes.

"Can anyone tell me where I can find Nadia Farkas?" I call out but I'm only met with blank stares. "A pinch of tobacco to anyone with information of her whereabouts."

Tobacco isn't commonly found in villages around these parts, being difficult to access, expensive to purchase, and somewhat regulated, but I bought a small pouch just for situations like this.

A small boy steps forward from the crowd that's gathered.

"Please, fine sir. There's a Nadia in the village, but she doesn't go by the name of Farkas. She's very old."

I have no doubt it's my Nadia, so I toss the tiny pouch to the child who runs off after directing me to the location of my boyhood home, on the outskirts of the village, past the meadow, nearly to the threshold of the forest. Did my father will his property to Nadia to reward her for a lifetime of service, having no other heirs except me who he never expected to see again? The sweet irony of living in my father's home with my beloved Nadia, my father now nothing more than food for worms. But the closer I get, the more nervous I am. Why should Nadia have a new name? Is it possible she hasn't been waiting for me and has married someone else?

Every drop of moisture in my mouth (which is little to begin with) seems to have traveled to my hands which feel slick with sweat against the leather of my reins. Sweat is a phenomenon I haven't experienced in fifty-five years, and yet here it is again, like an old friend. My breath comes fast and shallow, nearly impossible to catch, and though I need very little breath to exist, I can't summon even the small amount my body requires. A dark tunnel forms in front of me, narrowing my vision, as though I were looking through the wrong end of a telescope. Like a felled tree, I feel myself begin to topple from my horse's back.

As if my horse senses this, he slows to a halt allowing me to regain my balance by leaning forward and laying my cheek against his neck. I'm grateful for the warmth of his quivering flesh that reminds me what it means to be alive. His earthy scent. The rough bristle of his mane. After a few minutes I start to feel myself again. I'm so thankful to this animal that I drape my arms around his neck, embracing him while murmuring my appreciation. When I sit up in my saddle, a whoosh of vertigo overtakes me but after a brief time, this too is gone.

The familiar dense fog of terror has lifted and only then do I notice a woman standing by the side of the road. She's older and dressed in a drab garment, caked with mud at its hem which hides her shoes. Her hair is tied back in a kerchief but the strands that have escaped are silver and glint under the stars which are just beginning to emerge. Her face is etched deeply with lines carved from the weather over many decades. In her arms, she holds a small child propped on her generous hip. Another, more grown child stands nearby, his hand entwined in the folds of her dress. She doesn't say a word, simply stares at me as though drinking in my appearance and struggling to recollect a misplaced item but not remembering exactly what it was.

It's Nadia.

My lovely Nadia upon whom the sun still prefers to shine above all others, whom the moon chooses as the focal point for its orbit.

I need her to say my name. I can't be the first one to speak.

The child in her arms whimpers and then begins to cry. The child at her feet enfolds himself in her skirts until only one small hand is visible. Children instinctively recognize danger, and with a heavy heart, I realize the danger is me.

"Zoltan," she says at last. Her voice has been changed by age but underneath the years, I still hear the girl with whom I once lay, the moonlight awash over our nubile bodies. "Is that you?"

If I could cry, I would. I feel the familiar sting in my eyes, but my body is a desert now and I can no longer get the physical relief that crying provides when one's emotions are too much for the mind to clear on its own.

"It's me," I say. I know I should dismount and walk to her and take her in my arms at this very moment. But the children prevent me from moving. Who are these children? By the looks of them they're far too young to be Nadia's. And Nadia has given no indication she still desires me. She seems more pleased to have solved the puzzle of me than to be gifted with the presence of me.

"I knew you'd return," she says, "one day. Often, I said to your father, 'Bela, Zoltan will come back and we'll see him one more time before we die.'"

My heart sinks. Is Bela still alive? Is he here to ruin what I've been planning for fifty-five years?

"My father?"

Her breast which has grown more ample over the years, heaves from a sorrowful sigh. "Gone these past twenty years," she says.

Do I breathe a sigh of relief? I most certainly do.

"And the children?" I motion to the tot who has come out from behind Nadia's skirt to peek shyly at me.

"My grandchildren," she says, her expression turning thoughtful. "But what am I saying? Your niece and nephew!"

My heart falls off a cliff.

Nadia goes on as if she had just shared a lovely secret. "Your brother…my son…these two are his youngest children. Won't you come home? I have supper in the oven, and you look like you could stand to eat."

Has she forgotten what I am or is she just in denial? I decide the time isn't right to force the question.

"I've just eaten," I say. "But I suppose I can stop by for a few minutes before getting on my way."

"On your way?" Nadia seems surprised. "On your way where? You've come all this way to see me, no? So, stay and talk a bit for old times' sake. It's been…" Her brow furrows in concentration as if she's adding up the years in her head.

"Fifty-five years."

"Fifty-five years, is it?" she asks, not quite as shocked as I would have imagined she'd be upon hearing this very large number. I suppose the years have flown by for her. I suppose she hasn't thought of me once in all that time, busy as it seems she's been with grandchildren and children sired by…my father! "Then surely you can spare fifty-five minutes for an old lady."

I dismount from my trusty horse and take his reins to lead him while I walk beside Nadia down the dirt road towards my boyhood home. The young boy scampers ahead, constantly looking back over his shoulder at this unexpected stranger who has come to represent excitement more than danger. The baby is apparently capable of walking as well. She wriggles her way out of Nadia's arms and toddles off after her brother. This isn't the homecoming I had imagined; in fact, it is not homecoming at all. I find I have no words to say.

"The last time I saw you," Nadia says. "I feel I could have been kinder. I…I…Are you the same?" she asks. "Have you been…cured?"

"There is no cure," I say perhaps a bit brusquely. How naïve is this woman? Her questions cut me twice. Does she think my life a joke—that I disappeared for fifty-five years during which time I existed in a state of suspended animation only to return miraculously cured, but not a day past seventeen? All the while, she and my dear father were having

children and grandchildren? Living real lives.

"But it hasn't been too bad?" she says more than asks. "I mean, look at you. Look at me. I'm an old lady and you're still a young man. There's been more good than bad to it, I imagine."

She can't bring herself to say that word...vampire. She can't bring herself to comprehend the reality of my miserable existence. She probably couldn't live another day if she really understood all that I've lost. All that I've never been able to gain. How could I have loved this woman? How did I ever imagine there was beauty underneath her surface that matched the loveliness of her face?

"Truthfully, Nadia, there's been no good to it at all. Quite the opposite."

Our footsteps raise small clouds of dust as we make our way down the road. In the distance, I can see the home where I was raised. I think back on a day, long ago, when a stranger stopped by for a drink of water and left us with the pox, changing our lives forever in the worst possible way. I want to strike out at Nadia and hurt her as much as she's hurt me. But there's only one way I could do that and, although I actually consider it for a moment, I just can't.

I just can't.

I'm not that kind of monster.

As if she can read my thoughts, Nadia turns to regard me and, on her face, I see a sudden sharpening of her dull features. An understanding focuses her eyes. "You haven't..." she says, "come to do me or my family any harm, have you?"

Her question disgusts me but since the thought briefly crossed my mind, I let it go and answer with questions of my own. "How could you, Nadia? My father? How did you go from being my very own beloved to...to..." I place my hand on the velvet soft nose of my horse to ground me. The short hot pulses of his breath reassure that at least this one living creature doesn't instinctively recoil from my presence.

"Your father was a good man," Nadia says. "He provided for me and never beat me and never expected anything from me beyond just gratitude. I never loved him—not the way I loved you. But what was I to do? You were taken

from me overnight. We had no future anymore. I had no family to turn to. He was a kind man."

A pressure boils within me that seems impossible to contain. "He was a monster!" The very words themselves wound me. Scrape the sides of my throat. "A monster…and this is the man you willingly chose to share your life? Your bed?"

We've arrived at the cottage which has been expanded since I lived there. More rooms built on for children and grandchildren. Built by my father when he was alive, I suppose, or perhaps by the brother I'll never know. Suddenly, knowing what went on there, I can't bear the thought of entering. The children run inside, their happy laughter swallowed up by the walls. My horse stands between Nadia and me, a welcome barrier for both of us, I'm sure.

"Zoltan, look at you," she says. "This hasn't been all bad. You're still young. You're rich. All of you…money is never a problem for your kind."

"My kind?"

"Lord Istvan…he has money and power that very few possess. It's obvious from your clothes, your horse…you've also done very well for yourself."

I don't tell her how much this has cost me. Fifty-five years of scrimping and saving. My only revenge is the illusion of living well so I cling to the lie through my silence.

"He asks about you, you know," Nadia says. "Lord Istvan. He thinks of you fondly even after all these years. He would be very happy to see you again."

"I'd sooner drive a spike through my heart than see the devil again. Has he been making your life comfortable, is that it? Do you send your own children to him? Your grandchildren?"

Nadia's face reddens with the first true emotion I've seen on her face in fifty-five years. "Of course not! I would never. He's never asked and…anyway, you went to him of your own accord."

"Liar!" My horse, sensing my psychic calamity, rears his head up, nearly pulling the reins from my grip. "Bela sold me to Istvan for financial gain and to steal a young bride for

himself. The only good news I've received today is of Bela's death...a man I consider lower than the swine who feast on your feces and garbage."

"Zoltan! Don't speak of your father like that." A taste of the mother she's become. "I remember it that way," she says more softly. "I remember your willingly going to stay with Lord Istvan and when you returned...you were changed."

"You're a stupid old woman," I say. The hard lump in my throat has gravitated to my heart. What was I thinking by coming here? How foolish were my hopes and dreams? "And if you remember it that way, then I'll never have anything more to say to you nor you to me."

And on this day, this minute, this second, I stop believing in love.

And on that day... that minute... that second... I stopped believing in love.

CHAPTER TWENTY-TWO

I'M HUNGRY. SO HUNGRY.

I'm so hungry I can think of nothing else.

I'm so hungry my head throbs and my body is failing.

I'm so hungry I can't hear anything anyone says above the deafening roar of their blood rushing through their carotid arteries.

I don't know how much longer I can keep going.

I fear I may be dying.

***

Mr. X is sick, down with the flu.

Mr. X has never been sick before, and I fear he may be dying.

If Mr. X dies, then I shall surely die or return to my old ways.

I'd rather die.

***

Mrs. Dilliberato pounds on my door.

"Mr. Doe, I know you're in there."

"Mr. Doe, I haven't received this week's payment."

The jangling of her keys is like a steel spike through my brain.

***

Mr. Dilliberato comes to my door.

"Doe? Fred Dilliberato here. The wife tells me you're late on your installment payments. We know you're in there, buddy."

***

Miss Henrietta Devine knocks on my door.

"Johnny, is everything okay? I'm worried about you, honey."

"I'm fine," I say weakly, my voice further diminished by having to travel through the interior microphone to the external speaker of my coffin where I've been staying for the most part in order to conserve my energy. "Just a touch of the flu."

***

I skipped my last criminology class.

I haven't worked for four days.

I haven't answered Angela's texts in three days.

I haven't changed Clementine's water for two days.

I fear I may not last another day.

I fear if I let myself out of this apartment, I may attack the first person with whom I come into contact and heaven help me if it's Henrietta Devine.

***

I'm so hungry I'm prepared to trap the roof rat that runs along the ledge outside of my window.

I prepare to trap the roof rat that runs along the ledge outside of my window, consequences be damned.

Hantavirus, plague, salmonella, tularemia, and leptospirosis can't be any worse than death by starvation.

***

Hunger is a terrible thing—an evil like no other.

I'm being punished for my sin. The sin of being me. The sin of still taking a breath. The sin of still being alive.

***

I haven't worked for five days.

I haven't answered Angela's texts in four days.

I haven't changed Clementine's water for three days.

I haven't come out of my coffin in two days.

I fear Clementine is dead by now.

***

My phone battery is at four percent when the text finally comes in. Mr. X is feeling better and has returned to work. Mr. X will meet me at a location only five minutes from my apartment in... ten minutes. Can I be there?

Can a spider spin a web?

Can a hen lay an egg?

Can a...

I can be there.

***

I emerge from my coffin, sore in all places after so many hours of lying in one position. I have to hold on to the chair as I unfurl my arms and legs, being so weak as to find it impossible to stand without support. The few drops of what passes for blood in me whoosh out of my head and pool inside my feet and, for a moment, I feel as though I'm going to lose consciousness.

It's nighttime, thank God.

Clementine is alive and frisky. I toss more flakes into her bowl than are good for her with no time to waste on careful measurements.

"You're the only pure thing in my life," I tell her. "I don't deserve you and you don't deserve everything I put you through."

I open my door so quietly as to not make a sound. I creep down the stairs, avoiding the parts of the hallway I know from experience will creak under my weight. Outside, the air is so cold and dry that it burns and slaps at my face. I step carefully over the sleeping lady and her sleeping dog, using every bit of self-control I possess in order not to look at them. The dog wakens; I hear him whine and a puff of steam rises from his warm mouth before dissipating into the night.

I cannot look.

Food... sustenance... the red stuff... blood... is only minutes away.

I travel fast, the vampire way, although not nearly as fast as I'm normally capable of.

I arrive seconds before Mr. X.

I've left so quickly I forgot to bring money but I daren't miss him by returning home to get it.

Mr. X emerges, as always, like a magic trick, materializing out of the darkness, forming before my eyes.

"Sorry," he says. "It was a bad one. I haven't been that sick in years."

He holds two vials out towards me, and I greedily snatch them from his steady hand.

I turn my back to him and send the contents of the vials careening down my gullet in rapid succession. I wipe my lips and chin with the back of my hand and then turn around to face Mr. X, who has a look of pure disgust on his face.

"Get a flu shot next year," I say, already feeling my meager resources mobilizing. I burp quietly.

"Got one, man. They don't always work, you know."

He squints his face and angles it away from the lingering smell of my belch.

"I forgot to bring my wallet," I say. "Can I still take the rest?"

He hands over the bag and it's heavier than usual. He's brought me extra.

"Sure, I'll put it on your tab. I know you're good for it."

And I am. Good for it. I'm so darn grateful to this man and so happy, and for this moment I'm on top of the world. But then I think about Clementine and how she must be suffering from the fish food dump and three days without a water change. I think about the roof rat and how I had to force my gaze away from the old woman and her dog who sleep under the alcove in front of my apartment building. And worst of all, I question what I would have done had

Mr. X not come through for me and had I opened the door to Miss Henrietta Devine.

I could never.

I would never.

I don't think.

I need to get a back-up source in case something else happens to Mr. X.

> **MYTH: Vampires can exist on the blood of any mammal. Well yeah, and people could survive from eating banana slugs, but do they choose to do it? No. And, if they did, would banana slug meat provide all the nutrients a person requires? Again, no. And are there species-jumping viruses that leap from animal to human causing such catastrophic events as the Spanish Flu of 1918? Without a doubt. And are there times in one's life when a choice must be made but no available option seems acceptable?**

Enough said.

CHAPTER TWENTY-THREE

THE MORE TIME I spend around Molly, the less I see in her of Nadia. Initially, I compared her unfavorably to Nadia. Now I compare Nadia unfavorably to Molly. I know comparisons aren't fair, that we each have unique qualities forged through unique life experiences, but I can't help myself—they look so much alike.

Molly is what Calvin calls "good people." She came in as the new girl and never thought herself better than me or the busboys or dishwashers or anyone else lower in our restaurant's hierarchy. She never gossips. She works harder than anyone except me and, in fairness, I don't really work hard although I accomplish a great deal. She always comes to work in a good mood although I know that she, like anyone else, must have her bad days—but she doesn't let on at work when she does.

Molly is what I would call "good people" if Calvin hadn't beat me to it. If it didn't already exist, I would have invented the term for people like Molly. And Henrietta Devine.

Tonight, Molly plops down on the chair next to mine where I've escaped for a five-minute break.

"Phew," she says. "Tough crowd tonight. I need a breather."

I'm taking a breather myself, so I simply smile in response. Molly and I don't need to fill the silent spaces, but I do wonder if she's given any thought to my new look. Perhaps she's forgotten.

"You look deep in thought," she says.

I am.

"Do I?" I ask with a dismissive chuckle. "I guess I'm just tired."

Not true. I'm never tired.

I lean back in my chair, my legs stretched out in front of me, eyes closed. My knees have been particularly painful tonight, throbbing and swollen. My thoughts, as usual, consume me. I tap my right heel against the ground five times. I repeat this with my left heel.

"What're you thinking?" Molly's voice is like a knock on the door of my solitude. *Is anyone home?* Since she usually leaves me alone when I'm in a quiet mood, I know she must be more mentally than physically tired and probably in need of semi-intelligent conversation that doesn't have to do with hamburgers or shakes.

I need the opposite.

But Molly's good people so it's hard to deny her distraction in the form of semi-intelligent conversation. I open my eyes and look at her.

"Oh, I don't know. Nothing really," I say.

"Your book?" she asks, and I'm pleased to have her ask about my book. Pleased that she remembers it.

But I'm not thinking about my book right now, al though it would have been easy enough to answer in the affirmative. But if I tell Molly I'm thinking about my book, that could lead to questions about my book. Questions about the genre, characters, where it is in the publishing process (nowhere), what it's like to write a book (frustrating to the extreme). Questions I don't feel like answering at the moment. Or ever.

"Actually..." I draw out the word long enough to think through my answer. Truth or fiction? Does it matter to Molly? No, she's simply looking for a brief chat to clear her mind before going back to face the cantankerous carnivores. Truth, I decide. "My fish," I say. "I was just thinking about my fish."

"You have a fish?" Her eyes brighten and suddenly our

conversation is no longer mindless distraction, it's meaningful distraction. "Me too."

"A fish? You have a fish too?"

"Yes, actually I have three fish. A blue tang. A yellow tang. And a clown fish." She's turned her body to face me. Her eyes sparkle with interest, and sparkling eyes are a rarity at work.

"Ohhh, you have a saltwater aquarium." I'm jealous, although I love Clementine with all my heart and soul.

I know from past experience a saltwater aquarium requires expertise I will never possess. I tried once... operating one. My anxiety levels went through the roof. What with the constant testing of pH levels, nitrites, nitrates, ammonia, salinity. And the inevitable fish deaths that will come in spite of all that testing. The hours, days, months of guilt, wondering where you went wrong and which test you overlooked that could have prevented the needless suffering culminating in death. Which chemical you could have added that might have made a difference. I tried it once but will never try it again.

Clementine's care is easy by comparison but even that occupies most of my thoughts during most days.

"Yeah. Just a small one," Molly says, "a fifteen-gallon. I'm saving up for a forty-gallon and maybe some live coral and invertebrates."

Live coral and invertebrates are an even bigger challenge. "That's impressive," I say. "I tried once... a saltwater aquarium but it was too much... way too much. But they're beautiful. I envy you that you're able to maintain one."

"It's not too hard," Molly says. "Once you get the hang of it. You should come by and see it sometime."

The truth is I'd love to, but I also wouldn't love to.

"I'd love to."

"Tonight after work, then. You should come by."

I'd planned on editing my manuscript tonight, and I've been longing for my coffin all night... the dark calm it brings, the smooth, cool silk lining, retracting my limbs for a while to give my knees and elbows a much-needed rest. My meditation. My soothing mantra which seems all the more precious because of my promise not to disclose it to others. My incisors are growing back long enough to be seen when I smile (which I've avoided doing for the past few days). It's true they're needle thin but someone with sharp enough vision could see them if they stared into my mouth long enough... or so I believe. I'd been planning to do a bit of fang-filing tonight after work which requires intense concentration in order to avoid filing into the pulp of the tooth where the nerve-endings are.

"I have to deliver dinner to my neighbor. I usually take a doggy-bag home from work for her," I say. "She's older." This sounds like a good excuse and nothing about it is a lie, but Henrietta has as much energy as someone half her age.

"Then, just come by for ten minutes," Molly says. "Not everyone appreciates the work it takes to run a saltwater aquarium."

It's obvious this is Molly's passion and she wants to share it with me, a fellow fish enthusiast. How can I deny her? I don't.

"Sure, I'll stop by for a few minutes."

"What kind of fish do *you* have?" she asks "Zebra danio? Tetras?" She names off some of the more popular freshwater fish species that require a tank, a light fixture, and more work than I'm comfortable with.

"I have a goldfish," I interrupt. "Her name's Clementine. She lives in a... bowl."

"Hello?" Calvin's voice reverberates to the back corner where we've been trying to make ourselves invisible. "Enough with the yak-yak. Time to get back to work you two lovebirds."

"Aww, cute. I love the name Clementine." Molly ignores Calvin's insensitive jab. "And so sweet you're thinking about her at work."

If she only knew.

"Well, back to work," I say.

"Back to work. But I gotta feed my babies first."

Molly's babies are stray cats that come to the back of the restaurant. First it was cat (singular). Now it's cats—many of them. She sets out two dishes each night: one filled with water, the other filled with discarded meat from the uneaten servings of hamburger (the sauces carefully scraped away by Molly).

"Your babies have become a gang," I say only half-jokingly. Cats don't much like me, never have.

"Hey," Molly says. "You feed your strays and I feed mine."

I know she's referring to Peter and Fernando. At one time I might have argued that humans have more value than animals, but I'd never argue that now.

"First thing tomorrow, I'm calling the pound to come pick up those mangy animals," Calvin grumbles as Molly walks by with the freshly cleaned water dish.

"Calvin, you do, and I swear to God I'll quit."

That shuts him up. Calvin would never do anything to risk losing Molly.

"Let them get used to me and I promise, when I get them to trust me, I'll take them one at a time to get spayed or neutered," Molly says.

***

Molly's tank is small but impressive, just like her spiffy studio apartment, the walls of which are decorated with pastel prints of impressionist art. A snake plant stands at attention in the corner near a tiny round oak table and matching chair which, I suppose, is where Molly eats. Behind the table, the wall has been painted a warm peachy color. The long tendrils of a bright green fern cascade over the side of a lone chest of drawers, old but nicely refinished. A stack of books is neatly piled on the floor near her bed which is snugly covered by a cheery floral bedspread, the colors of which somehow make sense out of everything else in the room. A brightly woven rag-rug covers most of the floor, providing warmth and hominess. Molly has a gift. Molly can create beauty.

She's excited about our common bond and love for the Animalia Chordata Vertebrata (fish). I admire the inhabitants of her tank—there's much to admire. The layout of her rocks has been done with an artistic flourish. The crushed coral which lines the bottom of her tank is pristine white.

"They bring me so much peace of mind," she says. "I can stare at them for hours."

For me, it's the companionship. Definitely not the peace of mind.

"I've taken a few classes in ichthyology," I say. "Once thought of pursuing it as a career."

Did I not mention my equivalent degree in ichthyology? Hasn't done me a lick of good when it comes to my anxiety over Clementine. "It's nothing," I humble brag. "Just a few classes here and there. Four semesters actually. Advanced. Graduate level."

"Wow, very cool." Molly turns to look at me. "You know, John, when you told me about Clementine and how attached you are to her, I knew you were special. My mom always says that angels watch over people who love animals."

Am I over-reacting to the way she just looked at me with admiration? Projecting that look onto Nadia's face—the long overdue appreciation I still seek out in my dreams?

"Could I ask you a huge favor?" Molly blurts out. "I mean… I hate to…"

"What? You can always ask anything."

"Could you… would you mind… I have vacation time in two weeks and I'm going to visit my mom in Minnesota for a few days. That's the bad thing about a saltwater aquarium."

"You want me to feed your fish while you're gone."

"Would you mind? I mean, I know it's a huge favor to ask but you'd only have to come maybe three times—four max—while I'm gone. It's hard to find someone I trust with my babies."

I get that one hundred percent. Two hundred percent, as Detective Onslot would say. It's the source of my biggest anxiety and the reason I never go anywhere. Sometimes, even when I'm gone for just half a day, I take Clementine to Henrietta's. Thank goodness for Henrietta.

"No problem," I say. "Glad to do it."

"I can reciprocate anytime. If you ever need to go anywhere you can bring Clementine over here."

I don't tell her that Henrietta takes care of Clementine when needed because people like to feel they can pay you back for a favor even if they never will. They like to feel at least the option is there. An unspoken obligation.

"That'd be great. But I'm glad to do it, anyway."

Molly shows me where she keeps the food (frozen brine shrimp in her freezer). Explains that the light goes on and off automatically. And gives me her contact info in case any problems arise while she's gone.

I know I'm setting myself up for a week of intense worrying. If something happens to any one of these fine fellows while Molly's away, I couldn't bear it. But the tank is so well set up and a few days isn't a very long time. She said, three, maybe four visits—I know I'll be here every night at least twice checking on them. Probably three times, if I'm being completely honest.

"Oh, and John? I've been thinking about a new look for you and I think I got a good one. Johnny Depp."

Johnny Depp? But he's so old, well into his fifties by now. Does Molly think I look old? If she does, it's definitely time for an upgrade. I'm only seventeen, damn it!

"Isn't he kind of old?" Okay, maybe I'm fishing for a compliment.

"Oh, yeah, definitely. I mean like Johnny Depp from *21 Jump Street* days… let me show you some stuff I put on

Pinterest. I made a mood board for you."

I'm honored to have a mood board made for me although I have no idea what a mood board is. I'm also relieved she doesn't think I look old. My stage makeup adds a few years but what choice do I have? Maybe it's time to switch to a new mineral-based powder foundation. I've been giving it some thought but worry about its staying power.

Molly's thumb glides across the face of her phone until she's arrived where she wants to be, at which point, she swivels the phone so I can view the various images she's compiled.

I have to admit… I like it.

"Even the clothes could work," she says. "It's all coming back or if it isn't, it will be soon, and you can be cutting edge."

I like the idea of being cutting edge, so I nod and smile mirthfully.

"I can cut your hair for you and show you how to style it," she says. "I cut my own hair. All you have to do is wash all that gunk out of it sometime and come over. What's your natural color?"

She wasn't fooled by my dye job? And… gunk?

"Red," I say, but when I see the look of disappointment on her face, I add, "ish. Reddish."

"That could work," she says, and I see the wheels turning as she eyes my profile. "Reddish could work. Maybe auburn would work a little better. Has anyone ever told you that you kind of look like Johnny Depp?"

"No," I lie. "Never."

***

I take the fast way home because I need to deliver Miss Devine's dinner and there are only two things worse than a cold burger: cold fries and a melted shake.

CHAPTER TWENTY-FOUR

Onslot stops mid-sentence when I walk in five minutes late. "Mr. Doe. So glad you can join us!" Onslot's wearing a Tabasco sauce holster. An obvious case of *if you can't beat 'em, join 'em.*

"I'm coming straight from work," I say, perhaps a bit too defensively. I missed the last class due to my unfortunate externally imposed hunger strike. The class before, I left in the middle of a panic attack. I already have an unwanted spotlight on me, and I don't need Onslot to focus it even more intensely.

And besides... I pay to attend this class, which means if I want to walk in five minutes before class ends, it's my prerogative. Or to not attend at all.

"And besides—" It's good that my confidence is back. That I'm willing to go toe to toe with a bully like Onslot.

"Yeah, yeah, yeah... take a seat," he interrupts.

Angela leans across the aisle to pat the top of my desk as though I need coaxing to sit down. She smiles and points to a notebook where she's been writing. "Thoughts," she whispers. "About our first crime scene visit."

I've been having thoughts ever since we visited poor Myrna's home. Plenty of thoughts. I wonder what kind of thoughts Angela's been having.

"So, as I was saying." Onslot takes a seat behind his desk and removes what looks to be a giant burrito from a paper bag. He peels back the end paper as though peeling a banana and takes a lunging bite, like a python swallowing the head of a lamb. "T'night, yer gonna pair up 'n work on yer group projeck." His enunciation is dulled by a mouth clogged with burrito.

A collective groan floats up from the student body.

"When are we going to learn things?" Gus—the guy who sits right in front of me—asks. He's older than the rest of us, except for me, of course. He looks like the kind of guy who works at a job where nobody knows his name, someone considering a late-in-life career change. Something more rewarding, he probably imagines. Something more glamorous. I peg him for a guy with a wife and three kids at home right now, cheering him on. Kids who'll soon be requiring college tuition payments.

"Things?" Onslot works his jaw first on the right, then on the left, and after what seems like a full minute he swallows. I swear I can see that lamb-shape move down the python's gullet. "What kind of things you think you're going to learn here?"

"Like forensics... fingerprinting... blood spatter patterns... you know?"

"Yeah, I do know, and don't you forget it. I'm the one who knows and, when the time's right, I'll know that too. Remember. Me teacher. You student." He takes another huge bite off the end of his burrito.

Gus' ears turn bright red and he doesn't come back with a retort. It surprises me, actually. I'd have guessed he was the kind of guy who could stand up to Onslot but so far that seems to only be Angela, and Angela is deep into her notes, her pen tap-tapping out a Morse code message on her desk. I wonder if she's aware of what she's saying in code... probably not. I'd tell her but it ceases to make any sense after the words "sugar" and "fire," which are just the results of random tapping, like a monkey that can type out a novel if you give it a typewriter and enough time. I learned the code from Samuel Morse, himself, five years before his death in 1872, but that's another story for another time.

"But Gus is posing a valid question," I say, not quite sure where my bravery is coming from except out of pure spite. "We're supposed to be trained detectives within two months and, so far, we haven't learned much."

Gus turns around and smiles at me. I have to admit I wouldn't have challenged Onslot if Angela wasn't sitting mere feet away, even if she's not paying attention to this mutiny. A low murmur of agreement spreads among the other students.

"Did anyone ask for your opinion, Doe?" Onslot says. "I suppose you're going to sit there and tell me you haven't learned about partners and the importance of having your partner's back?"

"Well, yeah, but..."

"But, but, but. If ifs and buts were candy and nuts we'd all have a... have a... damn it! If wishes and buts were candy and nuts we'd all have a... *Merry Christmas*, that's it! Merry Christmas, Doe! Anyways, we'll learn all that stuff in due time. In the meanwhile, there's plenty of work for you to do, and I've got some work I need to get to tonight... court date tomorrow, you know."

This man is seriously mental. Candy and nuts! Merry Christmas? I scoot my chair over to Angela's desk and she finally looks up from her notebook.

"Hey! What's up?" she says.

"What's up? We practically just entered another dimension. You missed an entire alternate universe playing out courtesy of the twisted mind of Detective Onslot."

"I did? Darn. What happened?"

"He... ah, never mind. It's not worth repeating." As quickly as the fire flamed, it fizzled. Burning brain cells on Onslot is a waste.

"Oh well, it couldn't have been worse than last class when we had to watch *The Maltese Falcon*, which would have been fine if Onslot hadn't paused it every ten seconds to say, 'Now, that's how a real detective does it!'"

"I'll bet he goes home and play acts at being Sam

Spade," I say. "In fact, that's probably exactly what got him into trouble."

"Right? Then he'd rewind if anyone so much as whispered, just in case we happened to miss one precious second of the film."

"No wonder Gus is upset," I say. "It's insane that no one's dropped out of class yet. We're literally learning nothing. It's incredible none of us have demanded our money back. Or reported him to the Better Business Bureau."

"Shhh..." Angela bunches her eyebrows together. "He's looking."

"He's always looking at me," I say, perhaps a bit louder than I should. Perhaps loud enough for him to hear me even though he's thumbing through a thick stack of papers.

He sets the pile of papers down on his podium and his stubby fingers attach to the bottle of Tabasco sauce, which he mindlessly spins within its holster. For a moment I have a twinge of sympathy for him. He's a severely flawed man, but who am I to judge flawed men?

Even Gus is now engaged in serious work of some sort with his partner, a skinny little guy who couldn't weigh more than a hundred pounds on a good day. They make for an odd-looking pair but so do Angela and I.

"By the way," I say, "I did some internet sleuthing and apparently the good detective was let go when his partner turned him in for taking cash payments for protection money from shop owners in his district. So, this romantic notion of Onslot as some kind of a renegade hero fighting against the corrupt establishment is just pure BS."

"I know that, Doe." The corners of Angela's eyes lift impishly which, for some reason, makes me want to laugh out loud.

"You know?"

"Sure."

"How do you know?"

"You think you're the only one who can use a computer?"

So, Angela keeps secrets from me even while telling me that partners have to be completely open and honest with each other.

"No, but... you didn't say anything to me." I lower my head and a strand of hair falls across my forehead, the glue-like pomade holding it together in a thick clump. I push it back on my head and press it into place.

"I didn't want to burst your bubble," Angela says. "And by the way, I like your new nail polish color."

Today, I've painted my nails Gilded Gold, another color from Miss Devine's collection.

"I never had a bubble, so you couldn't burst it. No bubble existed. Therefore—"

"Okay, Doe. I just didn't want us to get distracted from our real objective. Onslot's a fraud, we both know it, but what do you expect for fifty bucks? He might have some useful information somewhere down the line. Anyway, he's innocent until proven guilty last I checked."

"Which means tomorrow," I say. "His court date is tomorrow. Then he'll be guilty."

"Or so you think."

"The evidence looks pretty compelling. Witnesses have come forward."

"Okay, so he's probably guilty. But if we get something out of this class that helps us catch more bad guys then isn't it all worth it?"

"By more, you mean other than Onslot?"

"Okay, yeah, have it your way. Isn't it still worth it?"

"But what have we gotten out of this class so far other than a diminished ego and maybe an appreciation for mid-twentieth century detective movies?"

The diminished ego, I know, is all about me. Angela's hasn't suffered at all.

"We've got each other, don't we?" Angela says, and her voice is so sincere I can't question it. "We're partners and we never would've been if it weren't for this class. We're both committed to bringing in the bad guys, particularly... you know who."

The thick stack of papers on Onslot's podium probably have to do with his court date. He's probably dreaming up an alibi or something he can say to the judge to defend the indefensible. He's probably seeing his reputation slip away with all its perks—his pension, his protection money, his job, his identity. Another twinge of sympathy for which I chastise myself.

The Gilded Gold isn't my favorite. It's too cute. Too gimmicky. I think I'll go back to my natural blue, which is pretty and, above all, easy.

"Back to work," Angela says. "Focus. Tell me what you think about Myrna's place. Any clues you feel were overlooked by the police? Anything that looked out of place?"

"Besides the murder?"

"Very funny. But listen, I had some thoughts. Beanie... can a cat carry the DNA of a human anywhere on its body? Chances are Beanie rubbed up against the perp because cats are always doing that, you know. Wonder if the cops dusted Beanie down."

"I have no idea," I say. "And I'm sure they're not going to share that information with us if they did."

"How do you think the perp got in?" Angela says. "No sign of forced entry. Did you see anything? I tested all the locks on both doors and all the windows, and everything seemed to be working—no weak entry points. You think Myrna knew him?"

"Again, I have no idea." I'm impressed that Angela did all that. While I was walking around Myrna's house sniffing out blood, Angela was busy checking the locks and who knows what else.

"Why do you think he cleans up all the blood with bleach? And then... changing her out of the bloody clothes after the fact. Weird, huh? A neatnik slasher?"

I look over at Onslot who's busily filling out paperwork. He seems to be completely oblivious to his students, his mind fixated on his upcoming trial. He holds a toothpick clenched between his teeth, rolling it masterfully from one side of his mouth to the other without ever touching it.

"He didn't clean the blood up with bleach afterwards," I say. "And he didn't change her clothes either. Those are the clothes she died in and..."

"And what?"

"There just wasn't any blood except for a few drops. I saw a few drops on the bedspread the cops obviously missed."

"You what? Why didn't you say anything?"

I splay the fingers of my right hand out in front of me as though admiring my nails. Then, I turn them back towards me as if to get a better view. My fingers are my best feature, the strongest part of me which I go to great pains to protect. My fingers can grip tiny indentations invisible to the human eye, allowing me to climb almost anything that has at least some form of surface imperfection. It isn't a skill I often use but it's a matter of pride, just knowing it's there. One of the few perks of being a vampire, along with speed, superior sight and strength, and that echolocation which can sometimes be a curse.

"I don't have an answer for that," I say. "I guess I was a little shaken up."

"Understandable," Angela says. "But what do you mean he didn't change her clothes or clean up with bleach. The cops said there was bleach residue all over the table, chair, and floor."

"Red herring," I say.

"That's a fish, right?"

"A smoked fish but also... a clue that someone leaves behind to purposely distract or mislead."

"Why would you think that?"

What can I say? I know it for a fact. I can smell blood —or the lack of it, no matter how much time has gone by or how many chemicals have been used to mask its existence, or in this case non-existence. But how do I explain that to Angela?

"Call it a hunch," I say. "It's just a feeling I have."

Angela stares at me curiously but, curiously, she does not challenge me.

Onslot suddenly looks up from the podium as though he's just remembered we're there. "For all of you who've been griping about being so-called forced to watch a black and white movie during our last class," he blurts out, "I'd like to inform you that next class we'll be watching *L.A. Confidential*. Got it? Color. Not black and white. So, I don't wanna hear any more of your bellyaching. Okay, you're all excused for today."

"Another movie?" Gus says in disbelief. "Is this a film history class or a criminology class?" He turns to his partner who merely shrugs. Onslot is holding his phone up to one ear, his finger plugging the other. He's speaking loudly to someone—his wife? Something about dinner and he hopes it's not meatloaf again.

"Do you think he completely missed the point?" I say to Angela. "Unbelievable the things people will accept without speaking out against it."

"C'mon, big guy. I didn't hear you saying anything." Angela gathers her papers, scoots her chair out, and stands up. "I'll tell you about my next idea while we're walking home."

CHAPTER TWENTY-FIVE

"Okay, here's my idea," Angela says. "I told you I knew the last victim of the Slasher... before he disappeared for a few months... before Myrna, that is. The guy was this nice, old, mild-mannered type of person, a widower. He collected samurai weapons because he said he could trace his roots back to a famous samurai family. He'd come in each week to see if we had anything new."

"So peculiar that both you and Lilibeth have this macabre connection to the Slasher."

"Not really, Doe. This city isn't as big as you'd think. You've probably got a connection to the Slasher too, if you only knew."

I shudder. "Let's hope not. What's your idea?"

"So... Mr. Watanabe, that's the guy I knew—"

"Yes, I remember the name from the news," I say.

"Anyway, his grandson called a few days ago. Said he wants to sell off his grandfather's collection. No one in the family is interested in antique weaponry and, in fact, they're all kind of skeeved out by it considering the violent way his grandpa died. So, he's going to come in tomorrow to talk to my boss, Stuart, and see what everything's worth if they decide to sell."

"And?"

"And I was thinking that you should be there. We can talk to him and see if we can flush out new details the cops might've overlooked. Maybe even take a look at the crime scene if he's willing to let us."

Another crime scene? This wasn't what I had in mind

when I envisioned a career in law enforcement—at least not a real-life grisly murder crime scene. I imagined it to be more cerebral and slightly glamorous—like Sherlock Holmes and Dr. Watson except without the pipe and hat. I imagined myself solving mysteries in the privacy of my home, puzzling it out at night while the rest of the world was sleeping. And then maybe swooping in for the arrest of a disgruntled but totally cooperative perp. But the Six o' Clock Slasher? Nope, not that.

"What's your boss going to think about interrogating his customer's grandson? Seems a little invasive."

"My boss is totally on board. I've told him all about what you and I are doing, and he thinks it's great. He hates that they haven't gotten Mr. Watanabe's killer yet."

"I wish I had a boss half as understanding about... basically anything."

"Stuart's a Los Angeles transplant," Angela says. "He's basically cool but he's Hollywood, if you know what I mean. He started collecting weapons when he worked on movie sets and got obsessed with it."

"So, why's he here? If he's so Hollywood?"

"He did location shooting here once and fell in love with the city. By then he was already making good money selling antique weapons on eBay. He decided to open a store and quit the movie business."

Why didn't I think about opening an antique weapons store? A missed opportunity, one of many.

"That worked out for you," I say. "And he's a nice boss so..."

"He's a little strange. He has a tanning bed in the basement where he bakes himself every other day even though he knows it's really bad for him... wants that Hollywood glow, you know? I guess it's like a drug and he's addicted. His skin's like leather and he looks like he's eighty even though he's only about half that." Angela suddenly looks over at me and I hope she isn't noticing my own leathery complexion. "He also grows weed down there," she whispers.

"Well, not my business what people do in the privacy of their basements," I say.

Who am I to judge? A serum-sipper like me.

Suddenly, I have that sense of being followed again. I want to wait until Angela's gone, but I can't—I must confirm it. I fake whistle a cheerful tune which earns me an odd look from Angela, and I quickly raise the pitch to beyond what even a dog can hear. With my lips still puckered, I must look frightfully strange.

"What're you doing?" Angela asks.

The confirming echo is a stabbing pain in my ear canal, and I whip my head around. Angela follows my lead, wanting to see what it is I see (or hear). No one. And yet there's someone.

"What is it?" she asks, but before I can come up with a reasonable explanation, we hear "John Doe."

By the time Fernando's finished saying "Doe" he's already upon us. The speed at which these boys move is astonishing, not to mention dangerous without helmets.

"Hi, Angela." Peter whooshes past.

"Hey guys!" Angela waves at their disappearing backs. Her grin is surprised and slightly sheepish, as though I caught her in the act of trying on my underwear.

"Angela?"

"What?"

"Angela? You're on a first name basis with the Wheelie Boys now?"

"Oh, yeah. Ever since that night... you know, your..." She doesn't want to say it and neither do I. Yes, the night of my terrible horrible panic attack. "They're everywhere. I'm always running into them."

"That's good. They can be helpful to you if you need to find out anything. Or get some news out fast. Helps if you have something to give them in return, though."

"They're cute kids," she says. "By the way, how are you feeling? I mean... after your flu last week when you weren't answering my calls, I was worried. Thought you said you weren't going to do that anymore."

She means Mr. X's flu, of course, although she doesn't know it. How could I possibly begin to explain? I can't. I pull the scarf so tightly around my neck it must resemble a noose.

"Sorry," I say. My temperature was sky-high, and I was throwing up day and night. Couldn't get out of bed and my phone battery died."

"Well, I gotta admit I was concerned. I know you're dealing with things and, if you hadn't told me about your neighbor lady who keeps an eye on you, I might've come over and knocked your door down, you know? Or maybe sent the cops over to do a wellness check."

A dagger-like icicle slices through my shriveled gut. Nothing frightens me quite so much as the possibility of something like that occurring. An unannounced and unexpected visitor forcing their way into my sanctuary.

"Please, Angela," I beg. "Please don't ever do anything like that. I assure you I'm fine."

She side-eyes me warily. Perhaps I've overreacted, arousing her suspicion.

"Okay, then..." she says. "Just text me if you're going to be out of touch for any significant amount of time. Then I won't worry. You don't have to talk... just text, okay?"

Our strides have slowed considerably during this past minute in the way people's strides slow when something of great significance is being discussed. I force myself to pick up the pace, which is a trick I've learned to take the focus away from something you'd rather avoid. People don't focus as keenly when they're gasping for breath.

"Okay, I promise," I say. "Now, you promise you'll never break my door down or subject me to the humiliation of a wellness check."

Humiliation is not quite the concern. Catching me in my coffin and exposing me as a freak at best or actual vampire at worst is a concern. Opening the door to allow in a beam of sunlight which might inadvertently kill me is a concern. At this time of year, a beam of sunlight will slice through my opened door from the window of the landing above sometime between the hours of 11:00 a.m. and noon. It varies according to the season and angle of the sun, and the cloud cover on any given day.

"Pinky promise." Angela is already huffing a bit with the exertion of my much quicker stride, which I will maintain until this issue has blown over when I'll resume a more normal, more conversationally appropriate pace. She hooks my pinky finger with her own.

I instinctively and fiercely yank my hand away. Was there time for her to feel the unusual texture of my skin? Does a person have nerve receptors on the underside of their pinky finger capable of sensing the leathery toughness of my hide?

"Sorry," Angela blurts out. "Boundaries, I know. I have a problem with boundaries but I'm working on it."

I keep up the pace. Her cheeks are pink with exertion, or perhaps embarrassment, or both.

"It's... okay. I'm sorry too. You just surprised me."

I back off, bringing my stride to a more forgiving pace. Angela's already on the defensive and the slower pace will facilitate forgiveness on my part, more defensiveness on hers, and generally moving on to other topics. One can learn a lot about body language in 317 years.

"So, you okay with my plan? Can you be there tomorrow when the grandson comes in?"

Her breathing has returned to normal.

"What time?"

"Probably late morning, early afternoon. I can text you a thirty-minute heads-up because he's supposed to call first."

Morning? Afternoon? No way.

"Ah, no, sorry. Can't make it then."

But Angela's not deterred, nor does she appear to hold it against me. She's willingly taken on the heavy load of our "partnership." That was settled long ago. My presence is my contribution—simply icing on the cake.

"Okay, I'll talk to him," she says. "And I'll ask about the crime scene. See what's going on with that. I'll let you know, okay?"

"Sounds good," I say. We've arrived at my apartment, and I know Angela will catch the bus from here to get to her place about twenty-minutes away.

"Answer your phone, okay? Or text. Just in case I have an update with important info," she says.

"Will do."

"Call if you need anything."

"Thanks."

"Talk to you soon, okay?"

"Sounds good."

"Anything... ever... I mean it, okay?"

"Angela. I'm fine. Really. Go home. Get out of the cold."

***

I've allowed a crack in my mask, made myself vulnerable. Angela's concern is endearing but it's also threatening. I've managed to travel solo since 1967 and in doing so I've managed to stay alive. In my experience, letting someone get too close has never been a good thing. Opening myself to Bibi is terrifying but seems necessary to my survival. She doesn't know anything about me—where I live, what I do for a living—and I plan to keep it that way. Henrietta Devine is different. She understands boundaries and respects them. We don't ask each other about our pasts, and I sense Henrietta has secrets of her own. More than once I've wondered if Henrietta escaped from someone or something in her past.

But I worry about Angela. She says she's working on respecting boundaries... but is she really?

FACT: Vampirovirus survivors value privacy above all else. For obvious reasons.

CHAPTER TWENTY-SIX

The Last Vampire

[REVISED: FIRST PERSON, PAST TENSE]

By John Doe

Chapter Twenty-Six

It's been ten years since I lost my dear

Present tense just wasn't working for me. Past tense seems more conducive to a memoir passing as a novel (or a novel passing as a memoir, depending on which side of the publishing business you stand). But now I feel that first person also isn't working. Third person is safer and allows me the separation I need from my manuscript—the separation Bibi and I discussed during my last appointment.

Right back where I started and so I shall proceed.

The Last Vampire

[REVISED: THIRD PERSON, PAST TENSE]

By John Doe

Chapter Twenty-Six

It was ten years since Zoltan lost his dear friend, Dr. Freidrich Ostentaysius, and everyone else in his life in whom he could confide. The Spanish Flu had done its dirty work, clearing the planet of those living with vampirovirus, and since nobody cared about them—in fact quite the contrary, they were despised by most—people began to feel that if there was a silver lining to the horrific pandemic which infected a third of the world's population, it was that vampires didn't seem to be around much anymore.

While most celebrated the end of WWI, Zoltan mourned the loss of his kind.

After Dr. Ostentaysius' death, Zoltan obsessively checked himself for symptoms, expecting to be slain by the new disease at any moment. Every tickle in his throat was a harbinger of his demise. Every extra beat or skipped beat of his vampire heart was an early symptom waiting to snowball. Every ache or pain was cause for extreme alarm. And then one day, in 1921 as the disease was waning across the globe, Zoltan woke up and realized he wasn't going to die. For the next few weeks he didn't know if that was a blessing or a curse. For the next few months, he tried to imagine life without friends. For the next few years, he crisscrossed the continent in search of survivors. Survivors who were already living with one incurable disease.

For the next hundred years, Zoltan would remember the feeling of terror triggered by his body's ordinary sensations (for even a vampire has sensations that are nothing more than the body adjusting or reacting to natural minor annoyances). His terror had long since carved out a pathway within Zoltan's brain which led directly to the primordial port, that reptilian center that acts as conductor to the orchestra of one's life. The pathway—a scar that refused to heal—no longer required Zoltan to have an actual cause for worry. Worry simply settled in just like the vampirovirus and became his constant companion.

***

By the middle of the decade, Zoltan was hearing stories about America and the Roaring '20s, and he determined to leave the continent behind forever and cross the Atlantic to continue his search for survivors. By now, a cloud of gloom followed him wherever he went, and he hoped not only to find more of his kind, but also for a new beginning. He longed for the magic of flappers, and their "new world" exuberance, and yes, even their decadence, that might lift him as a rising tide lifts all boats. Besides, he'd heard rumors of a community of vampires flourishing in a town along the eastern seaboard of Florida, gathered originally as a kind of joke response to the Fountain of Youth that early Spanish explorers sought in that same location. If anyone could lay claim to the Fountain of Youth, indeed it was the vampires.

Zoltan stowed away on a trans-Atlantic ocean liner which was quite an easy thing for someone of his capabilities. By the time land was in sight, many a passenger complained about monstrously itchy spider bites, usually on their necks or arms. Zoltan put on a nice cushion of weight during that week, having no problem with seasickness and a captive supply of the red stuff on board. But he also added to his burden of worries—possible viruses he may have ingested, although he chose only the healthiest (by appearances, at least) to sup upon.

At the very first sight of the tall green lady lifting her torch into a darkened sky, Zoltan jumped ship, literally diving from the deck into the ocean. It was a starless and moonless night with a thick cloud cover, not even a breeze. He swam to shore bypassing Ellis Island, an immigration facility which would have spelled the end for him.

MYTH: Vampires cannot swim. This isn't exactly a myth as there's some truth to it. Because the amount of water in the body of a vampire is only 5% relative to the 50%+ in humans, we're far less buoyant and are prone to sinking. However, our superior strength and quickness makes up for our lack of buoyancy as long as we keep moving and don't try anything foolish like floating on our backs. It's true, we can't cross a river or any other body

of water with a current; however, it's perfectly fine to ride a current (i.e., swim to shore by catching a wave).

I'm actually an excellent surfer although I have to be towed out beyond the break via jet ski. I enjoy the water as much as the next person, and maybe even more since I don't take the fluid in my body for granted. And, yes, there is one place a vampire can float—the Dead Sea, because of its high salt content. How do I know? I've tried it myself.

New York City in 1926 might have been a dream-come-true for many but Zoltan's bleak mindset followed him wherever he went. The sale of alcohol, banned in the United States since 1920, was booming. Bootlegging liquor created overnight millionaires and propped up powerful criminal cartels. Money seemed to be everywhere. People were making it, spending it, wasting it. The young partied every night like there was no tomorrow.

"And maybe there won't be a tomorrow," Zoltan thought. "These careless people have no idea how quickly a life can turn around." He couldn't wait to leave New York and continue his search for his own kind but since much of city life took place at night (daytime being the hours people slept off their hangovers) it was a perfect start for Zoltan to get a feel for the new world and mingle without danger to himself.

Months later and after many interesting experiences

As a reader, this screams out to me to be filled in with more detail. How have I not realized this until now? Many interesting experiences indeed. Note to self... fill in *some* of the interesting experiences, not all are required. Walter the pickpocket, for example. The evening I spent with Zelda and F. Scott at a speakeasy where we celebrated the success of the recently published *Great Gatsby*. Benny the Enforcer always makes for an entertaining anecdote. Dorothy Dangerous' Death Defying Acts of Debauchery, absolutely!

Maybe not Dorothy Dangerous.

Florida wasn't much back in 1926, not like we think of it today with its crowded beaches and Disney World. Back in 1926, Florida was malaria-infested swamps, unbearable heat and humidity. There was no air conditioning back then—at least not outside the fancy movie houses of New York City. There were sharks and alligators and sand flies and fire ants that didn't bother Zoltan but the bite of which caused excruciating pain in tender human flesh.

There are still sharks and alligators and sand flies and fire ants that cause excruciating pain, so delete that line. Malaria wasn't eradicated until the early 1950s, so leave that in.

It was on a lonely stretch of beach where Zoltan awoke one evening, sick, penniless, friendless, and having found no thriving community of vampires where he'd chased down rumors and pinned all his hopes. Not even one single vampire did he find, although there was much evidence the community had existed as recently as ten years earlier.

Whispers from folks he met along the way about "those kind" but "you know, they all died off from that foreign sickness." And "wasn't it maybe for the best...who knows that they didn't bring it upon themselves, exposing everyone else in the process." There were rumors of a mass grave where "those things" were put to rest once and for all.

With his broad-brimmed straw hat, Zoltan hid his features from the folks he encountered along the way. Everyone had leathery tough skin, courtesy of the relentless sun, so Zoltan fit right in. He traveled at night, seeking out those who cooled themselves on their front porches, perhaps partaking in an after-dinner cup of tongue-loosening moonshine which made them more likely to share information with Zoltan, the stranger in their midst.

But if talk could break a person's heart, Zoltan's would have shattered at the soul-crushing words that came out of the mouths of the locals.

Vampires were victims. No one chose to be infected by the vampirovirus, but once infected their natural instinct for survival took over. As for the Spanish flu which really had nothing to do with Spain, vampires were victims twice-fold. The most vulnerable of the vulnerable without any natural defenses to survive it. Except for Zoltan, of course. Zoltan who now found himself on a moonlit beach with puppy-warm wavelets lapping at his ankles, a death-blue crab perched on his hand, its color perfectly matching his fingernails, its pincers reaching skyward as if pleading for its salvation.

Zoltan hadn't eaten for weeks.

"Y'all okay?"

A shadow darkened the inside of his eyelids, blocking the golden beams of a fat full moon. The voice, at first, he mistook for a voice in his head. He sat up slowly, pushing off from his elbows, groping for his hat which he planted on his head. He brought a hand up to wipe sugar-white crystals of sand from the side of his face. He was weak as a kitten. Dizzy. Nauseous.

"Ya look like death warmed over," she said and now he could see it was a real-life person talking to him—not some auditory hallucination. She looked...tempting...delicious.

He hated himself. And she was probably way too strong for him.

She wore a loose cotton dress, sleeveless. Her skirt was tied up in a knot between her legs which changed the dress into a pantaloon, more appropriate for the beach. Her hair was long, loose, brown. Her skin darkened by sun. Her eyes, lit by the moon, were a midnight blue—compassionate yet frank. Everything about her radiated strength, both physical and psychological. He wanted her to pick him up in her powerful arms and cradle him.

He began to cry like he hadn't cried since he was a child and still had a mother to tend to his needs.

"There's no need for that," she said, and he felt her embarrassment as he felt his own. "You prob'ly just need somethin' to drink."

Whereas he hadn't noticed it before, she pulled a machete from a bag she'd been carrying and aimed it square at a coconut she pulled out of the sane bag. With one swipe, the top came off and she brought the hairy fruit to his lips.

"Drink," she said. "You'll feel better, I promise."

And he did, surprisingly. The electrolytes and chemical makeup of coconut water, being somewhat similar to human blood—at least for a vampire's immediate needs. But the high didn't last long—minutes perhaps. Enough time to stop his tears. Enough time to give him hope.

After that, the girl did pick him up just as though he were a baby.

"You're light as a feather," she remarked. Then, with the heavy bag slung over one shoulder, she shuffled through the sand of the beach and plunged into a pine forest lit only by strips of moonlight which hung from the branches.

He gave himself over to the girl, manly pride being a luxury he could no longer afford, humiliation being an infinitesimal torment compared to survival.

"You smell bad," she said. "Real bad. By the way, my name's Marie. You?"

"Tom," he said. "Tom Smith."

And this was the first time he used the name he would come to adopt as his own. A new world required a new name. Zoltan would only make him stand out and standing out was not something he wished to do.

"Well, we'll get you to bed, Tom Smith," she said. "And you can rest up until you get back on your feet."

Perhaps an explanation is in order here. I have consistently used real names throughout my memoir but for obvious reasons my main character's name cannot match the author's name. But I digress. Back to the story.

By then they'd arrived at a sprawling cabin built in the space of a clearing where he could see trees had been felled all around them.

"Pa and my brothers are gone for a bit," she explained when she lay him down on a rustic cot made of wood beams and topped by a delightfully soft feather mattress Marie had beat with a broom to fluff before settling John into place. "They'll be back by and by, then you can meet them."

But Tom didn't want to meet Pa and her brothers. No

good could come from Pa and her brothers, who, given the family genetics he could surmise from Marie's sturdy appearance, must surely be brutes.

Marie continued to tend to him, bringing him cup after cup of coconut water which was the only thing he allowed beyond his lips. He had great difficulty keeping his gaze from the vibrant pulsating carotids on the sides of Marie's neck. She was healthy, he could see that beyond a doubt. But she was strong, so strong...and he was so very weak. Besides that, she was the first person to show him any real compassion since Dr. Ostentaysius passed which was a very long time ago. A very long time to survive without the milk of kindness, human or vampire.

So that night, after Marie had extinguished the kerosene lamp and retired to her room, Tom drank the coconut water she'd left by his bedside and half-staggered, half-crawled on all fours towards the scent of human blood which was in a cabin several miles away. He supped that night on the blood of a young man and his wife, being careful to leave them as healthy as he found them, but not being fully satiated until he'd fed from both.

It had been a very long time since Tom Smith had eaten.

After that, he traveled the vampire way back to Marie's cabin and laid himself down on the feather mattress where he stared into the darkness, his thoughts temporarily happy ones, grateful for the windowless room in which he lay.

Over a period of days and many long hours of talks, Tom Smith convinced Marie that he still wasn't well enough to leave his bed. During the day, in his windowless room he was safe. "Marie must be terribly lonely," he thought. Out in the woods all by herself with Pa and her brothers away for so long. She's lonely just like me.

And away they were for much of the time. From Marie, he learned that the men in her family were rum-runners—traveling to Cuba where alcohol was still legal and returning with a boatload of inventory to sell off. Pa and the boys had a very fast boat. Their ancestors were pirates along these same shores, so for many generations her family had been outsmarting the law on the high seas.

Whenever they returned from their rum runs, their pockets would be stuffed with cash and treats for Marie and they'd have a grand old time until the next run. The next lonesome stretch of days and weeks. Marie lived for the times when her family was together although she had no sisters and her mother died from the Spanish flu years ago. For weeks at a time, sometimes months, Marie was on her own, protecting the family assets (cash, gold, and jewels buried in a steel box hidden beneath the floorboard of the cabin under a woven rug near the kitchen).

Marie didn't know that Tom knew this, but one night he observed her retrieving the box when she thought he was sleeping. She had nothing to worry about when it came to Tom, though. He was not a thief. Well, maybe a blood thief but nothing more than that. And Marie was a formidable young woman who most people wouldn't dare tangle with.

One day as Marie sat in a chair by Tom's bed reading to him from a favorite book of poems that had once belonged to her mother, she abruptly closed the book and set it in her lap.

"I know what you are," she said softly. "You're one of 'em, aren't you?" Her eyes narrowed and every nerve in his body electrified. It was daytime. If it came to a showdown, he couldn't run away from her or he'd die from sun exposure. But he couldn't kill Marie who had saved his life and become a dear friend in such a short period of time. He never thought he'd see the hateful look on her face that he'd seen on so many others in the past.

"One of...?" he prompted, hoping beyond hope she'd say something...anything...other than what he feared most.

"A sapien sucker," she said. "I knows'd it from the minute I first saw ya."

He sprang from his cot and backed into a corner, frightened like a wild animal.

"And you're just a blood bag." He spat out the ugly words so angrily.

Yes, I'm ashamed to admit that I used that crude phrase. It was the first and only time those words ever came out of my mouth.

"Ease up," Marie said. "I have no fear of you. When I was just a small fry, I played with a girl...Missy...who was one of ya. She were my only friend I ever had outside my family. She never harmed me and I was sad to see her gone from the foreign sickness that took my mama too."

A tear as big as a marble slid from her eye straight down her cheek. She dabbed it away with the back of her hand and snuffed up the tears that hadn't yet escaped.

"We can be friends," she said. "Like I did for Missy, I can do for you too if you promise not to harm me."

Tom felt ashamed that he'd seen hate in Marie's eyes when she was offering him the most generous gift a human can offer a vampirovirus patient—the gift of her blood. As long as he promised not to take it too far, which he never would. He wasn't that kind. Never had been. "Thou shalt not kill" had always been his guiding principle. He would rather die than take the life of another.

Marie and Tom had an entire month to themselves, the happiest time of his life since he romped in the fields with Nadia. Far from the maddening crowd they became fast friends and exchanged every secret. They read poetry and told scary stories in the dark, and Tom had plenty of scary stories to tell. They took long walks in the moonlight and breathed in the scent of pine cones and ocean fizz.

He was happy at last.

Then one day Pa and the boys showed up at the cabin. Marie and Tom had been talking and laughing, so preoccupied they didn't hear the footsteps approaching, nor the door opening.

Thank goodness it was nighttime.

When Pa saw his daughter's hand playfully stroking the arm of the stranger in his house, he slammed the door against the wall with such ferocity, splinters flew through the air.

His eyes were filled with murderous rage.

The boys coming up behind him were as tall and strong as a team of oxen.

"What in tarnation?!" Pa spat an angry gob of tobacco juice which seeped into the wood floor like a blood stain.

What it must have looked like to him. To them.

What Pa must have looked like to her. What they looked like to Tom.

"It's…it's…not what you think," Marie sputtered and for the first time she seemed delicate. Weak, even.

Whack! Pa's response sent Marie careening across the floor, crashing into the wall where she slid down, hugging her knees with one arm, her free hand…

Her free hand with finger outstretched pointed directly at Tom Smith.

"He's one a 'em, Pa." The words tumbled out of her mouth like dice into a terrible void but even to Tom they sounded unconvincing, choked with tears, defeated. "Get 'im, Pa," she said, "for what he done to me."

Tom's heart broke for Marie, for he knew what this betrayal must cost her. But he also knew that Pa and the boys would require no convincing. He bared his fangs and growled in a mockery of what humans believe to be predatory vampire behavior. He crouched into the classic vampire attack pose, popularized in movies—elbows drawn back, fingers curled, upper body bent forward. It's a terrifying image which renders most humans weak at the knees, paralyzed by irrational fear.

In this case it had the desired effect, buying Tom the few precious seconds he needed to escape. The men froze in their tracks while Tom leaped through an open window, landing outside on his two feet and one hand. By the time Pa and the boys recovered from their initial shock, Tom was almost out of sight. He said a prayer for Marie while a bullet whizzed by mere millimeters from his left ear, but he never looked back as he disappeared into the forest. The vampire way.

He still cared for Marie and didn't blame her. How could he?

She chose survival just as he had chosen survival time and time again.

I learned a hard lesson that day.

No matter what they might say and how badly you might want to believe them, humans can never be trusted, and I've never completely trusted one since then.

Now, Angela Ruiz is trying to get close to me, and I have an overwhelming sense of danger in spite of my fondness and gratitude to her. She swears she'll always have my back, but she doesn't *know* my back.

I need to find a way to break it off with her.

CHAPTER TWENTY-SEVEN

Reflections on Blood

A Personal Essay by John Doe

Although it may seem like a silly thing to reflect on the value and meaning of blood to a vampire who is the last of his kind, one day, if I don't survive, I hope my writings will lead the world to a better understanding of those living with vampirovirus.

With understanding, at least in hindsight, I hope for forgiveness. No, not forgiveness, for we've done nothing wrong. I hope that history will rewrite the dark chapters of this terrible pandemic brought upon the world by the few—the sadists among us—who purposely infected the innocent for their own despicable purposes. Who wanted others to share their fate. Who gave new meaning to the adage that "misery loves company." There were others who purposely chose to be infected—not wishing to part with a child or a spouse who would otherwise face eternal life without their families by their sides. Of these two groups, I belong to the first, an innocent taken against my will.

Perhaps with this understanding, should another similar virus arise in the future (for viruses are always lurking, waiting for the perfect confluence of events to assert themselves) perhaps humanity will behave as the name implies: Humanely.

Blood. Who loves it more, vampire or human? I suggest human in spite of the fact they give very little thought to it, being so fortunate as to take it for granted. Think about it...

A red-blooded American

My heart bleeds for you
Bleeding heart liberal
The nosebleed section
Bad blood
Bleed someone dry
Blood brothers
Blood in the water
Blood diamonds
Blood curdling
Blood on your hands
Blood, sweat, and tears
It makes one's blood boil
Hemorrhaging money

All of these expressions have one thing in common. They carelessly apply the imagery of blood to the most mundane actions or descriptions.

Everything with humans is about blood. Blood, blood, blood. And yet they have an endless supply of the red stuff. Within their very bones, they operate tiny blood factories that function around the clock. Should anything happen to diminish their supply, transfusions are readily available to humans at their local hospitals. A person may cut themselves and bleed which causes an instinctive alarm because loving blood is human at its core, but they know it's not the end of them unless the accident is major.

For a vampire, losing even a drop or two is cause for great concern, spelling a possible serious consequence, because blood is so hard to come by for us. We don't love blood. We don't brag about it or find a way to fit it into every sentence we utter. We never worshiped it through blood sacrifices. We simply realize its importance in the same way we learn to avoid the sun. We learn to hunt for it. Hunt or die.

And yet for the vampire, there are no blood luxuries although our needs relative to humans is infinitesimal. Throughout history we've been hunted, scorned, hated, blamed for every conceivable evil, and yet, for the most part, we've done nothing wrong beyond trying to survive. There are no transfusions available to us although a true transfusion would last us many months, possibly up to a year.

It's just not an option.

We're forced to either steal from others, leaving them alive and healthy; purchase it on the black market, as do I; drain an innocent person resulting in their death; or, as happened to me, infect a victim by leaving them barely alive in only the technical sense of the word—drinking all but what is absolutely essential in order for them to carry on in vampiric form.

My suggestion? Let vampires come out of the literal darkness to seek blood legally. This would help put an end to unfounded fears, discrimination, and prevent unnecessary deaths.

Do I think this will happen in my lifetime? Absolutely not. And now with no more vampires to agitate on our behalf (except me), there's not even a point to this essay.

But I do feel better having gotten it off my chest.

FACT: They say the Inuit people have more than fifty words for "snow." Persons living with vampirovirus (commonly, and for the sake of simplicity, called vampires) have more than fifty terms for blood. The red stuff. Serum. Jolly juice. Cranberry cocktail. Sapien sap. Clotting claret. Fairy fluid. I could go on but let's leave it at that. Unlike the human metaphors which contain within them a form of braggadocio, our phrases apply only to the actual substance.

CHAPTER TWENTY-EIGHT

"Meat Tree!" Calvin bellows. "What's going on? Waiting on those shakes anytime now."

I'm wiping down the chopping counters with a piping hot rag, but I can see the flush on Dimitri's cheeks from where I stand. He sticks a knife into the underside of the shake machine which tells me there's a mechanical issue. Lucky thing Calvin's back is turned because right about now he'd go ballistic if he saw what Dimitri's doing. I know enough about fixing things (quite a bit, in fact) to know that sticking a knife in something is probably never a good idea, particularly when said thing is plugged into the wall. I'm just about to tell Dimitri to hold up when Molly sweeps in.

"Let me have a look," she says.

"You're still on break," he counters, even though I'm sure he's desperate for help.

"It's fine," Molly says, unplugging the shake machine from the wall. "I was getting bored just sitting over there by myself."

She opens the top and jiggles a few things, turns the machine on its side to rotate something manually underneath, turns it upright again and reaches into the well to feel for something which she twists, then puts the cover back on and plugs it into the outlet. A snap of the switch and it purrs to life.

"Thanks," Dimitri says, two shades pinker now. Not only is he embarrassed but I'm pretty sure he's fallen for Molly—and who could blame him.

Me? I'm still tearing myself apart over how to back out of my "partnership" with Angela. This particular self-torment has been ongoing since last night and it's not getting any better. It's madness, this childish dream of hers that we're going to solve a series of homicides that have stymied the police for two years. Absolute madness. I rap on the back of my skull five times with the knuckles of my right hand. I lose track and start again.

Not only is it foolishness but it's dangerous to both her and me. I'm not doing her a favor by encouraging her with my tacit approval which she assumes if I don't speak up.

I tap my right heel against the floor five times, and then an additional five at a slightly greater intensity.

Marie had my back once upon a time too. And where did that lead? To my discovery and near miss encounter with my own demise.

I tap my left heel on the ground five times. And then another five for good measure, again with added intensity.

"Doe, what the hell?" Calvin barks out from behind my back, bringing the argument I'm having with myself to an abrupt halt. "You auditioning for *Dancing with the Stars* or something?"

How did he see me from way over there?

"Just love that you've gone back to your blue nail polish," Calvin says. "It's so... so... *you*, you know?"

"Technically, you're verbally harassing your employee when you say that," Dimitri says. Dimitri who is so sweet and kind and idealistic and so unprepared for the real world. The ugly world.

"*Am I?*" Calvin says. "I did not know that. Thanks, Mother Teresa. Thanks for enlightening me."

In many ways, Calvin reminds me of Onslot with a few exceptions, one being that I know for a fact Calvin likes me. I know he likes Dimitri too, although he has a twisted way of showing it. He just has an odd (albeit cruel) way of entertaining himself while he's churning out beef patties by the hundreds, night after night after night after night. It's enough to drive a person mad, I imagine. I switch to blinking.

Three fast. Three slow. Three fast.

I can drop out of class. Tell Angela I'm sick or a family member is dying. But she knows where I work. She knows where I live. She's threatened to come over and kick my door down or call the police in for a wellness check.

Three VERY fast. Three VERY slow. Three VERY fast.

"Contacts?" Molly asks. She's moved on from Dimitri to my chopping station.

"What?"

"Are your contacts bothering you? Mine are too... I think it's all the smoke in here," she says, blinking her own eyes.

Oh, God.

Now my heel begins tapping of its own accord.

"I'm just... allergies," I say. "To onions."

This is an obvious lie.

And then I remember.

"You're leaving next week, right? I guess you should give me the key to your apartment."

"Thanks, I was just going to ask if it's still okay. I'll reciprocate anytime with Clementine. And I mean *anytime*. Okay?"

"No problem," I start to blink but stop myself. My hand sneaks up to the back of my skull and I rap five times, trying to make it look like an innocent head scratch.

"You okay? You seem a little jumpy today."

"Who's Clementine?" Dimitri asks.

"I'm fine. Just..."

"His fish."

I need to have it out with Angela, but what should I say? The truth? Not the real full truth because that would involve... you know... *the truth*. Just the truth without the other stuff, the vampire stuff. And what exactly is that truth? It's a futile childish endeavor? She cares too much and is getting too close? I can't possibly tell her the truth. It would either break her heart or make me seem like a complete imbecile or reveal me for who I am. Or perhaps all three!

My innards churn and feel suddenly loose.

Molly's still messing around with her keychain and she finally removes two round silver keys on their own separate key ring.

"Here's my spare set," she says. "One for the building and one for my apartment. Can you start Tuesday because I'm leaving Sunday night? Anytime Tuesday night is okay."

"Who's Clementine?" Dimitri apparently didn't hear Molly's response the first time.

"His fish!"

"Tuesday. Tuesday's fine. Good. Thanks." I pocket the keys. "Have a great time if I don't see you before then."

"Doe! There's a couple of kids at the back door asking for you. Those same boys again."

Three fast. Three slow. Three fast.

SOS

Save me!

CHAPTER TWENTY-NINE

"I'M GLAD YOU CALLED, Mr. Doe," Bibi says. "Take a seat wherever you're comfortable."

"John," I say. I thought we'd already settled that. I bypass the divan and settle on the white leather recliner. I raise my footrest just a smidge.

Bibi squints at me with her normally wide, intelligent eyes. She opens her notebook and begins to write. I wonder if she's making notes about my appearance. Something she noticed during her initial assessment. Why is she squinting with such disdain?

"What're you writing?" I blurt out. "I haven't said a word yet."

"Just recording the time and date."

She continues to squint and then looks up from her notebook and squints some more.

"How've you been?" she asks. "Since the last time I saw you."

Squint.

The last time I saw you. Not the last time we saw each other. This immediately puts her on a level above me. She's claimed the power. But I'm willingly giving her the power, aren't I? Aren't I here for her help?

"Why are you looking at me that way?" I asked, unnerved by her disapproving stare.

"Like what?"

"Like I disgust you somehow."

She jots something in her notebook. "Why would you say that, John?"

"Because I can tell. You're looking at me in a whole different way. Like suddenly I'm a horrible person."

"Can you demonstrate what you mean, please?"

I squint my eyes, screw up my face, and thrust my head forward in a ridiculous exaggeration of the way she's been looking at me since I got here. I suddenly feel like a child and wonder how someone 317 years old can regress so quickly to an emotional 7-year-old.

She stares at me for a second and I wonder if I've gone too far.

"Oh," she says. "Sorry. I lost one of my contacts, so I took the other one out. I can't see you very well... you're like, all fuzzy."

She stands and walks to the desk where she's left her backpack, rummages around in it, and when she withdraws her hand, she's holding a pair of oversized eyeglasses. She puts them on and returns to her seat to face me. "Better?" she asks.

"Sorry," I mumble, deeply ashamed.

"How's the writing coming along?" she asks. "Any progress?"

I squirm. "I don't want to talk about my writing today, if that's okay."

"Perfectly okay. This is your hour. Talk about whatever you want to talk about."

"Do you have any new patients?" I ask. "Since last time?"

Last time I was her only patient.

"I did get one call." My face must drop because I can certainly feel my shoulders sag. "But they hung up before I could schedule an appointment."

"Oh, that's too bad," I say, with an inward sigh of relief. I hate the pettiness in me, but the truth is I don't want to share Bibi. I want all of her attention. I don't want to be just another one of many patients with a litany of problems she has to keep notes on, lest she forget. "I'm sure you'll have others before too long."

She ignores my comment and instead focuses her unyielding gaze on me once again. Somehow her glasses make her eyes appear to be twice as large. Twice as searching. Twice as demanding. I prefer her fuzzy squint to these glasses that turn her eyes into tools of inquisition. But if I ask her to remove the glasses...

"Shall we talk about your fish? You mentioned the fish just as we concluded our last session," she says.

"I don't wish to discuss my fish today," I say, looking off to the side, surrendering to her merciless gaze. It's a game of eye-contact chicken, really, and I just lost. Perhaps I *should* ask her to remove her glasses.

"Why are you here today, John?" she asks. Is it my imagination or do I hear an exasperated sigh punctuating that question? Has she already had it with me so early in this session? If she looks at her watch... please don't let her look at her watch. "What brings you here tonight if you don't want to discuss your writing or your fish."

I reach down for the button on the side of my chair and bring my footrest up another few inches. I feel around for the second button and recline the back of my seat slightly.

"Actually, I have something else I want to discuss today," I say. "Something that's been bothering me."

"Okay, good, proceed."

Proceed? That's a little cold, isn't it? Normally, she says "let's talk about it" or something encouraging along those lines. Proceed indeed. Is she already tired of me? Have I tested her patience and found it lacking?

Please don't lose patience with me, Bibi.

I bring my hand to the back of my skull and rap in my best imitation of a head-scratching.

"I, uh... I've been having a problem with a classmate. A boundary issue."

I look over quickly to see how she'll react to this.

"Male, female, non-binary?"

"Female. But... that has nothing to do with the boundary issue."

"So, it's not a sexual harassment thing?"

"Certainly not!" I told her it had nothing to do with gender so why would she go there right away?

"Not that I'm saying it'd have to be a girl to be sexual harassment, you understand."

"I said, no."

"Okay, okay... just trying to set the stage a little. Sometimes I might ask a question that doesn't seem relevant but I'm just trying to color between the lines, you know?"

"Good... metaphors," I say. "I get it."

I didn't mean that to come out so dismissively. I hope she doesn't think I'm talking down to her. Maybe I should apologize. I *will* apologize. I raise my head to look at her and she doesn't look angry or upset. I actually can't imagine Bibi looking angry or upset. I hope I never see her looking angry or upset.

"Ah yes, metaphors. A writer like you *would* notice that." Her lips purse together in a private smile like she's just figured out the punchline to a joke. "So, your writing isn't bothering you anymore?"

"Not... at the moment."

"And your fish? No longer an issue?"

"Again, not at this time."

She chuckles to herself.

"Are you laughing at me?" I ask.

"No, no, no." She shakes her head twice for each no. "I will never... *ever*... laugh at you, John. I was just thinking about something funny my karate teacher said to me today. My sensei."

"You have a sensei?"

"Yes, I'm a brown belt," she says.

I don't see any reason to tell her about my black belt.

"What did he say that was so funny?"

"Well. We were sparring and I put my arm up to block her punch and *she* got me right on the bony part of my arm, which actually really hurt. Look."

I raise my head again to see what she wants me to see. She hitches up the sleeve of her shirt to reveal an oblong bruise that's beginning to darken. I don't like to see bruises or anything else that reminds me of the red stuff in between feedings. I lower my head back against the recliner and look away. My stomach cramps, the result of a hunger pang. Or distress.

"Sorry," I say.

"No sorry necessary. It's part of the learning experience. But when I complained to my sensei that my arm hurt, she stepped on my foot. Hard. Then she said, 'Bet your arm doesn't hurt anymore, does it?'"

Bibi laughs at the memory and suddenly I know where she's going with it.

"So, whatever it is that's bothering you now... the boundary issue with your classmate... at least you're not upset about your writing or your fish, are you? Amazing how the human brain, as complex as it is, has limited capacity to focus on more than one problem at a time."

I stare stony-faced at her, waiting for an apology that doesn't come.

"Well, isn't it?" she says. "Amazing? I mean, you said those things weren't bothering you."

"At the moment," I say. "We may get back to them at a later date."

"Okay, well at least for the moment. At least you know there's a theoretical end to your worrying, even if it's temporary. Go on. Sorry to interrupt. This classmate... the girl... what did she do to you?"

My hand reaches up to the back of my skull again. Another knuckle-thumping disguised as a head scratch. My other hand finds the chair buttons to lift my legs a bit higher. This lowers my torso. I'm now completely out of Bibi's direct line of vision.

"How do I tell someone... to back off? My classmate is trying to get too personal in a way I'm not comfortable with and, in fact, I find a bit threatening. So, I want to know how to let her know... in a nice way, you understand... to basically leave me alone."

"In a nice way?"

"A nice way."

"If you find her threatening, why do you care about being nice?"

"Because I'm a nice person. If there's a nice way to do something, I'd rather do it that way instead of a not-so-nice way."

"I see. Threatening, you say?"

"Exactly."

"Can you describe the way this girl, let's call her Tiffany for the sake of convenience... how Tiffany has threatened you?"

"Tiffany? I can't even begin to imagine her as a Tiffany."

Angela being a Tiffany. Hah!

"Then you pick a name, John Doe."

Is Bibi making fun of my own name? Does she not believe it to be true? My hip and shoulder sockets feel like they need a good cracking. I squirm into a slightly more comfortable position.

"Tiffany's fine."

"Okay, then. How did Tiffany threaten you?"

"I didn't say she threatened me. I said that I found her to be threatening."

This is not going as planned.

"And in what way is Tiffany threatening?"

"For instance... for instance she threatened to break my door down."

Well, she did! That's not a lie.

"That's alarming. Did you call the police?"

"No, heavens no."

"Why not?"

"Because. It was said in reference to checking up on me when I was home sick with the flu."

They say "the truth will always out" but that didn't

take long. I'm looking for tools to handle the problem of Angela, not an analysis for the reasons behind it. I already know everything there is to know about that (see *The Last Vampire*, Chapter 26). I lack wiles, that's always been my problem. The ability to successfully carry out a lie although one might say my entire life is a lie. But there's usually an element of truth to each of my successful lies that doesn't seem to work with Bibi.

"Oh, I see. So, she's a friend or am I missing something? I mean, she knows you're home sick with the flu. Couldn't she just call you?"

"She didn't know. Exactly. She just knew I didn't show up to class." I leave out the part about not answering her numerous texts and calls.

"I see."

My hand creeps up to the back of my head. I perform a stealth knuckle-rap. I lower my torso and raise my feet until I'm almost parallel to the ground.

"She's... just tell me what to say to her," I blurt out.

"You probably already know this, John, so I feel a little silly telling you... but there isn't a nice way of telling someone who's concerned about your well-being to leave you alone. No matter what you say to them, they're bound to feel a little rejected. You could ghost her but that probably won't work if you're classmates. It's also quite cowardly."

I know that. I know that. That's why I was hoping for...

"I was just hoping—"

"I'm sorry but I don't have a magic bullet to avoid hurt feelings and have you come out of it smelling like a rose. You're just going to have to deal with Tiffany face to face."

"Nice metaphors," I say.

Bibi ignores that. No more compliments forthcoming about my being a writer.

"Is there something about her, John? Does she have bad breath or bad politics or does she hate koala bears or something?"

"Not that I know of."

"You're an introvert," Bibi says. "I get that. Start by being honest with her. You don't have to socialize with anyone just because they want to socialize with you. You get to pick, okay? So just be honest with her."

This is going nowhere. I wish I hadn't brought it up. Another knuckle-rapping against the back of my skull. Angela prying into my life feels perilous. Her trying to drag me into her life feels dangerous. Bibi doesn't get it but how can she? Was I expecting a magic bullet that would have me smelling like a rose? Absolutely.

"That thing you do," Bibi says. "Knocking on the back of your head. That's a ritual, isn't it? Something to calm you when you're wound up."

"Knocking? What? I don't even know what you're talking about."

I practically have to hold my right hand down with my left hand to stop myself from performing another round of knocking. I blink instead.

Three fast... three slow... three fast.

"It's okay," she says. "If you ever want to address it, I've been reading up on it. And asking my mom about it too."

"Your *mom*? Why on earth would you ask your mom?"

"Because I've noticed you doing it from the first time we met, and my mom happens to know a lot about it. Remember, she's a real therapist. You also have a blinking thing you do too, and a heel tapping thing. It's fine if it helps you but if you ever want to talk about it there are things—I mean, we can just talk about it so at least you don't have to try and hide it from me."

I let out the most impatient, loudest sigh I can muster. There's nothing really that I want to say about that right now.

"It's part of obsessive-compulsive disorder, you know?" Bibi says just as plainly as if she was observing the weather.

I know that. Of course, I do. I've had hundreds of years

to learn everything about it.

But no one to talk to until now. At least no one I trusted.

And yet, now... now that I have my chance, I find I have nothing to say.

"Obsessive thoughts lead to compulsive urges to perform rituals to deal with the anxiety. Mom says it's a glitch in the brain... chemical or biological, nobody knows for sure. Maybe it was something useful for early man's survival that we don't need anymore. But you know what I think it is, John? I think rituals are a way to bring order to a world that seems out of control."

My world *is* out of control.

"John, what's your dad like?"

"Dead."

"Okay... what *was* he like?"

"Mean."

I can hear the scratching of pen against paper.

"How about your mom?"

"Equally dead."

"And what was she like?"

"Weak."

More scratching.

"Brothers? Sisters?"

"None."

Silence.

"John, you sure I can't read your manuscript?"

"No offense, but I've never been so sure of anything in my life."

"No offense taken. It sure would help me though. I can only go so far with your therapy if you're not willing to open up to me."

"Understood."

"We can continue to work on things, working on an issue here and a problem there... isolating things in your life like they have no connection to each other and are just random events. But as you can see, that's not going to produce great results."

Nope. This is not going at all the way I intended.

"I understand that, truly I do. But let's not forget that I'm just here because you offered to listen to me, and you *don't* have professional therapy credentials like your mom. If you don't want to listen, I won't bother you anymore."

I feel like crying. If Bibi doesn't want to listen to me anymore, who will?

"I do want to listen, John. That's what I *can* do... listen. But are you sure you're not wanted by the law or anything like that?"

"I can at least assure you of that," I say. "If nothing else."

"Hang on, I gotta pee. BRB."

Bibi disappears into the adjoining room where there's a mini-fridge and a private bathroom. I really didn't need to know what she had to do in there—TMI, as they say these days. But I need a minute to collect my thoughts. Perhaps I should leave when she returns. I'll come back when I'm in a better mood and not so likely to alienate her. In the meantime... Angela. Bibi's right. Face to face, I need to bow out. Maybe I should drop the class.

A loud crash from the next room. I position my chair into an upright sitting position to make sure I heard what I heard.

"Bibi?" I call out.

Another crash and then a moan.

I spring from my chair and walk into the break room.

"Bibi, are you okay?"

No answer.

A much louder moan.

"Bibi!"

I knock on the door. No answer.

"Bibi. Bibi, are you okay? Please answer me."

Silence.

More knocking. Louder. More pleading.

I notice the tiny hole in the doorknob and rummage through the drawer under the microwave. I find what I'm looking for—a paper clip, which I straighten.

"Bibi, I'm coming in," I say after a few more knocks with no response.

My hands are shaking so much I can barely push the paper clip into the hole. I feel pressure and then a click when the lock releases. I open the door cautiously in case she's lying on the floor. I wouldn't want to hit her. I hope beyond hope she's not bleeding.

And there she is. Fully clothed and sitting on the toilet with the seat down. Just sitting there staring at the open doorway. And me.

"Are we friends, John?" she asks, her eyes as enormous through those glasses as a barn owl's.

"No, we're professional acquaintances."

"Exactly. And yet you broke down the door to make sure I was okay. Well, technically you didn't break it down because it's a paper-clip friendly door. But you would've."

I stare at her. Speechless. This girl.

"All I'm saying is that caring isn't necessarily threatening. But you can certainly tell Tiffany that you want your space. People understand more than they're given credit for."

"You don't understand," I say.

"Then help me to understand."

"Is this session over?"

"If you want it to be. Maybe it's a good place to end until next time, okay?"

I mumble "okay" so quietly she probably doesn't hear. I'm mad at myself but also so grateful she said there *will* be a next time. She's not giving up on me. Bibi doesn't give up. I turn to leave when something makes me stop. I look back, and she's still sitting there on that toilet seat just watching me walk away.

"Bibi," I say, "I'm glad you're okay. I was worried."

"I know," she says. "Thanks, friend."

CHAPTER THIRTY

Ken Watanabe is a serious man with a serious job, and yet he's taken time from his busy life to meet with us, such is Angela's persuasive power with people. We're standing inside the last home of Mr. Watanabe's grandfather (who the family called Jiji, a shortened version of the Japanese word for grandfather). This is where the murder took place three months ago—an in-law unit some fifty yards behind Ken Watanabe's main house.

"We didn't hear a thing," Ken says. "It was horrible. When he didn't show up for breakfast the next morning, I came over and knocked on the door. When he didn't answer, I kicked it open and…" He shakes his head like he's trying to shake away the memory. "Anyway, it was thoroughly searched by the police. We thought about renting it out, but honestly, who would want to live here after what happened? So, now we use it for storage. One day, we'll tear it down altogether."

Another door busted down, I think, *by another person who cared.*

Tonight's the night I'll break the news to Angela. I at least owe her my support for this one last inspection, which must be hard on her since she actually knew Jiji. After that, I'm out, and I've made up my mind to drop the class which I never should have signed up for in the first place.

"Is it okay with you if we just poke around for a few minutes?" Angela asks.

"Sure, no problem. Take your time," Ken says. "Sorry

about all the boxes. A lot of what's in them are the weapons. You know... his collection."

Angela nods earnestly. "Did he have any pets?" she asks.

"A cat," Ken says. "But it was feral. Lived outside and Jiji only put food out for it. He was working on making it a house cat, but I think the cat had different ideas. Anyway, I just got home from work, so I'll go say hi to the kids and be back in fifteen minutes to lock up."

"Pets?" I raise my eyebrows once Ken is safely out of earshot.

"You never know, Doe. Myrna had a cat too. Maybe there's a connection."

"Like maybe the Slasher's a dog?" I say, then immediately regret it when Angela responds with a hurtful look.

"Same backstory as Myrna, since you missed my first meeting with Ken. Jiji was sitting at the little card table where he used to play solitaire. He'd gone out to lunch that day, so he called over to the big house and said he was going to skip supper since he usually ate with them."

"Blood?"

"None. Again. And his clothes were clean. And again, there was evidence of a major clean-up with bleach. Weird, huh?"

"Weird."

"So, if he's collecting all this blood in a bucket or something, what the hell is he doing with it? And why's he going to such trouble to clean it up? I don't get it. It's like... it's like what people do when they slaughter animals, you know? Cut their throats and drain all the blood out."

I walk away from Angela into the next room. All this talk of blood and cutting throats is too much. Another reason for me to get away from her. It's too much. I told Angela the clean-up with bleach was just a red herring in Myrna's case. That there was no blood on the floor or the table to begin with. Angela didn't argue with me, but I guess she completely discounted what I said because now she's back to talking about the bleach again. Well, why should she believe me? I can't exactly let on as to how I know that for a fact.

"Where was the card table?" I call from the next room. "Where they found him."

"Over here if you want to help me move these boxes out of the way."

I go back into the room where Angela is poking around, testing windows and the front door lock (which appears to be very sturdy and is equipped with a deadbolt and peephole).

"I wonder if this deadbolt was here before," Angela says. "Obviously, they had to replace the door after Ken kicked it down." She points to a pile of boxes in a corner. "Right under where those boxes are now," she says. "That's supposedly where he was sitting when the body was discovered."

We carefully move the boxes one by one to the other side of the room so we can get a better look and draw a mental picture of how the murder unfolded all those months ago. Once the last box has been moved and the wood floor has been exposed, we see it—the discoloration where someone scrubbed at the wood, with what must have been almost pure bleach to strip away the stain and varnish, leaving a pale amoeba-like shadow of what was once (supposedly) a blood stain.

Only, there was never any blood in that spot.

If there had been, I could have seen it, smelled it, even after all this time and even under all that bleach residue. We stand and stare at the spot as though we'd just come across the victim himself. As if we were watching Mr. Ken Watanabe busting down the door and being greeted with the horrible sight of his murdered grandfather.

"Ugh," Angela says. "I hate this guy. He's evil, pure evil. We have to get him, Doe. You and me. We have to get the Slasher, or nobody will."

Angela feels injustice in the world as we all do. The

difference between Angela and a lot of other people is that she wants to act on it. Root it out. Right the wrongs.

All I want to do is survive.

I decide against telling Angela what I know to be true, that there was never any blood to begin with. What would be the point of telling her if I can't reveal how I know? I wander off to inspect the other rooms: a small bedroom big enough for a single bed; a tiny bathroom with shower; a kitchenette with a microwave and one of those little bar refrigerators. There's nothing here. Nothing, not even tiny droplets or splashes of blood like in Myrna's place. I know it's been cleaned—thoroughly—but I would've smelled it. Seen it.

"Weird," I hear Angela say from the small living room where she's moving the boxes back into place. I walk through the bedroom door to where she's standing, peering into one of the boxes which has been opened, no doubt, by her.

"Should you be doing that?" I ask. "I mean, he didn't give us permission to open the boxes."

"I didn't open it... exactly. The tape was loose and—"

"You helped it along," I say.

"A little."

"So, what's weird?"

"Probably nothing," Angela says. "But I noticed the same flyer in Myrna's house." She passes a leaflet to me that has the tell-tale holes on top where a staple once held it to a utility pole. A flyer requesting signatures and addresses to put legislation on the ballot to provide public funding for animal rescue no-kill shelters. A website where supporters of the legislation can sign up.

These are the flyers Peter and Fernando were posting when I saw them near Uncle Ramon's house.

"So, we're back to cats again, are we? Anyway, I've seen these flyers all over town... Fernando and Peter have been posting them. I don't know how it could be significant. Myrna and Jiji were both animal lovers, after all."

I think about what Molly's mom says—how angels watch over people who love animals. Where were the angels when Jiji Watanabe and Myrna were slaughtered in their own homes?

Angela purses her lips. Then she returns the flyer to the box which is filled with papers and photos and some books. She presses the tape back into place and sets another box on top.

"Check out the wood crate in the corner," she says. "I recognize the Gurkha Kukri on top. He bought it at our store."

Even from where I'm standing, I can see inside the large crate packed carelessly with various swords, daggers, and even an antique pistol is visible through the wooden slats. The samurai swords themselves (I spot a splendid katana and several magnificent wakizashis) must be worth a small fortune. It's obvious that Ken Watanabe wants nothing to do with this collection, and who could blame him? Although these weapons haven't seen action in decades or even centuries, the stink of blood and death is still upon them.

But it's the kukri that most bothers me. A curved dagger from what is now Nepal, popular folklore claims Dracula was killed when his throat was on the receiving end of the kukri blade, his heart simultaneously welcoming a Bowie knife. Although Dracula is a fictional character, there were always the yahoos out there just dying to make a name for themselves by using a kukri to slash the throat of a vampire, and if you've ever seen a kukri, you know what a disturbing thought that is. Historically, vampires made light of it, inoculating themselves against fear by owning one of the loathsome daggers, a sort of reverse lucky charm. Lord Istvan himself possessed one and hung it above his hearth but, of course, I knew nothing of its significance to vampires or Lord Istvan's true nature until it was too late.

Now just thinking about poor Jiji Watanabe and

Myrna, the kukri feels like a dangerous animal—a caged cobra in a wooden crate just waiting to strike, although I know it hasn't been used for centuries. One can tell these things if one is a vampire—relatively new blood versus ancient blood. There's nothing but ancient blood in this home. In the meantime, the Six o' Clock Slasher continues to foil everyone on his tail.

Ken Watanabe appears in the open doorway. "You two about ready to wrap things up? Sorry to rush you but it's date night for the wife and me and the babysitter's here."

"Mr. Watanabe, there was no sign of forced entry, right?"

"That's correct."

"Was Jiji the kind of person who would've opened the door to an unknown person at night?"

"It's possible if he thought it was one of my kids… his grandkids. But he wasn't a stupid man. Quite the opposite, in fact."

***

"I don't know, what d'you think, Doe?" Angela asks once we're back out on the street. "It's pretty amazing we've gotten this kind of access to two crime scenes, but I don't think we're going to get this lucky again."

"Lucky?" It's time for me to tell Angela what's on my mind. I've lived with death for far too long and can't take any more. I need calm in my life. Peace. When I signed up for a criminology class, I was thinking of petty crimes—smash and grabs, burglaries, identity theft. I didn't sign up to be hot on the trail of the Six o' Clock Slasher, for heaven's sake. I can barely cope with worry about Clementine's safety and health. I can barely cope with rejection from a literary agent. How can I possibly continue to cope with images of Jiji Watanabe and Myrna, their heads slumped over as if they were napping instead of nursing a mortal wound.

"You know what I mean," Angela says. "I mean, we

have to take what we've been given and try to see what everyone else has missed so far."

"I need to talk to you," I blurt out. "Now."

Angela signals me with her go-ahead look.

"I've been thinking about dropping Onslot's class from day one," I say. "But I was worried he'd cancel the class, and everyone would blame me."

Angela doesn't say anything, just nods for me to go on.

"But now I think I'm going to drop—" I stop when her face drops at the same time I say the word. "I can't—"

"Look, I know you can't stand him," Angela says. "But please just hang in there. Skip the next class if you need to. I'll be your buffer because I know he bullies you and I won't let him get away with it. We're partners, remember?"

"It's not just that. It's... you know I have anxiety issues."

Angela nods.

"I can't deal with it anymore. The mayhem. The violence. At night when I go home, I can't get the... those images out of my head."

The blood, I don't say. The scent of it. The waste of it. The devastating appetite I have for it that will never go away as long as I roam the earth. Even just talk of it. Thinking about it. I'm not strong enough to resist forever. It's like being an alcoholic and working in a liquor store.

"I get it," she says. "I totally understand you need to do what you need to do to protect yourself, and I'll still be there for you. Once a partner, always a partner."

"What about you? Does this ruin everything?"

"I still have support," she says. "Lilibeth does brainstorming sessions with me. And maybe you could at least be there if there's something I wanna run by you?"

"Always."

"So, will you come to class tomorrow to say goodbye or do you want me to tell Onslot."

I can at least do this on my own. There's no way Onslot can add to my troubles, and I don't want Angela getting the wrong impression. I *am* capable of many things, just not *everything*. And 317 years has taught me to distinguish between the two.

"I'll be there," I say. "And thanks for understanding."

CHAPTER THIRTY-ONE

"WHAT ARE YOU DOING out here?"

My last class with Onslot which I've been dreading the entire day. Dreading so much, in fact, I'm late. And here's Angela leaning against the side of the building on the most bitterly cold and damp night of the year, backpack slung over her shoulder, slowly shaking her hood-covered head. Her frustrated sigh comes out with a breath-cloud.

"No class," she says. "I've been waiting for you for like..." She checks her watch. "Fifteen minutes."

"He canceled class tonight?"

"Class canceled. Permanently. Like no more class ever."

It just takes a second to put two and two together. "His trial... guilty?"

"As charged." She pulls a crumpled paper from her pocket and thrusts it at me. "I brought it for you to see since everyone else has already seen it. Thought you'd want to know."

SORRY TO INFORM THAT THE POWERS
THAT BE SAW FIT TO UNJUSTLY CHARGE
AND CONVICT THE ONLY GOOD
COP ON THE FORCE.
SORRY NO REFUNDS.

"Wow," I say.

"Surprised?"

"Nope. I only wonder if they'll let him keep his Tabasco sauce in jail."

Too soon? I couldn't resist.

"Hey!" Angela pats her own Tabasco sauce holster which is always strapped to her hip. "No cruel and unusual punishment, remember? Food is worthless without it."

"You know he only started carrying it to get in with the cool crowd, i.e. you. But let's not waste any more breath on Onslot. What will *you* do now?"

"Let's walk," she said. "I gotta catch the bus."

Angela's nose and cheeks, normally a warm beige, are red from the extreme chill of the night. A blue wool scarf is wrapped around her neck to just under her chin. Her upper lip shines with moisture from her dripping nose. I notice these things. Cold. Damp. Breath-clouds. Leaky noses. None of this affects me although I pretend it does by mimicking the actions and dress codes of humans. I can shiver along with the best of them.

"Of course," I say. "I'm sorry for you, and I hope we'll see each other—"

I'm trying not to look too happy, but this solves all my problems. The search for the Slasher is off and I'm personally off the hook. Sometimes fate really does intervene in a good way.

"We'll see each other, don't you worry," Angela says. "I know where you work, so I'll be dropping by. And don't feel sorry for me because there's no way I'm giving up now."

So maybe this wasn't the complete separation I'd hoped for. I have to admit I've grown accustomed to having Angela around but would have preferred her company without all the other baggage.

"You know the flyer that Myrna and Watanabe had? The animal rescue thing for the no-kill shelters?" she asks. I nod my head. "When I went home, I Googled the organization and went on their website. It's legit. But when I called the number on the website, they didn't know anything about the flyer. The guy on the phone said he didn't think they'd ever put up flyers."

A cold chill of the type I *do* experience crawls up the back of my neck. I don't want to hear any more about the Slasher. I want to go home and be done with this whole episode of my life. When I signed up for Onslot's class little did I know I'd be making one of the biggest mistakes of my life.

"Interesting," I say in a tone I hope conveys quite the opposite. Indifference. Boredom, even. I can't feed into her obsession or she'll drag me back down with her. "Maybe it was just an intern or a new worker. You can't assume the guy who answers the phone knows everything."

"That's what I thought too, Doe, so I asked how many people they have on staff and you know what he said? Three. They have three people on staff. This isn't some huge charitable organization or anything. It's just a tiny group of dedicated animal lovers working for free."

"Okay. Your point?"

"I'm getting to my point. I tracked down the boys you call the Wheelies, you know... the blondie and the Latino kid."

"Peter and Fernando," I say. "The Wheelie Boys."

"Exactly. And I asked who hired them to put up those flyers, and you know what they said?"

"I think you're about to tell me." I never dreamed that when Angela asked me to share my contacts, she'd actually use them.

"They said an older guy... forty-something. He gave them each a hundred-dollar bill to cover the city."

"Maybe he's a supporter... someone who loves animals and is trying to help spread the word."

"Could be." Angela nods thoughtfully. "I know they've tried to get the initiative on the ballot before. The guy I talked to on the phone said this will be their third attempt and he asked me to help spread the word because they think they have a real shot this time."

"There you go. See."

"I was just thinking, Doe... that an animal lover might open their door to someone at night. Someone claiming to have found a lost cat or someone who wants them to sign a petition. Animal lovers have big hearts, you know?"

"That's pretty far-fetched," I say. "Besides, what are you saying... that someone in this well-meaning poorly funded organization is a serial killer?"

"Not at all," Angela says. "It's just that with a list of names and addresses of people who are obvious animal rights supporters, a person with an evil mind could use that information to talk their way into someone's home. It's just a thought, and you said it's okay if I bounce stuff off you. Oh, shoot. I forgot to show you the biggest thing." She pulls a flyer from the pocket opposite the one that held Onslot's notice. "Check out this website address."

"Did you take that from Watanabe's house?" I ask, prepared to scold her.

"Nope. The wheelie dudes had a stack they still had to put up. They gave me one."

I glance at the URL which doesn't seem like anything special. "So?"

"So, see right there." She points at the last letter right before the dot org. "Right there it's missing an S."

"Typo."

"I tried it and it works. Fully functioning. I even entered a fake name and address to test it out. And there's no phone contact like there is on the real website."

A dread is growing inside of me—I call it the black dog of my despair and it's back to hound me, so to speak. Its sudden appearance is alarming as it gnaws on my heart. My stomach. My detestable intestines. I feel the urge to defecate which is something I normally only do two or three times a year.

"Anyway, there's my bus so I'd better run. Talk soon, okay? Think about what I said."

But I don't want to think about what Angela Ruiz just said. As I watch the bus door slide open with a hiss, engulfing her into its cavernous mouth, I'm suddenly seized with a paralyzing fear.

"Be careful!" I call after her although, to my ears, it's a pathetic squawk and beyond the reach of Angela's ears. "Don't do anything stupid."

***

No sooner do I return home than there's a light rap on my door.

"John, it's Henrietta. Can I come in, honey?"

Rarely have I denied entrance to Henrietta and tonight is no exception even though I haven't had more than a few seconds to check on Clementine's well-being.

"You're home from class awfully early tonight," she says. "I was wondering if you're not too busy would you care to accompany me on my rounds tonight?"

"Of course," I say, taking another furtive look at Clementine who's wiggling with joy just at the sight of me. "Let me give Clementine a few flakes first."

"Not a problem," she says. "You take your time and when you're ready just come on by. There's quite a bit to carry tonight so I'm grateful for your help. Don't think I could've managed on my own."

The "quite a bit to carry" turns out to be blankets, jackets, gloves, toothbrushes, soap, socks, hairbrushes, canned goods that don't require cooking, energy bars, bottled water, and more. Miss Devine has been busy collecting donations, both from neighborhood stores and the people who live in apartment buildings up and down our street. With her preference for doing the rounds at night, and my ability to only be out at night, we make a perfect team. The added benefit of our nighttime hours is the very low risk of running into Mrs. Dilliberato who never leaves the manager's apartment after 5:00 p.m., barring an unforeseen emergency such as a broken water pipe.

I pull the wagon loaded with the donations, trailing behind Miss Devine, who stops to chat with each person. She knows their names, their afflictions, the names of their children, parents, spouses living and deceased. She remembers where they came from and what chain of events brought them to the point where a cold, hard sidewalk replaced a warm, soft bed. We stop to chat with the old lady with the spotted dog who's wearing my sweatshirt. Henrietta gives her a small bag of dried dog food.

If Henrietta has a gift to share, it's not the blankets or jackets or energy bars or even the bottled water, although those are vital and greatly appreciated. It's her smile, the way she laughs with them and helps them dredge up fond memories, the way she looks in their eyes while she listens. It's the way she becomes a human mirror, reflecting back their own humanity and reminding them of their worth.

Henrietta's greatest gift is to make the invisible feel visible, if only for the few precious minutes she has to share.

I look away, pained by reminders of my own loss of self. What I would have given for a Henrietta during my darkest times when the black dog was nipping at my heels, threatening to pull me down into the netherworld. Those times, after the loss of Dr. Ostentaysius, after the loss of Marie, when I thought nothing would ever again coax a smile from my face or plant a seed of hope in my heart.

***

All night, my ears have been burning. Someone's been following us, of that I'm sure. By the time I get home I have a headache of massive proportions and anxiety to match.

"Lock up, okay," I say when I part company with Henrietta at her front door.

"I will, Johnny. You know I always do."

"All four deadbolts," I say. "I'm going to stand here until I hear you do it."

She laughs in that rich husky way she has, and I stand outside her door until every single lock has clicked into place.

And then I go home and collapse into my own private hell.

CHAPTER THIRTY-TWO

The Last Vampire

[REVISED]

By John Doe

Chapter Thirty-Two

The Roaring '20s for many was a time of great excitement and vibrancy, where everyone seemed to be young, beautiful, and rich. But for me, the Roaring '20s—the Jazz Age—was like a two-ton crystal chandelier hanging from the ceiling by a single silk thread. More alone than ever before, I seemed to be pulling pebbles from a basket only to toss them into the sea—each pebble, a reason to live. It wasn't long before my basket was empty, my existence having outlived any rational purpose for life. Those were the years when I first met the black dog of despair. The eternal life I'd been granted through Istvan's toxic bite became nature's cruelest punishment for the only survivor of what was meant to kill us all.

The decade that came in with a roar went out with a crash—that is, the stock market crash of 1929. Overnight millionaires became beggars. The shameful waste of the 1920s was now not only unthinkable, it was disavowed by the masses who claimed to have witnessed it but never partook of it themselves.

This new decade, which would come to be known as the Great Depression, marked the end of my own great depression. Whereas I'd barely been treading water for years, scarcely coming up for air, now I could finally swim to shore—a shore that was suddenly plainly visible to me. I'm not sure why it happened, although I have my theories. All I know for sure is that the black dog finally put its tail between its legs and slunk off to its den to be heard from no more.

With unemployment at 25% no one paid much attention to me, which was exactly what I needed. I was just another person looking for work, riding the rails, crisscrossing the country in search of it. No job was beneath me so I took whatever I could get. And I admit to feeding off the most vulnerable—others, like me, who never turned down an honest day's work and more often than not, never turned down a dishonest day's work either, if the opportunity presented itself.

But I never hurt anyone, I swear on my mother's long-lost Bible. I never took more than I needed to live. And I always left behind a few coins—as much as I could spare—for those who provided. Sometimes I stuck around long enough to see the joy on their faces when they opened their eyes in the morning and saw a few nickels or dimes scattered on the ground next to them, scooping them up with one hand while scratching the itchy bites on their necks with the other. So, for those people, at least, I did good, buying them a second meal on a day when they were destined for only one. In any case, I can safely say I did no harm.

Did the idea of ingesting germs bother me back then? Most certainly. But the idea of starvation bothered me more. Constant movement, constant work—it has a way of smothering the worry out of you. I'd always assumed that vampires were tortured beings and there was no other way for us to be, but those years, that decade, those were happy times for me. Even if I had no actual peers, I had real friends who didn't judge my otherness. Comrades together in our plight of "us against the world." The fellows I befriended—hobos they called them back then—they were fine fellows doing their best to survive under very difficult circumstances. I made many friends working odd jobs here and there. Most of them would be gone by now.

When WWII came along, everything ramped up into high gear. Once again, I found myself left behind. Once again, living in the shadows. Once again, alone.

CHAPTER THIRTY-THREE

"Back so soon?"

I don't wait for Bibi to ask. I head straight for my usual chair, collapse into it and recline myself as close to 180 degrees as I can get.

"I have a problem," I say to the ceiling.

"Your classmate again?" she asks. "With the boundary issues?"

"No, that's been resolved. It's something else."

"For my own education, can I ask how you resolved it? It might come in handy one day with another patient."

I prop myself up on my elbows, raising my head to look at Bibi. "Do you have a new patient?"

"No. Not yet. But when I do."

I collapse again, a little too hard, and I worry for an instant about a vertebral fracture in my neck, my bones being as porous and susceptible to fracture as they are. I wait for five seconds. No pain. I blink at the ceiling. Three times fast. Three times slow. Three times fast again. I no longer care if Bibi witnesses my rituals.

"I resolved it in two ways," I say. "First, class is over. It's been canceled permanently so we're no longer classmates."

"That's convenient," Bibi says.

"Second… an amicable friendship divorce."

I hear Bibi scratching—pen against paper. It no longer makes me nervous to know she's taking notes. In fact, I've come to find it reassuring.

"That's a new one," she says once the scratching has

stopped. "And how did your classmate... *former* classmate... take it? The amicable friendship divorce."

"She... uh... I'm not sure she realizes it yet."

More scratching.

"But that's not my problem today."

"Okay, so what's your problem today?"

I take a deep breath. "I think I'm being followed."

There, I've said it out loud. At last.

"Followed, as in...?"

"Followed. Like someone is following me." Try as I might (and I am), I can't completely erase the impatience from my voice. Fortunately, Bibi ignores it.

"Are you? Being followed, that is."

I bring the back of my hands to my eyes as if to block out the world, but it doesn't work. The world is still there.

"No, of course not. It's my anxiety. Aren't you supposed to talk me through it?"

There's a brief silence but I don't hear any scratching, so I calculate Bibi's either thinking about my question or she's angry with me. I dearly hope it's the former.

"Well," she says and, from her even tone, I can tell she's not angry. "What if you came in here and told me you were coughing up blood and I knew for a fact that you had health anxiety."

"Which I do."

"Which you do. Should I just tell you it's all in your head, or should I first make sure you're not coughing up blood?"

I sigh deeply in lieu of crying. I press the backs of my hands so tightly against my eyes, I begin to see stars.

"Open your eyes, John," Bibi says. "You're safe."

"Am I?"

"You're safe right now," she says.

I move my hands back to my sides but keep my eyes shut.

"Let's get back to this feeling you have of being followed. Would it necessarily have to be a bad thing?"

"Of course. It's never a good thing to be followed. If someone wasn't intent on harming you, why would they follow you? If they wanted to do something nice for you, they'd just come out in the open and do it."

"Are you thinking of harming yourself, John?"

"No, no. Never." After 317 years of far more despair than delight, the thought has never once occurred to me. I cling to my life like a dog clings to its stinky, spitty, chewed-up rag toy. "Why would you ask that?"

"Because I have to."

Scratching.

"Have you ever had this feeling before? Like you're being followed."

"Yes," I blurt out a tad too quickly.

I've had this feeling many times over the past three centuries. It started not long after I returned to see Nadia and learned of my father's death. But it's not really a feeling, it's a fact. I *am* being followed.

But the reality is we're all being followed by someone. Someone is always behind us and often going in the same direction. Normally it's a stranger with no connection to us, so why can't I just let it be? I rap on my skull five times.

"Okay, let's just play this out. If you think you're being followed and you're sure it's not true but just the result of your anxiety... in other words, it's all in your head... can we make the fantasy play out so that it's actually someone who wants to do you a good deed?"

I prop myself up on my elbows and try not to glare at her, but I do glare at her, although I have enough self-restraint to keep my mouth shut.

"Why not?" she says, shrugging her shoulders, her wise-child eyes taking in mine. "If your mind's capable of creating a stalker with evil intent, isn't it just as capable of creating one with good intentions. We could work on it right now. A Santa Claus type character who maybe... wants to see what your daily life is like, so he knows just the right kind of present to give you for Christmas."

"Are you making fun of me?"

"No. I mean... I think it's worth a shot, don't you? We can play with it. Do it together. See what we come up with."

It seems utterly ridiculous but what's worse: diving into an utterly ridiculous brain game or living in terror?

"I suppose so," I say.

"But before we start, there's something I need to tell you. I'll be gone next week. I'm going to Hawaii with my parents."

This is unexpected. Unacceptable. Un... *intolerable.*

"But... but... you'll miss school, won't you?"

Yes, that should do it. It's not yet winter break, or is it? Children don't just go running off to Hawaii while school is in session, do they? That couldn't possibly be permissible. Her parents wouldn't allow it. The school wouldn't allow it.

"No biggie. We do it every year and it's just for a week. My teachers are cool with it."

No biggie or a precursor to the fall of civilization? In my day, we'd be beaten with a stick if we ran off to play instead of showing up for class. Of course, most days our parents needed us at home, so we actually spent very little time in class. Almost none at all.

"But... what if I need you? Can I call you?"

"No, I'll be on vacation, remember? You don't really need me. You figure everything out on your own. I'm just a sounding board."

But Bibi's so much more than a sounding board. Bibi is wise. And I am... I am smart but not wise.

"Can I text you if I need to?"

"No... okay, yes. But only if you really need to."

I'll do everything within my power not to bother Bibi on her vacation, but just knowing I can is a huge relief. Knowing I can is probably the thing that will keep me from doing it.

We play out the good-guy fantasy for another fifteen

minutes, coming up with everything from a lost fuzzy bunny looking for someone to take it home and feed it a carrot, to a stranger who saw a twenty-dollar bill drop out of my pocket and is trying to return it to me, to an agent from a modeling agency who loves my look and wants to sign me. It succeeds in tamping down my anxiety and I vow to use this tactic the next time I get that special pain in my ears.

When I finally maneuver my chair into an upright sitting position, I'm this close to hugging Bibi—if only I was the type to hug people. Which I'm not for obvious reasons, not the least of which is my hard exoskeleton (formerly skin) that would be difficult to explain. And so many other reasons having to do with boundaries and professional doctor-patient relationships and a myriad of others including I'm just *not* the type to hug people. So, I don't but I'm grateful, and I know I'll miss her terribly even though it's just for a week.

"John," she says once I'm standing and she's gathering up her things. "Be careful okay? Just in case you really are coughing up blood."

CHAPTER THIRTY-FOUR

I WASN'T HOME FIVE minutes before self-bargaining kicked in and despite Bibi's parting words, which troubled me not only for its reference to the red stuff but also for the implication of a real threat that might not be the product of my over-active imagination, my worrying self won out.

It went something like this:

Self: Molly leaves sometime tonight, doesn't she?

Self: Yes. So what?

Self: Her fish are all alone and the power might have gone out. If so, the aquarium heater would not work, and the water would become too cold to sustain the life of a tropical fish.

Self: Why would the power go out? The weather is very cold but not at all windy.

Self: Other things could happen.

Self: Such as?

Self: Perhaps Molly left in such a hurry she forgot to feed her fish.

Self: Molly would not do that. And you're not even sure what time she leaves tonight.

Self: It's better to be safe than sorry, isn't it?

Self: Really?!

Self: What if she left earlier than expected? Yesterday, even.

Self: She said I only had to feed them three times. Four max. And besides, you were planning to work on your manuscript tonight.

Self: And whose shoulders would it fall upon if something bad were to happen to her fish?

Self: Yours.

Self: Mine.

I'm an annoyance to myself to a far greater degree than I could possibly ever be to someone else. With an exasperated sigh, I grab my jacket—not necessary for my comfort but totally necessary for being a believably dressed person in this cold snap we're having. I wrap a scarf around my neck twice and pull on my knit beanie for good measure. Then I'm out the door.

This is one of those occasions when traveling vampire style is in order. I want to get in and out as quickly as possible so I can go home and devote a few hours to the final edit of my manuscript. I've been making good progress, so now my next question is whether to re-query the agents who rejected me more than a year ago and may not have kept a record of my initial query, re-query with the disclaimer that this is a newly revised version of a previously submitted manuscript, or search for new agents or agents I may have previously considered beneath me but no longer would.

A block away from Molly's house, I slow to travel the normal way. This makes me vulnerable to the possibility of being followed and even more vulnerable to thoughts of being followed. I think about the bunny and the twenty-dollar bill and the talent scout in love with my sleek looks. They aren't working so well out here in the real world.

Instead, I imagine myself as the leader of a marching band. A drum major smartly dressed in a red jacket and white pants with red stripes down the side. Fringed epaulets accent my wide shoulders. Shiny black boots nearly up to my knees. A tall white hat adorns my head, its chin strap cupping my jaw, drawing attention to the chiseled masculinity of my natural bone structure. In my right hand, an ornate baton is tucked under my armpit. I bring it forward, drawing it back and forth in the air to direct the music. I high-step to the tempo. All eyes are on me waiting to see where I'll go, what pace I'll set for those who follow me. I feel a surge of power and self-confidence and notice that I'm indeed lifting my feet higher. Holding my back straighter. Swinging my arms confidently. Bibi would be proud of me.

Everyone behind me is just part of the band.

I march the remaining half block leading to the front entrance of Molly's building where I use the building key to let myself in. I march through the lobby (decidedly nicer than my own) to the staircase. I march up the stairs, shortening my pace to align with each step. When I reach the second landing, I march down the hall towards Molly's apartment number 212 as if I were Harold Hill, himself. It's impossible to feel helpless when you're leading a marching band, especially one as big as my own. It's impossible to feel…

I whistle a John Philip Sousa marching tune which I raise to an ultrasonic frequency with the greatest urgency. The homecoming echo rushes through my ear canals like a scream that's just broken the sound barrier. With a sudden and complete loss of balance I reach for the only support around, Molly's doorknob, but it's not enough so I lower myself to the ground, trying to recapture my balance in the palms of my hands which instinctively cover my ears. The hallway continues to spin around me like a whirling dervish. I squeeze shut my eyes and breathe in deeply, my head supported by my drawn-up knees.

Only supersonic motion can disturb my hypersensitive radar in this manner, but the hallway is empty, and the movement isn't approaching me, it's receding. Way too fast.

With my balance only partially restored, I struggle to my feet and shove the apartment key into the hole, but it doesn't work. Something's jamming the other side. How many more red flags do I need? Without a second's thought, I pull my leg back and with all my considerable strength (and no thought to my porous femur) I kick open the door.

The violence of my forced entry belies the peaceful scene before me—peachy earth tones and cool pastels, surprising greens of healthy houseplants, books neatly stacked, floral bedspread draped over a hastily-made bed, the soft, homey rag rug, jewel-colored fish gliding across the aquarium, pink anemones swaying in their wake. Molly, sitting in a chair, her head resting peacefully on the tiny table, her rust-brown hair blending perfectly with the oak stain, her pale, white hand inches from her phone.

Her gray eyes are wide and glassy. Like a dead fish. Staring at nothing.

There's no point in yelling or shaking her. I hold her limp wrist and feel for a pulse but don't feel one. Self-bargaining kicks in.

Let Molly be alive, and I'll never complain about anything again as long as I live.

I move my fingers to the side of her throat. I can feel it, the faint beat of a heart struggling with all its might to squeeze life back into its host. I know the signs of hemorrhagic shock all too well. Her brave heart is straining to push what's left of her blood through her body, beating as rapidly as if she'd just run a marathon. I feel for her breath on the back of my hand; it's weak but rapid.

Molly, please live. Molly, please don't leave me. Molly, I'll do anything. Anything, if you just don't die.

I hear footsteps coming up the stairs. In a matter of seconds, I'll be discovered leaning over her near lifeless body. I'll be arrested and taken to prison where my true nature will be revealed. They'll blame me for this terrible thing. I don't care what happens to me, but I couldn't bear it if anyone thought I did this to dear Molly.

I pick up her phone and dial 9-1-1, pitching my voice high and breathless. Faint. Whisper-light.

"Help me," I say into the phone. "I need blood...Six o' Clock Slasher...212."

I check to make sure the phone's GPS is turned on. The footsteps draw closer.

I leave no fingerprints because I have no fingerprints, so there's nothing to wipe down. I remember the plugged keyhole and pull the wadded-up paper that's been stuffed into it from the inside. A torn piece of the animal rescue organization flyer. The very same one that has Angela on the move. In the small waste can by the door is the rest of the flyer. I put it on the table next to Angela for the cops to find.

The footsteps are almost upon me and now there's yelling in the hallway as well. Someone has spotted the broken door; they must have heard the noise I made when I entered.

The window is already open which I only just notice. It's large enough for someone to have made an exit, so this is how the assassin escaped and how I will escape as well. A ledge outside the window is only about four inches deep but that's wide enough for me. The stucco exterior is rough enough for my hands to grip. I could easily jump from the second floor with only the possibility of a painful, fractured leg that should eventually heal, although it would take many years. Or I could climb down the face of the building clinging to the stubble of its exterior like a free climber, easy enough for me.

But I stay as near to Molly as I can until I hear sirens approaching. I hope it's too dark for anyone to notice my silhouette pressed flat against the wall, and in any case the first responders will be looking forward, not up.

"John Doe," someone calls up to me from the street. Some twenty feet beneath me are Fernando and Peter, idling on their scooters. "What the hell, John Doe?"

Tonight, of all nights, they're finally wearing helmets… helmets with headlamps, the beams of which merge to focus a painful spotlight on me.

I draw a finger to my lips and point to the approaching police cars. Then I point to the entrance of Molly's building. They turn to look, taking their spotlight with them.

One police car screeches to a halt, and then another. An ambulance comes next.

"Over there!" Peter hollers to the first cop out of his car. He points to the entrance of the building.

"We heard yelling coming from there," Fernando adds.

The police move quickly to the entrance, guns drawn. Someone's already at the door, holding it open for them, motioning them towards the stairs. The EMT's follow cautiously at a safe distance.

Once they're all out of sight, I scurry down the side of the building like a spider, jumping the final ten feet with a landing that sends a painful jolt up my spine. I gulp down a few breaths before straightening into an upright posture. The pain is fading which means no fracture. Peter and Fernando stare at me in disbelief. Peter's holding a stack of flyers and Fernando has the staple gun, as if they were about to hang a flyer on the post outside Molly's house when everything went down.

"Give me those," I hiss, and Peter wordlessly hands them over. I dump the whole batch in the garbage receptacle attached to the post. "Did you see anyone come out the window before me?"

They shake their heads solemnly. They're stunned and I feel sorry to be the cause of their distress.

"Okay, go pull down every last flyer you've put up and when you're done come see me at the diner tomorrow. I'll give you each a hundred bucks and as much food as you can eat for the next year."

"What're you going to do, John Doe?" asks Fernando, as though he's a bit frightened of me and my next move.

"I'm going to get the person that did this," I say.

"Did what?" Peter asks.

I can't afford to have them hanging around and I can't afford to be seen.

"Just go," I say. "Do what I asked and please don't tell anyone you saw me," I say. "I'll explain later, I promise."

I have no idea how I'll explain it to them since I can't even explain it to myself.

"Is it the Slasher, John Doe?" Peter asks.

"Go! Please hurry. It's not safe for you here and please... no one. You never saw me here tonight, okay?"

Without a word, they turn their scooters and zip off into the night, their new helmets lighting the way. I don't think it's entirely fear that makes them leave so quickly without pressing for answers to their questions. I think it's the purpose they feel of being involved in something much bigger than themselves.

I wait across the street in the shadow of an overhang until the emergency responders come out of Molly's building, carrying a stretcher through the door, then sliding it into the back of the ambulance. A drip bag connected to Molly is attached to an IV pole.

The attendants are moving fast which is a good thing, right?

An IV bag is a good thing, right?

I didn't know Myrna and I didn't know Jiji Watanabe but I do know Molly and I know one thing for sure: Molly *would* open her door to someone on the other side with a plea to save an animal in need. Molly would do that.

I also know something else. When I felt for Molly's pulse on the side of her neck, I saw something—two red, raised bumps (like mosquito bites) right over the carotid artery. I must have caught her attacker in the act which is why Molly was still alive. *Is* still alive—it must be so because I can't bear it any other way. I caught him before he successfully drained all the blood from her body.

FACT: The Six o' Clock Slasher is a vampire.

FACT: I'm not alone.

I watch the attendant leap into the back of the ambulance and pull the door shut behind him. The ambulance races off with sirens blaring.

Sirens blaring is a good thing, right?

There's only one thing left to do. I pull my phone from my pocket and punch in Angela's number.

"Doe?"

I've never called her before, so I understand the surprise in her voice.

"Angela," I say. "Where are you on the Six o' Clock Slasher case? I want back in."

CHAPTER THIRTY-FIVE

Before I see Angela, I have to see Molly. The nearest hospital is also the nearest trauma hospital, so I have no doubt that's where they're taking her. I could beat her there but what would be the point? I need to bide my time until she's been admitted and treated, and I can (hopefully) get more information. It's hard to restrain myself from going back to her apartment to check on the fish but the police are still there. And I did get a glimpse of the fish. They seemed fine.

I have a long dark night ahead of me and at least a few hours before I can check on Molly. I can't bring myself to go home. Editing my manuscript right now seems like a joke. I wonder if I'll ever be able to return to it with the intensity I had before. All that worrying I did about getting an agent, feeling rejected, wondering if my story would ever be read by anyone other than myself—it seems so silly right now. So insignificant when compared to Molly's life. And catching the Slasher.

Angela and I agreed to meet tomorrow before my shift at the Gobble-Down-Suck-Up. In the meantime, I need to come up with a plan or hope that Angela has one. I'm not confident on either account.

The police will be baffled by Molly's case. No slit throat. No bleach residue on the floor demarcating a fake blood stain. They won't understand the significance of the mosquito bites. Because vampires disappeared a hundred years ago, police these days aren't trained to look for their bites. And yet, there will be the recording of the 9-1-1 call where Molly (me) whispered the name of her attacker. There will be her near complete blood loss, probably a good two-thirds of it from the way she looked. Right about now the cops will be dusting for fingerprints, but they won't find any useful ones. They'll be checking Molly's computer files but probably won't find anything useful.

Except the website. If she signed up on the phony website, they might at least investigate further. Or not. Maybe Molly opened her door to someone claiming to be collecting signatures for the ballot initiative. I left the flyer on the table where the cops can't possibly miss it, but will they make the connection to Myrna and Mr. Watanabe the way Angela did?

I wish I could tell them what I suspect but, of course, that's not an option.

I walk so far and I'm so deep in thought, I scarcely know how I got where I am. It's a neighborhood park, in name only. In reality, it's the Grand Central Station of drug deals in this city. No one would think to bring their children here to play but plenty of junkies come here to buy and then, without being able to wait, shoot up and pass out within twenty yards of the spot where money and drugs exchanged hands. I find an empty bench which is surprising. Most benches in this park are occupied by now for those who have the presence of mind to put distance between themselves and the damp ground before surrendering to their chemical dreams.

All the years I've dreamed of finding another like me. All the years I've imagined how my life could be transformed if only there was someone—anyone—even just *one* other who would understand what I was going through. Someone who wouldn't judge me for being who I am. And now my wish has come true. He's out there somewhere and probably aware of me, if not tracking me.

It wasn't my anxiety that perceived the rapid movements only a vampire can make. It wasn't the Wheelie Boys throwing off my radar. It was him. And if it was him and he's following me then that means he purposely targeted Molly. He would have seen me at her home. He would have known we work together. He selected Molly to get to me. And what kind of a monster would do that?

Come get me, you bastard! If it's me you want, then come get me instead of attacking a defenseless human who has more value in her belly-button lint than your whole stinking, rotten, miserable life.

Molly's alive only because I interrupted the Slasher. How easily things could have turned out differently. How easily I could have settled into editing my manuscript and skipped the visit to Molly's apartment. All the years I hoped and dreamed, and this is who I get? The Six o' Clock Slasher? Be careful what you wish for, they say.

"Mind if I share this seat with you, bub?" An old guy with a gaunt face partially covered by a beard so sparse there are entire patches missing. His eyes slide to the back of his head and with effort he brings them back before they begin to slide again. He's shivering and I can see what looks like decades worth of needle tracks on his arm where he hasn't even bothered to roll down his sleeve. I take off my jacket and hand it to him and when he doesn't take it, I drape it over his shoulders.

"Be my guest," I say. "I was just leaving."

By the time I reach the edge of the park, he's horizontal and far away from the ugly reality of his life.

It's been hours since Molly should have arrived at the hospital. In another few hours, day will break, and I have to be home well before that. But I can't go home without at least trying to see her. I need to know if she's alive.

I walk around the building looking for the Emergency Room entrance which is where she would have been taken. This might very well be the busiest place in the city this time of night. In the waiting room I count two children and three adults, all coughing, all with glazed, feverish eyes (bad memories of the Spanish flu); I see a young woman, her expression stoic, her leg wrapped in gauze, a bright red patch of blood flowering from beneath her generously bandaged wound (I turn away); I eye a man, doubled over in his seat, moaning, insisting to anyone who passes (me) that he's sure he has appendicitis and can't I get someone to help (not a chance). I edge my way forward to the front where the receptionist has triaged everyone who's still waiting—the more serious cases, I know, are already behind the swinging double doors.

"A young woman," I say to him, "by the name of Molly Givens. She would be here at the hospital, I think. Brought here maybe two or three hours ago."

The receptionist stares blankly at me. He must have to ration out his compassion or risk running out of it ten minutes into his shift. I get that. I've seen my share of tragedy and it can wring you dry if you aren't careful. It can harden you to empathy. "Are you family?" he asks.

"No, a friend," I say and then curse my honesty. I should have said family. "I just want to check on how she's doing."

"Sorry, I'm not allowed to give out personal information."

"I know. I understand. Could you just... can you tell me at least if she's here?"

What I really want is confirmation that she's here as a patient and not in the morgue.

"Sorry," he says and looks down at the keyboard where he resumes typing whatever he was typing before I interrupted.

But I can't have waited all this time just to go home without knowing if she made it. For a moment, I consider busting through those double doors, running from room to room calling out her name—but she wouldn't still be in the ER. She'd be admitted by now. Or in surgery. Or wherever they take you to pump you full of blood again.

Or in the morgue.

I can try the main entrance and this time I'll say I'm a

relative. A cousin, I'll say. Visiting from out of town. Staying at her apartment while I'm visiting. I came home from the movies and found police swarming her apartment. They told me what happened. Told me to check at the hospital for information.

Outside the ER, I see an ambulance idling at the curb. The driver is looking at her phone, perhaps waiting for the next call. I recognize her. The EMT in the seat next to her is leaning back in his seat, his eyes closed. I recognize him too. This is the crew that brought Molly to the hospital. I rap on the window of the driver's side. She looks over at me and the window slides down. She looks tired.

"I was wondering," I say. "They told me you were the two who brought Molly Givens in a few hours ago. I'm her cousin and I… can you tell me anything? Anything at all?"

"We're not supposed to," the driver says. When I said she looks tired, I mean she looks *really* tired.

"Please," I say. "Can you tell me if she made it? Is she… alive?"

The guy opens his eyes and looks over at me. The driver looks over at him and they have a meaningful, yet wordless, exchange. The driver looks back at me.

"She's alive," she says. "At least she was when we brought her in. Thank goodness she had it in her to call 9-1-1 before she passed out. Another minute or two, she might not have made it."

"Thanks," I say. "I'll go to the front desk and see if I can visit."

I must look exceptionally pathetic because they suddenly seem more willing to talk to me.

"Probably not much chance of that," says the driver. "They assigned a cop to stay with her right when we got here. Police investigation, you know. They've probably got someone posted outside her room."

"Weird," her partner says. "Really weird. But we probably shouldn't say anymore."

"Sorry," the driver says. "About your cousin. That's

rough."

She's alive! Or at least she was when they brought her here. I hear a bird singing although the sun's not yet out. I need to be home, safely tucked away in my coffin.

I need my coffin tonight more than I ever have before.

CHAPTER THIRTY-SIX

My phone starts ringing first thing in the morning—only two hours after retiring to my coffin. It's Calvin and he doesn't text, he calls, and when he calls it's significant and something one should not ignore. But today I know why he's calling. The news has hit the wire. The police have probably already contacted him to find out what he knows about Molly and who might be trying to kill her. I know all this, but I don't want to discuss it with Calvin just yet. I'll see him later tonight and meanwhile I need more coffin time. More time to get my head wrapped around what's happened. I go one step further than muting my phone, I power it off.

***

"I'm so glad you're back," Lilibeth signs to me. "I love Angela, but I'm not cut out for this." Her silvery curls glisten under the flickering light of the fast-food joint where we're meeting for coffee. The smell of grease permeates the walls, rancid and old. The coffee is bitter but hot. One sip is all I need or desire.

"Hey, not too fast," Angela signs clumsily. "I'm improving but I can't keep up with you guys."

For my part, I'm not sure how to respond. *Glad to be back*, doesn't quite cut it. I'm desperate. Desperate to be back on the trail of the Six o' Clock Slasher, and this time with my whole heart and whatever part of the soul that still resides within me.

"I've had bad news," I say and sign. "Terrible news. I have to be honest, if it didn't happen, I probably wouldn't be here right now."

"The Slasher?" Angela asks as Lilibeth's eyes widen. "We heard rumors there might have been another victim last night. Do you know something we don't know?"

"No... I mean, yes to the rumors. No, I don't know anything more than what you heard on the news, but the victim, who I guess managed to save herself by calling 9-1-1 before she passed out... I know her well. Very well."

"No! Who is it, Doe?"

"You've met her," I say. "The waitress who served you that time you came to see me at work. Her name is Molly."

It's surprising how hard I have to work to keep my voice and my heart from cracking into a million pieces. Sometimes you don't know how badly something's affected you until you try to explain it to another person.

Angela turns to Lilibeth and begins to sign. "We... know—" But Lilibeth cuts her off.

"I know," she signs. Her shoulders slump forward. She has already lip-read what I just told Angela.

Angela turns back to me. "I'm sorry if this is hard for you to answer, or if you even know the answer... but why didn't he kill her? I mean... you know... like the others."

She doesn't want to come out and ask why he didn't slash her throat and I don't even want to think about that.

"I have no idea," I say. "Maybe something scared him off."

I realize this isn't the total and complete honesty Angela expects from her partner, but my hands are somewhat tied. I'll do all I can in every other way.

"Do you have any new leads?" I ask. "Anything at all we can go on?"

"Well...actually yes," Angela says. "I've been racking my brain trying to think of something... *anything*, and I kept coming up blank. I thought about the flyers but that might have been coincidence. I thought about whether someone might have come into the shop where I work and established contact with Watanabe... someone I didn't know because most of our customers are repeat customers. It's been driving me nuts because I wasn't getting anywhere."

Lilibeth nods. "She was not fun to be around," she signs and rolls her eyes.

"Then I had the idea to visit Onslot since you weren't around, and I needed a different perspective."

Ouch! That hurt. The fact that Angela had to turn to Onslot because I abandoned her? Unforgivable.

"But... isn't he in jail?"

"Yeah. I went to see him in jail. You can do that, you know, if he puts you on his visitors list. Anyway, he didn't think the idea about the flyer was that crazy. He thought it was worth investigating. And... here comes the good part... he suggested I ask those boys, Fernando and Peter, what the guy who hired them looked like... which I'd already done."

"I remember you said an older guy in his forties."

Laughable to think a guy in his forties is older. Try 317.

"Yep. And Onslot said that if I hired an artist maybe I could have the boys describe the guy and get some kind of likeness made up."

"A likeness. Good idea... I should've thought of that myself."

I'm a poor partner. A terrible partner, in fact. Angela deserves a way better partner than me.

"Me too. Seems so obvious, right? Anyway, guess what? I didn't have to hire an artist because Lilibeth's an amazing artist."

I'd almost forgotten that. The drawing she did of Angela was an uncanny likeness.

"So, we interviewed Peter and Fernando and they were actually really helpful in terms of coming up with a facial composite. That's what you call it, Doe—a facial composite."

"I know," I say. "And?"

"Young people have pretty good memories it turns out."

"Yes. That makes sense. So?"

"So..." She reaches for her backpack from the corner of the chair where it was hanging and puts it on her lap. She unzips the backpack and pulls out a large envelope. She opens the envelope and removes a white sheet of drawing paper. She places it face-down in front of her. She scoots our coffee mugs out of the way and then wipes the surface of the table with a few balled up napkins. Finally, she turns the paper right-side-up and places it in front of me.

"Guess what?" she says. "I *have* seen this guy in our store. He bought a kukri exactly like Mr. Watanabe's. In fact, they bonded one day in the store over their interest in the kukri."

I stare at the paper. It's drawn in pencil but may as well be in living color. It may as well jump off the page and grab me by the throat.

Because, guess what? I've seen him too.

MYTH: People who say they never forget a face are either lying or exaggerating or giving themselves more credit than they deserve. It's impossible to remember the faces of everyone you've ever known whether intimately or casually.

FACT: One never forgets the face of their murderer.

CHAPTER THIRTY-SEVEN

THE MOOD IS DOOM and gloom at the Gobble-Down-Suck-Up. The first thing I notice is a sign out front that says:

CLOSING EARLY TONIGHT (8 PM)
PRAY FOR MOLLY

Calvin looks up from the extra-large industrial skillet when I walk in.

"John," he says, and his voice is so subdued I almost check to make sure it came out of his mouth. Also, *John*? Calvin's never called me anything but *Doe*. "I tried to call to let you know but from the look on your face I guess you've heard."

"I heard," I say. "Horrible. I don't have words."

"She's alive," he says, and I notice he's not paying attention to the burgers sizzling away on the grill. I walk over, take the spatula from his hand, and flip a dozen patties which are already close to being burned on their undersides. Calvin looks bad, the usual bags under his eyes dark with sleeplessness. "I called the hospital just now and she's alive, but they won't let anyone see her except family. She has a police guard in front of her room. Twenty-four, seven, they said."

"Well, thank goodness for that at least," I say and hand the spatula back to Calvin who seems unaware to be holding it. I scan the kitchen and spot the regular dishwashing crew, but I don't see Dimitri.

"Where's Dimitri?" I ask. I'm most concerned about Dimitri of everyone here.

Calvin motions over his shoulder with his thumb. "I told him to take a break. We're just going to cook up this batch and then close down for the night."

Calvin hasn't closed the Gobble-Down-Suck-Up once in the fifteen years he's been in business. Not even when his children were born.

"I can't see the point of flipping burgers tonight," he goes on. "You know? Something like this makes you think about what's important in life, and it sure ain't cooking burgers."

"Don't talk like that, Calvin," I say. "People love this place. And you provide jobs for your employees so we can pay our rent, buy clothes, eat." He nods mournfully but I can see his heart isn't in it. "Who's waitressing?" I ask, and Calvin mumbles something I don't catch but don't want to ask him to repeat.

I get my answer when Doris walks in carrying a few empty plates. "Hey, John, long time." She never got to know Molly since they didn't overlap. Doris just up and quit one day and the next day Molly started. It wasn't a bitter parting, from what Dimitri overheard. No hard feelings as evidenced now by her willingness to cover for Molly. But by the look on Doris's face I know she can tell Molly's impact on the rest of us has been more significant than hers ever was.

Even though it looks like there are enough prepared French fries for ten meals, I need to get busy with tomatoes for the salads. But first I want to check on Dimitri. He's off in the corner where we take our breaks, sitting in a chair, leaning back with his head resting on the wall behind him. His eyes are closed but I can see dried tear stains on his cheeks, and it doesn't surprise me. Dimitri loves Molly. I leave him be.

No sooner are the tomatoes chopped than Dimitri is standing beside me.

"Those boys are at the back door asking for you," he says.

He looks defeated as he makes his way towards the shake machine, shoulders slumped forward, a shuffling walk.

"How you holdin' up, buddy?" Calvin walks over and places a hand on Dimitri's shoulder. "I just want you to know I'm real sorry because I know you're sweet on Molly. And another thing... I know I can be a jerk but that's all gonna change. Something like this just makes you think, you know?"

I worry for a minute the burgers are burning again but I see Doris scooping them up and sliding them onto the open-faced buns.

I shed my gloves and go to the back door where Fernando and Peter are waiting. I have a hundred-dollar bill for each of them. It was supposed to go towards my rent payment, but now Mrs. Dilliberato will have to wait a little longer.

"Did you take all the flyers down?" I ask.

They both nod and I notice they're looking at me in a whole new way. Almost as if they're in awe of me.

"Every one we could find," Fernando says. "Some of them were already torn down but we looked really good everywhere we posted."

"Thanks boys. Oh, and you haven't said anything to anyone about what you saw, right?"

They solemnly shake their heads in unison.

"Not even to Angela... I know you guys are friends now."

Peter and Fernando exchange glances as if to decide who should answer me.

"Don't worry. You were our friend before she was," Peter says. Fernando nods his agreement.

"And you give us fries," Fernando adds.

"And shakes," Peter says, although I've never given them shakes before and they seem to be testing the limits of how far I'm willing to go. Today, I'm ready to go as far as they want so I'd better get rid of them before it gets out of hand.

"Okay, thanks again." I nod first at one and then the other. "I don't have anything to give you tonight. We're closing early so there's just enough left for our paying customers."

"That's okay, John Doe," Fernando says. "We know what happened."

"John Doe," Peter says. "How did you climb down the side of that building?"

I'm ready for this question.

"Free climbing," I say. "It's called free climbing and I'm an expert. Something I do in my spare time."

"Oh, like that movie about the guy in Yosemite?" Fernando asks. "I saw that movie."

"Yep, just like that."

"Cool," Peter says. "I didn't know you did that, John Doe."

"Okay, you guys better get going and I better get back to work. We're closing soon and Calvin needs my help."

They look at me again with awe and... is it admiration I see in their eyes? It's so rare I'm tempted to bask in it, but I don't because admiration is a fleeting thing. External. It has nothing to do with how I feel about myself. But it does feel good for a brief moment in time.

FACT: If a kid likes you, they're more than willing to believe almost anything you tell them.

CHAPTER THIRTY-EIGHT

TWO DAYS OF TORMENT go by with very little to distract me.

Angela and Stuart—Angela's pot-growing, tan-loving boss—remember Istvan as someone who comes into the store to occasionally buy something with cash. The funny thing is they do have a security camera in the store and Angela's been poring through saved files (which are kept for thirty days but rarely looked at). She can't find a clip of Istvan although she swears she saw him in the store just a few weeks ago. Stuart swears it too. Usually Istvan comes in just before closing time, they both recall. When it's already dark, due to the winter time change, I make note.

I can't say it, of course, but they'll never find Istvan on camera. We vampires don't photograph well... or at all.

Since I now know Istvan's been following me, I worry about anyone close to me. If he went after Molly to get to me, he could go after others. I remind Angela not to answer the door to anyone but she's already wary and savvy. I have the conversation with Henrietta over and over.

"I'm just here to check that your door's bolted." I say every night to her locked door, which she opens immediately.

"Of course, Johnny. Don't you worry about me."

"But you just opened the door."

"Of course, I did. I recognize your voice."

"Someone could've been holding a gun to my head. Don't open it unless I text you first."

She sighs. "If you say so, Johnny. If that will make you

sleep better at night."

"It will. And don't open it to someone claiming that someone on the streets needs your help right away."

"But if someone really does..."

"You see. That's exactly what the Six o' Clock Slasher would do to trick a kind-hearted person like you. Just text me if someone knocks and I'll come out and check."

Another sigh.

"How about this?" she says. "I just won't open the door to anyone who knocks around six o'clock."

"No! The Slasher can change his methods. I'm not even sure if that name is accurate, it's just one of those catchy monikers some newspaper came up with for click-bait."

"Clickbait?"

"Just... don't answer to anyone. Even me. And don't ever ever invite someone into your home if you do open the door which you never should."

"But if I opened the door to a mass murderer, I don't think he'd much care if I invited him in or not," she says, completely baffled by my erratic statements.

And I can't explain the whole thing about vampires not being allowed in unless they're invited.

So, it's been like that the past two days with me and Henrietta. I wish Bibi were here because I need her more than ever, but I made a promise to her and I'm trying my best to keep it.

On the third day, tucked away in my coffin which has changed from a place of repose and meditation to a place of brainstorming and worrying, I have an alarming thought, followed soon afterwards by another alarming thought.

Alarming Thought #1: Is anyone feeding Molly's fish? How could I have forgotten? I am a self-centered being and a worthless friend.

Alarming Thought #2: Does Angela ever work the closing shift at Up In Arms on her own? Of course not. She couldn't. Wouldn't. Stuart would never allow that.

I text.

Me: You don't ever work the closing shift on your own, do you? After dark?

Angela: Ya, don't worry I can handle myself

Me: That's what everyone thinks. But you absolutely cannot.

A long pause

Angela: It kind of offends me that you would say that

Me: I just mean...

Angela: And don't forget where I work. We have protection here

Me: Like what? Your Tabasco sauce?!

I wish I hadn't said that last thing. It can only sound rude.

Another long pause. Three dots and then nothing. Three dots and then nothing.

Angela: Okay that kind of offends me too. We have weapons here in addition to the antique kind if you know what I mean. And I'm on the alert for the guy in Lilibeth's drawing

Me: You mean a gun?

Angela: No comment

Me: Have you ever fired a gun?

Angela: No but

A gun would be useless against Istvan even if she did know how to fire one.

Me: When do you close next?

Angela: Tomorrow. And I don't need you there, okay? I'm a big girl and can take care of myself

But *there* is exactly where I plan to be.

Later in the afternoon, I receive a group text from Calvin to all the employees. The Gobble-Down-Suck-Up will be closed for the next week with full pay for all employees.

***

When it's dark enough to get to Molly's place, I find the door has been replaced. I knock quietly to make sure her apartment isn't occupied by a visiting relative but, with Molly still in the hospital, I imagine any visiting relative would want to avoid this place where such horror unfolded only days earlier. Lucky for me, when they replaced the door, they didn't replace the lock. My key still works, and I enter as quietly as possible, so as not to arouse the suspicion of neighbors.

To my absolute delight, the automatic light setting of the aquarium is functioning and I count each and every one of the fish as they swim by, ecstatic at my unexpected presence. I feed them and they eat frantically, obviously famished but in good health from the looks of them. I water the snake plant and the fern before letting myself out, quietly locking the door behind me.

There's another stop I need to make before going home: the hospital. I know they won't let me see Molly and they haven't publicly shared any information about her, but I leave a message at the front desk which they promise to relay. Although they don't let on as to whether Molly is in any condition to receive my message.

"Please tell her from John that her fish are being fed and her plants are being watered."

CHAPTER THIRTY-NINE

As has become my habit of late, I whistle a tune as I make my way home—"On the Sunny Side of the Street" because I've always appreciated a good irony. After a minute or so I raise the pitch to echolocation levels. My echo-whistle is very much my own, every vampire having one as personal to them as a fingerprint is to a human. Since Molly's attack, every ultrasonic whistle I've sent out comes back empty; in other words, it doesn't come back to me at all.

This time it does.

The receptor cells in my ear canals feel like stinging nettles in my brain. I stop walking, perform a test whistle, and the stinging stops. I take a few steps and send out another signal which comes bouncing back at me full force. I stop again and take a deep breath. He's closer. Walk. Signal. Movement. Stop. Signal. Nothing. Each time I move, he moves closer to me like the children's game, Mother May I (where the "children" attempt to move closer and closer to the "mother" without being detected).

I don't want to face Istvan. Not yet. Not without a plan in place. And yet... and yet I want to see him more than anything I've ever wanted in my life. More than Nadia's love or Dr. Ostentaysius' friendship or Marie's understanding and compassion. Istvan's existence validates my own in its most primal and urgent need. For, if I am not alone, then I am someone. I mean something. I count.

I slow my step and continue to emit my echo-whistle. He draws closer and closer with every second until I can feel he's only a few feet behind me. I stop but don't look behind me.

We're in a dimly lit alley I've walked in to, by choice. No windows overlook this alley, no garbage dumpsters are rolled out here for collection, no dogs claw at chain link fences. I know this alley well, having used it once or twice as a rendezvous with Mr. X. Tonight, a heavy fog fills it up like an empty trough.

My heart is near bursting as if it could be the end of me, but my heart doesn't betray me. It never will, however shrunken and irrelevant it's become over the past 300 years.

"Hello, Zoltan."

Zoltan. The name elicits an involuntary laugh from me, as if someone is discussing the main character in my book with whom I have no personal connection.

I turn to face him and am shocked by the ordinary man in front of me. Without the trappings of his castle and his fancy clothes and servants and expensive carriages, he's just an ordinary man—perhaps in his forties when he was infected by who knows who. He's older than me, obviously. Not just older in years when he stopped being human and was infected by vampirovirus, but probably much older, perhaps centuries. No one in the village remembered a time when he wasn't there, living in the castle, presiding over us all.

But now I notice the little things: the thinning hair, the paunch, the beginning of jowls. These are things I would have been too scared to notice when I was just Zoltan.

"I don't go by Zoltan anymore. That's from a past I no longer belong to. Now I'm just John."

And now it's his turn to laugh—a high, tinny peal of laughter which ends as abruptly as it began. "I know that. But you are Zoltan and always will be Zoltan. A person can't change who they are, can they? A leopard can't change its spots."

Where did the courage go that I felt only seconds ago?

Why do I feel like the village boy trembling in the presence of his master? What is Istvan's hold on me? And why does hate now feel so much like love?

"You look well, Zoltan," he says, ignoring my preference for John, and I hate that his compliment has injected an extra beat into my heart. "I have so much to say to you. So much time has passed."

My emotions are like a pendulum swinging wildly. I hate the unfathomable hold he has over me, but I can't deny its existence. "What could you possibly have to say to me?" I ask. "Other than throw yourself at my feet and beg forgiveness for the fate worse than death you've bequeathed to me."

He takes a step closer and I can see that if he bothers with makeup, he hasn't bothered tonight. His skin is a ghostly white—paler than the fog that engulfs us. "Is it death you would have preferred?" he asks. "I would have preferred that for you as well. But your father exacted a promise from me that I'd spare your life, and so I did. I'm not a man who goes back on his word."

My father... Bela. He knew what he was condemning me to and thought he was doing a good deed by forcing eternal life onto me instead of a quick death?

"In all my life," Istvan says. "You're the only one I've spared." And the most amazing thing to me is that he speaks these words with great tenderness.

"You don't have to convince me of that," I say. "I've seen the results of your handiwork, or at least the ruin you've left behind. Unluckily for your killing streak, Molly survived without infection."

"And she has you to thank for that, doesn't she?" Istvan says. "Small matter. It was you I've wanted to see all this time, but I admit I've been afraid of the day we'd finally meet face to face."

"And here we are," I say. "Now what?"

"And here we are," he repeats dreamily.

"*What do you want from me?*" I scream the question

until it feels like my vocal cords will rip in two. In any other part of the city, people would call 9-1-1. Dogs would bark. A nearby cop car would flash its lights. But here in this abandoned alley nobody hears me. Nobody except Istvan whose eyes are moist but not from the fog.

"I want what you must want," he says. "Companionship. Understanding. I feel... you're like a son to me. I've tracked you throughout time only to have lost you and found you again and lost you again. But I've never had the courage... or perhaps the desperation to make contact until now. And now... now, my fondest hope would be if you felt for me what I feel for you. If I could be a father to you, like the father you deserved."

He holds his arms out to me and, since we're only inches from each other by now, I fall into his clutch and bury my head against his shoulder, hard like mine. I recognize his scent—like mine it's the scent of a decomposed corpse long after it's finished emitting the foul smells most repugnant to humans. Undetectable to a human but as plain as day to me. A tear rolls down my cheek, the release of moisture from my body a rare and precious event.

"How did you survive the 1918 flu?" I brush away the tear with the back of my hand. If Istvan survived there could be others. Maybe Istvan even knows where they are.

He gently pats my back. "I survived because of you, how else can it be explained? When I *turned* you, we became a part of each other, forever inseparable."

"But I... I survived because of the trial injections I was taking at the time and continued to take for years after. Dr. Ostentaysius—"

"Say no more, I know all about that practitioner of quackery and a good riddance to him, looking for a cure as if what we have somehow makes us monsters. We're no more monsters than the so-called philanthropic pillars of our society who give with one hand and rob with the other. We're immortal. We're gods, you and me. You survived because of a fluke in your genetic composition and I survived because you and I are one. For that I'm eternally grateful."

If I survived the 1918 flu virus because of a genetic fluke while tens of thousands of my peers perished... if Istvan is right and it's just the two of us for all eternity... well, as a connoisseur of the absurd, this would be one irony I just couldn't bear.

"As you know, I've been watching you," he continues. "So, I know you buy your blood from a vendor. We need to change that. We'll work on it together. It's an unhealthy practice and you must take your nutrients fresh from the source in order to be strong."

I pull away from his fatherly embrace and try to see beyond my own selfish need for his approval.

"Bela recognized this about you," he continues. "He said you were weak, but I know it's not weakness. It's fragility. I understand you as he never did. And I'll help you get over it. I'll teach you to be a man and not a boy."

"I have to go," I say, so deeply ashamed of myself that I can't bear being in anyone's presence, let alone Istvan's. What would Bibi say if she knew what I was feeling? What would she tell me to do if she could even bear to give advice to someone as toxic as me?

"When will I see you again?" Istvan asks.

I look at the time on my phone. "I'll meet you here in two days," I say. "At this same time. In the meantime, don't come looking for me and don't follow me. If you do, I won't ever speak to you again."

Istvan has power over me but I also have power over him. We both want what only the other can give. Understanding. Acceptance.

"You have my word and—"

"And don't ever come after one of my friends again," I say. "If you think that's a good way to get my attention, you're right."

The look of bemusement on his face says it all. A father's pride in his son tempered with the knowledge that the child has some "growing up to do." Weakness. Fragility. Things a strong father will tolerate for only so long.

CHAPTER FORTY

ALTHOUGH SHE TOLD ME not to come, here I am at Up In Arms checking on Angela just before closing time. Part of me wants to know that Istvan has taken me seriously enough to stay away from my friends (he knows Angela is my friend). Part of me wants to see if he's following me (he wasn't). And part of me just needs to talk to Angela, even if I can't tell her what's on my mind.

Some buddy. Onslot would not approve.

"Oh my God," she says when I walk through the door. "You really don't listen, do you? I appreciate your concern and don't mean to sound ungrateful, but I already told you I can handle myself."

"Okay," I say. "I just wanted to hang out with you."

"Alright, Doe." Angela lets loose with a big whopping sigh matched in drama only by her accompanying eye roll. "Let's just pretend it's that. Take a look around as long as you're here. We've got some pretty cool stuff."

I mosey through the aisles, peering into the glass cases looking for that Wogdon dueling pistol that's eluded me for 200 years. Given to me by none other than Alexander Hamilton's widow who wanted nothing to do with it, I have no idea what happened to the mate—only being certain of one thing, the pistols which are currently touted as the real thing are not. Did I mention I was a loyal manservant in the Hamilton household? I was let go a month after he died with only the pistol as my parting compensation. When the master was alive, he never minded that I performed my domestic duties at night when the family and household staff were sleeping, but after his death the missus couldn't take it. She woke at night thinking she was hearing ghosts when, in fact, she was only hearing an industrious vampire busy with his dusting and polishing.

There's no sign of the dueling pistol, or any other pistol from that era, but I'm fascinated by the vast array of the simply odd and the wildly extraordinary. I can't imagine how long it took Stuart to build up a collection like this. Istvan possessed many weapons of this sort in his manor. I saw them hanging from the walls. Balanced on mantels. I didn't pay them much attention, but now I can see what drew him to Up In Arms. I understand how a person could get caught up in this type of collecting.

From the corner of my eye, I can see Angela writing down figures. Counting cash. Doing the normal things people do when they close down a place of business at night. Finally, I see her flip the sign from OPEN to CLOSED and deadbolt the door from the inside by using a key.

"Come downstairs, I wanna show you something cool," she says while she's bent over a gun locker where she places a handgun which I suppose is normally kept at the ready behind the counter. It's shocking to see it in the midst of all these terrifying instruments of death, which were equally as terrifying in their day as the pistol she carefully locks up is today. I suppose it shouldn't shock me. She spins the dial of the combination lock and motions for me to follow her down a dark, narrow staircase. She carries a large vinyl zipper-bag filled with what I imagine to be checks and cash and credit card receipts.

At the bottom of the staircase are two doors, one to the right and the other to the left.

"That's where Stuart's tanning bed is." She points to the door on the left. "And also where he grows his weed. Pretend you didn't just hear that."

"Have you ever seen the inside?" I ask.

"Sure. He comes down to turn the grow lights on and

off and obviously he comes down to tan himself. It's locked but the key's right under that brick. I could go in and help myself to some weed if I ever wanted but I never would. I'm too honest and definitely not into drugs. Plus, you'd never catch me in a tanning bed."

It should go without saying you'd never catch me in a tanning bed either, UVA being more than detrimental to my health to put it mildly. Angela turns to the door on the right which is also locked.

"This is where he keeps the coolest collection," she says, stooping to retrieve the key from under the brick. Apparently, this key works for both doors. "The most expensive things."

Inside she flips on the lights and I see a spectrum of weapons and armor from medieval Europe. A true spectacle, swords and shields that would make King Arthur envious. And all the way in the back, set up on a dummy against the wall is a full suit of armor just like you'd see in the 1500s, way before even I was born. I draw in a sharp breath. The craftsmanship alone is awe-inspiring, not to mention the thought that a real-live person actually wore this while riding a horse into battle or jousting. The metal made from iron or steel plates has been burnished to a soft glow.

"Incredible," I say. "How did the knights get all these separate pieces on?"

"Easier than you think," Angela says. "Stuart did it once with his wife helping him. In the old days the knight's squire helped him. There's an exact order for putting on each piece. That's what the sheet taped to the wall describes."

"Hard to imagine you could see well enough out of those eye slits. Or breathe through those tiny holes."

Being a coffin-dweller myself, I'm not prone to claustrophobia, but I can imagine what it would be like if you were.

"Anyway," Angela says. "I gotta lock everything up in

the vault so you'd better leave. I mean... I trust you, but Stuart trusts me so, ah, just get out of here so you don't see me spinning the combination."

"As if I would look," I say, trying my best to sound offended. I wouldn't look. Truly. I'm not a thief and anyway, money doesn't interest me except for my immediate needs which are few and basic.

But a seed has been planted in my brain and it's growing out of control like one of Jack's beanstalks. I take the stairs up three at a time, calling behind me, "When do you work next?"

"Friday," Angela answers, her voice now muffled by the floor in between us. "Why?"

I don't bother answering. I saw Angela drop her keys in her purse after locking the deadbolt from the inside. Angela has a key ring that could rival Mrs. Dilliberato's—God knows what all those keys are for.

She won't miss just one little key.

CHAPTER FORTY-ONE

TWO NIGHTS LATER, I'M at the same alley at the same time.

Two nights ago, my next move wasn't clear to me. Two nights ago, I fell into Istvan's arms dry-sobbing like a lost child who's finally found his father. Two nights ago, I meant it. For a minute. Or two. For up to five or ten if I'm being honest. If I'm being completely honest, I still feel it... this unbearable but unbreakable connection.

But tonight, I'm out for revenge. Tonight, I'm here to avenge Molly and Jiji Watanabe and poor Myrna who would go to any lengths to reunite a lost pet with its owner. I'm sure of that now.

It surprises me how calm I am. I remember Bibi's story about her sensei stepping on her foot to make her forget the pain in her arm. I haven't blinked or knocked or tapped once in the last two days. Somehow, something is holding me together—but it's precarious, that's for sure. It's as precarious as a poorly knit sweater with one loose thread; all it takes is a hard tug for the whole thing to unravel. But I need to maintain my calm in order to pull off my plan and, for that reason, I don't send out an echo-whistle. I simply wait in the inky darkness trying to focus instead on when it was I last had something to eat.

I wonder what Istvan would say if he knew about my rituals. I wonder if I blinked or knocked or tapped in his presence. Istvan would have noticed. And, if he noticed, he most certainly would use it against me. Will use it against me. Fragile, he'd call me. As if.

"How lovely to see you again." A disembodied voice in the dark. I turn to face him, not having heard his approach. "I'm so glad you're here, my boy."

Istvan's voice is solid. Confident. A reassuring baritone. He places a hand on my shoulder in a very paternal way, but I steel myself against any feelings his touch might stir. I have to keep a clear head. I have to disconnect Istvan, the murderer, from Istvan, the second-to-the-last vampire in the world.

"Not here," I say. "There's a place we can meet and speak privately where we won't be seen. You know the Up In Arms? I'm cleaning the place while the regular janitor's on vacation, so I have a key."

I suffer a moment of panic as I realize there may indeed be a janitor. There could also be an alarm with a code I don't know. But Angela didn't set an alarm when we left the shop two nights ago. As for the janitor, the place was pretty dirty, so I have to trust in fate. Still, I turn my head away and blink out a silent SOS.

"I know the place," he says. "Shall we walk there together?"

"Too dangerous," I say. "For the two of us to be seen together. And I have to stop by my apartment first to feed my fish and do a few other things."

"Ah, your fish?" Istvan arches an eyebrow. "Fish make delightful companions for a single person. I recently saw a lovely aquarium with exquisitely colored tropical fish..." He trails off, probably realizing that was Molly's aquarium and, judging by the tightening of my jaw, a subject better left alone if he wants to make inroads with his "son." "I've been thinking of starting one myself," he says instead.

Now that it's planted, I can't get the image out of my head. Istvan stopping to admire Molly's aquarium after incapacitating her with his bite.

"I'd like to see your apartment, if you don't mind," he says. "Perhaps I could come with you and see your fish as well."

Never! Never! Never would I let Istvan anywhere near my Clementine. Or Henrietta.

"That would be a bad idea," I say. "I have a very nosy landlady and she might start asking questions if she sees you with me because I never bring friends home. I think we should take things slow. Get to know each other first."

He takes it in stride, his face never revealing any emotion after so many centuries of practiced composure. I look for signs of skepticism that I fear might be there, but I see none.

"Of course," he says. "I suppose we don't really know each other, do we? Although I often feel like I know you very well. When shall I meet you?"

"One hour from now."

I hope that one hour will buy me all the time I need. I travel the vampire way straight to Up In Arms. My hands tremble so violently when I insert the key to open the door that I'm afraid I'll use the entire hour just trying to get in. But I do get in with no alarm going off, and I call out to make sure no one's there. No response. So far so good. Now I have to work fast.

I hurry down the stairs and, when I get to the bottom, my foot crashes into the brick, sending the hidden key skittering across the floor. I have no doubt I've broken my toe. The pain is so intense I literally see stars—or more accurately, lightning bolts. I double over to breathe through the nausea, realizing that haste and anxiety are costing me precious minutes. I think about my meditation mantra, put it on a mental background loop, and fumble in the dark for the key.

With key finally in hand, I unlock the door on the right and flip the light switch. There it stands, as impressive and beautiful as I remember. Behind the suit of armor, taped to the wall, instructions for how to don this fifty-pound beast. Oh, what I'd give for a squire right now. I skip the instructions, which I'm too nervous to read, and do my best just based on common sense. First, I wiggle into the main section which covers most of the torso, then the legs, then the arms and hands which include armor for each individual finger. Finally, I settle the helmet over my head just to see how it feels. It might not be perfect, but I'm basically covered with steel from head to toe which is all that matters.

I clomp over to the locked door on the left and am barely able to turn the key without removing my hand armor. I'm grateful for my vampire's superior strength—the weight of this thing is nothing to me—but the loss of agility is tough. Vampires rely on their superior agility and it's not something we easily surrender. But in this case, it's a necessary trade off. I pull down the face cover of my helmet which leaves only the narrowest slits for vision, and I open the door.

There's Stuart's weed crop and there are the full spectrum grow lights beaming down on the marijuana plants. I turn my head to take in the entire room through the slits of my helmet and spy the tanning bed pushed up against the wall. I clomp over to the plants and disable the grow lights by pulling a single plug from a wall outlet—these lights aren't powerful enough to hurt me, but long-term they won't do me any good.

The room is dark, which is what I want. I'm able to see in the dark, but the eye slits limit my vision. I pull up the face cover and lean over to read the instructions for the tanning bed. It's not rocket science. There's a timer to set for when you want the bed to turn on, with one minute the minimum—two seems to be a safe choice. There's a selection for the light intensity level, and, naturally, I set it to the most powerful.

I've left the front door of the shop unlocked so that Istvan can enter. Now all I have to do is sit and wait for him. By my calculation he should be here in about twenty minutes.

But time with nothing to do is never my friend, and the heat of this suit combined with my natural anxiety has me drenched with sweat within minutes. Sweat is not my friend either, having such little bodily fluid to spare. And less now because it's been over a week, by my calculation, since I've eaten. I could be heading for trouble.

I bring my steel-gloved knuckles up to my steel-covered head and start to rap my requisite five times. The sound this creates is neither pleasant nor especially reassuring, considering how sensitive my ears are to even the slightest noise. After the first rap I question the necessity for the following four and discover to my immense pleasure that I'm able to do without. A small victory, certainly, but it feels like so much more.

I have no idea how many minutes are left to wait and wonder if I'll faint from dehydration before Istvan arrives. I clomp back to the room on the right to retrieve my phone so I can see the time. Ten minutes before he arrives. Even ten minutes of unbridled anxiety feels like an entire lifetime. I begin my mantra again and it helps. Until I start to think.

Self: Angela is my partner. A great partner, completely unselfish.

Self: I'm a bad partner. A bad person. A selfish person.

Self: Angela would do anything for me.

Self: I've done practically nothing for Angela except share my contacts (Fernando and Peter).

Self: Angela keeps no secrets from me.

Self: Almost everything I've told Angela—everything significant—has been an utter and total lie.

Self: Angela trusts me implicitly.

Self: I am undeserving of Angela's trust and have proven that by stealing the key from her keychain. This is in addition to the many lies I've told her.

Self: Angela wants nothing more than to stop the Six o' Clock Slasher and she's never wavered from that goal.

Self: I abandoned Angela when she needed me to help track down the Six o' Clock Slasher. I only rejoined her efforts when it affected me personally.

Self: Angela would never understand if she knew who... what I really am. She would turn on me just like Marie did.

Self: I should give Angela the chance to prove who she really is. If Angela turns on me then so be it. It wouldn't be the first time I'd be forced to move to a new city and it certainly won't be the last.

I pick up my phone and dial Angela's number. She answers on the first ring.

"Doe! What's up?"

"I've done a terrible thing," I say. "And I need to tell you about it."

Silence.

"Where are you, Doe?"

"I'm at the Up In Arms. Inside."

"What the... stay where you are, I'm on my way."

Knowing the distance to Angela's home and the scarcity of public transportation this time of night, I know it will be a good thirty to forty minutes before she gets here. By that time, Istvan will be dead. At that time, I can tell her that we've accomplished what we set out to do.

That *I've* accomplished what we set out to do.

CHAPTER FORTY-TWO

When I hear Istvan's tap on the shop door, I stand at attention. After a few more knocks, he'll try the door and, finding it open, come in. It's just human nature, or even vampire nature.

I go over my advantages and disadvantages when it comes to doing battle with Istvan. I have the advantage of surprise. I have youth on my side which means I have better reflexes and superior strength and speed. I definitely have the advantage of weight while I'm wearing this suit of armor. I only hope I'm mentally strong enough for what will come next.

I wait for Istvan's second and third (louder) knocks and then for the door to open just as I knew it would. I enter the room on the left and set the tanning bed timer to two minutes. Then I position myself in the hallway between the two doors at the bottom of the stairs.

"Zoltan?"

"I'm downstairs," I call up to him. "Come on down, I have something to show you I think you'll love."

The seconds tick by in my mind as Istvan makes his way to the back of the store and then down the steps. I've closed both doors so it's dark, but that doesn't affect Istvan or me. When he's near the bottom of the stairs he can finally see my full figure encased in the shining suit of armor. I've calculated forty-five seconds have gone by.

"Magnificent," he says, taking in the dramatic sight of me. "Truly magnificent. Is it for sale because, if so, I'll buy it for you."

I suppose this is Istvan's idea of the most perfect gift a father could bestow his son, instead of… I don't know, a baseball glove for example. This is Istvan's idea of male bonding just like I hoped it would be.

"Follow me," I say. "There's more that you'll love. Stuart keeps his special collection in this room, and I have the key." I hope I sound conspiratorial. My steel-plated hand points the way to the room on the left.

Istvan descends the final three steps, and I open the door to allow him to enter first, closing the door behind me and blocking it with my armored body. It's still dark in the room but the timer should go off in seconds.

"What is this?" Istvan asks.

"There's something about me I want you to know," I say, hoping I have time to finish before the timer goes off and my plan is exposed. It's something I wish I could have said to Bela before he died and now I want Istvan to take it with him to his grave. "What you and Bela mistook for weakness, for fragility… well, that's something most people call morality. Something you'd know nothing about, which is why I'll go on living and you'll die tonight."

"What's the meaning of this?" Istvan's fear is palpable even through the thick armor that surrounds me.

And right on cue, the tanning bed lights up like a spaceship.

Instantly, Istvan claws at me, panicked, trying to make his way through the door, past my metallic bulk. He pummels me with his fists, but I feel nothing. I grab him around the throat with one iron glove and grab ahold of his arm with the other. I push, drag, and pull him towards the bed, his screams barely reaching my ears through the metal helmet.

The painful UV rays penetrate the gaps in my armor, and there are many. My face suffers most in spite of the minuscule size of the slits and breathing holes. Other areas admit more light but at least those areas are slightly protected by my clothes—but not for long. If I don't get

Istvan into the tanning bed as quickly as possible, I could be the one to die tonight and Istvan would be loose upon the world with no one the wiser.

I push Istvan to the ground, then lose my own balance. We heave ourselves at each other like two wild animals, reduced to grunts and moans with only survival on our minds. But my suit of armor feels like a cage from which I can't fight my way out of, and I'm beginning to think I badly misjudged how this would play out. My bulk is losing out to Istvan's agility while my body betrays me—burning on the inside from my trapped body heat.

When it occurs to me that I could die, my life passes before my eyes just like they say happens at the moment of death. But when it comes to the frame where young Zoltan arrives at Istvan's manor only to be forever changed, the movie of my life hits pause and a sudden surge of energy transforms me into a looming avenger with enough strength to lift Istvan from the ground and forcefully thrust him into the tanning bed. I clamber on top to hold the lid down and remove myself from further harm.

I have no idea how long this will take. No idea at all. Believe it or not, I've never seen a vampire die by sun exposure and I'm not even sure if this is close enough to the real thing to do the job. His screams tell me it is, but I hope it happens soon.

With whatever strength he has left, Istvan gives one hard upward shove with his legs, and I slide off to land on the cement floor with a crashing thud. Taking the opportunity to escape, Istvan drags himself towards the door, howling like a wounded beast.

My sight, already hindered by the narrow slits, is limited even more by the painful burns around my eyes. I pull myself up and plod clumsily after him, lunging at the last minute in an attempted takedown. I miss, and he reaches the door just as it opens wide to...

Angela?

"What the hell? What the blooming hell?" she says, the final "hell" morphing into a piercing scream which I won't soon forget.

Istvan shoves her aside and lurches up the stairs. By the time he reaches the top of the stairs, I've caught up with him. I wrap both arms around his waist, this time in a successful tackle. We slide down the stairs, me on my back holding Istvan face-up from behind. Angela side-steps us at the last second.

"It's him, Angela!" I yell. "Get something to hit him."

I'm thinking a club or a sword or the brick on the ground. Anything.

But Angela pulls the Tabasco sauce from her holster and, with a powerful jabbing motion, she lands a perfect shot in each of his eyes. The tanning bed induced screams are nothing compared to the tortured cries coming out of Istvan post-Tabasco.

I hold on for dear life with every bit of strength I have left. I hold on until Istvan stops moving. Until Istvan crumples in my arms. Until Istvan is soft like a down pillow. Until Istvan is nothing but a pile of ash.

Only then do I fully comprehend the extent of my pain, a thousand red-hot needles piercing my eyes, my mouth, my groin, my armpits. I'm on fire.

I get up and run.

EPILOGUE

To my dying day, if that ever comes, I don't think I'll be able to explain why I ran. But it's a known fact that an animal or other living creature will run for no reason other than panic—fight or flight, it's called. Even a burning man will sometimes run until someone takes him down to smother the flames. Whatever the reason, physical or emotional or both, I ran straight out of the store at my vampire speed, reduced only slightly by the suit of armor that couldn't quite keep up.

To Fernando and Peter, who'd been waiting outside for Angela after serendipitously running into her while she was waiting for the bus and offering her a ride to Up In Arms on Fernando's scooter...

To Fernando and Peter, who saw only the blurriest of images, a knight in shining armor moving at lightning speed, vanishing into the fog before their brains could make sense of what their eyes were seeing...

To Fernando and Peter, the knight who slew the Six o' Clock Slasher (with Angela's help, of course) would become the stuff of local legend... and soon the whole city would know of him via the mouths of boys who could spread a story faster than 5G.

I eventually came to my senses and eventually came back to Up In Arms. Angela, having sent the Wheelie Boys home, was waiting for me to do a whole lot of explaining. And believe me when I say there was a *whole lot* of explaining. When I was done, I wondered why I hadn't trusted Angela in the first place. How did I not recognize a true partner when one was looking me right in the eye?

***

Now, I knew I truly was the last vampire on Earth.

***

Although, never say never. I'd made that mistake once before.

***

It was good to be back at work at the Gobble-Down-Suck-Up after taking a few weeks off to recuperate from my UV burns (flu, I told Calvin). Calvin kept his word about changing his ways. He was much nicer to everyone, although he could get a little prickly when business was brisk.

Peter and Fernando continued to show up in the back for their promised one year of all the food and shakes they wanted, at my expense of course. They leaned on me to teach them free climbing and, although I promised I would if they relinquished their right to fries and shakes for a year, it never happened. Truthfully I have no idea how to teach a human to free climb vampire style.

One day we got the news we'd all been waiting for. Molly was well enough to have visitors. She no longer had a police guard since the Slasher was dead. I was proud that I'd kept her fish alive and healthy and her plants too. I prevailed on Lilibeth to help me with just one thing before I went to visit Molly.

"Can you make me look like him?" I signed, holding up a photo of Johnny Depp from his *21 Jump Street* days. She eyed the photo and then me and, after a few back and forths, she nodded enthusiastically. And I have to say, when we were done, with the haircut and style using only a light holding spray, and with a much more natural mineral-based foundation, Molly was right. I did look like young Johnny Depp.

"You look amazing," Molly said when I sat on the chair

beside her hospital bed. "I knew it. I knew that was you."

It wasn't me, but it felt good to see the smize in her eyes again. Every time someone thinks someone is me, it's really someone else. But I know who I am, and now so does Angela. I'm good with that. I'm good with who I am, even if I'm really not young Johnny Depp.

"Thanks for everything," Molly said. "For looking after my fish. For being my friend. For everything."

Molly still thought she'd saved herself by dialing 9-1-1 and no one would ever tell her differently, certainly not me. But Molly *had* saved herself when it came right down to it. It's hard to take the life out of a girl who has so much life in her.

***

A month or two passed before Angela approached me with an idea.

"I was thinking of starting a business," she said. "And I was wondering if you wanted to be my partner."

There was a great deal of hemming and hawing before she got to the point. "I think we have what it takes to be great detectives. We've been through trial by fire and... well how about we keep our regular jobs and just dip a toe in the water?"

"What about your school?" I asked.

"I'm staying local so nothing would have to change."

"Could we keep it to misdemeanors and cheating spouses?" I asked.

"To start with." She smiled cheekily. "We can see where it goes."

Truthfully, I didn't really want to do it, but Angela's my partner and a partner's gotta have his partner's back. The next thing I knew, Peter and Fernando were blanketing the city with flyers.

IS THERE A MYSTERY IN YOUR LIFE?
DO YOU NEED SOMEONE TO SOLVE IT?

FOR A SERVICE THAT'S CHEAP, RELIABLE & DISCREET

CALL [...]

Angela and I were officially in business.

A few days later I was lying in my coffin contemplating what I'd just gotten myself into when I heard the familiar sound of mail sliding under my door. More bills. More catalogs. More of nothing good. When I arose from my coffin an hour later, I swept up the mail into a pile, mindlessly thumbing through it, dropping everything into either a recycle pile or a to-be-paid pile, when I came across a letter addressed to me by hand with a return address I didn't recognize.

Dear Mr. Doe,

I'm sorry to be writing you via snail mail but I'm responding to a written query you submitted eight years ago. At the time we weren't using electronic submissions, so I don't have an email address for you. Without any further ado let me get straight to the point. An intern picked your manuscript out of our slush pile and fell for it immediately. When she put it in my hands, I read straight through without stopping until the end. Your imagination is so vivid and your voice so unique. If you haven't yet found representation, I'd like to extend an offer via this letter which I pray will find its way to you. Please call or email me at [...]

Best,

Best indeed.

I called.

FACT: If you keep trying and never give up, your dream will eventually come true. Of course, it helps to have eternal life.

***

There was just one final thing I needed to do. I hadn't

seen Bibi since the events. Since… everything. I thought I was fine and had no need to see Bibi anymore, but I came to realize that I did need to keep seeing her. And maybe it was even more important to see her when I was doing well, to keep up my coping skills for a time when I might not be doing so well and would need them to fall back on. So, I picked up the phone and called her. She was surprised to hear from me, said she thought she'd heard the last of me, that maybe I hadn't forgiven her for abandoning me when she went to Hawaii. But that wasn't true at all.

When I showed up at her office at our appointed time, I came carrying a packet under my arm.

"What's this?" she asked, eyeing the heavy packet I held out to her.

"It's my manuscript," I said. "I won't be staying tonight."

"Will you be back?" she asked, sounding slightly hurt.

"Yes, I will. But I want you to read this first."

***

It feels good to be in business with the best and truest partner a guy could ask for. We don't have any customers yet, but it took a while before Bibi got her first call from the sad and desperate person I used to be before I found her. And Angela. Before I was accepted and loved for who I am and not who I pretended to be. I know I'm blessed to have Angela and Bibi in my life for as long as they're here on earth. I'm grateful for Henrietta and Molly too, although they know me in a different way.

Angela and I are walking down the street. It's springtime now but the weather is just as cold as if it was winter. We spy one of our flyers which never ceases to deliver a thrill.

"Wow, just look at us," Angela says as she casts a careless arm around my shoulder. "Oof, you're hard as a lobster."

"Boundaries," I remind her, although I have no more to fear from her touch.

"Okay, sorry, I'm working on it, promise I am."

I nudge her with my elbow to let her know I was kidding. "You were saying?"

"Doe, I think this is the beginning of a beautiful friendship."

"*Casablanca*," I say.

She cocks her head and side-eyes me appraisingly. "High five! I never took you for a film buff."

"I don't mean for this to sound like a boast, but I did attend the world premiere... New York, 1942. A night I shall never forget."

Angela glances at me again as if trying to separate fact from fiction.

"I can see we have a lot of catching up to do," she says. "Hey, did you really get to meet Johnny Cash?"

ACKNOWLEDGEMENTS

Geoff Habiger, thank you for turning your attention to this story of my heart and ultimately throwing your full support behind it. Lisa McCoy, thank you for helping to make it a better version of itself.

Cherrita and Moshoula you were John Doe's earliest cheerleaders. Macy you're my "write or die".

Deborah, we've talked through just about every scenario over the past three decades. Here's to another three decades.

Thank you to my writing posse: Vera, Melissa, Grace and Agathe. It's true we've ventured into other territories but we were there when it mattered and we're still here after all these years. And it still matters.

A million thanks to my family for their unwavering love and support... Jeremy, Hilary, Lucas, Nishita, Corey and Samantha.

To my grandchildren who add the necessary sparkle and joy to my life... Greyson, Charlotte, Leo, Bria, Arlo and Ellie.

To my husband, George, who selflessly gives his all to me, a gift I am blessed to receive each and every day.

***

If you or someone you know is struggling with obsessive compulsive disorder, you're not alone and help is available. Reaching out to a mental health professional can be an important step toward understanding what you're going through and finding effective ways to manage it.

Please don't be afraid to take that first step even if it's just reaching out to a friend, family member or trusted member of your community.

In addition, there are online resources such as https://www.nami.org

The Last Vampire

[LASTVAMPIRE_DoeEDIT4.5]

By John Doe

Chapter Forty-Three

They say a person has three great loves in their life. The first is pure and true. Love only for love's sake. The second is for financial security. The third and last is for the sake of companionship. If this is true, then Tom Smith lived his life accordingly.

Nadia. They were babes in the woods. Literally. Until greed and power and the other worst vices of humanity scorched through their innocent bliss, leaving it in ruins, they believed there would never be anything ahead of them except their longing to be together and the day that dream would finally come true.

Humans seek financial security for the peace of mind that it buys. Vampires seek a reliable source of blood for the same thing. So, one might say that a reliable source of blood, willingly given, is precisely the equivalent to financial security for a human. That's what Marie was for Tom.

But many years later, Tom had his third and final encounter with love. Of course, he hadn't expected to find love in the human sense. His opportunity for that had long since passed, physical love no longer being an option. But he ached to experience the merging of souls that humans expound upon in poetry, literature, songs. A love so true that kissing and petting and the ultimate act was simply an afterthought, if even that. If humans could have this, why couldn't he? He wanted it desperately. One especially warm day in the autumn of 1965, his prayers were answered by Clara.

Tom had crisscrossed the country for years and knew most every right angle of the bigger western states and every peculiar twist and turn of the smaller eastern states. His preference for wide open spaces and the greater respect shown to strangers and loners out west eventually led him to a ranch a hundred miles outside of Reno, which was then considered "the biggest little city in the world." Tom applied for, and was hired as, the job of a ranch hand. Although he'd never worked with horses and cattle before, he did have experience with donkeys, sheep, and pigs, and after all, how different could a donkey be from a horse, or a sheep from a cow? He loved the work and took to it well, keeping his distance from the other ranch hands who respected his solitary nature. He asked for, and was immediately granted, nighttime watch over the herds, keeping them safe from prowling cougars and rustlers while perched on top of his ink black pony.

Although Tom didn't technically need a hat at night, he was never seen without his wide brimmed ten-gallon hat which was much admired by the others and which did a decent job of hiding his unusual complexion, eliminating the necessity for wearing makeup. During the day, he stayed in a small dark room built behind the hay loft in the barn, which he locked carefully from the inside. It was a noisy place during the day, and the other hands marveled how Tom Smith could sleep through anything.

Then one day, there was a knock on his door, and he called out to see who was there.

"Clara, the cook," came the answer. "Brought you some breakfast 'cause the other fellas say you sleep away the day."

Tom could open the door a crack, maybe more than a crack, without a shaft of direct light hitting him in the airless loft built high above the stalls where the horses slept. So, he did.

"I already rustled up somethin' for myself," he said, trying his hardest to sound like a tough cowboy. "But I most appreciate the courtesy, ma'am."

If he'd been wearing his hat, he would have tipped it to her at that point, but he wasn't, so he just looked straight into her round blue eyes, as blue as Lake Tahoe which wasn't too far from the ranch. And when he did, he felt like he was drowning in that beautiful snow-fed mountain lake. Like he was drowning but he didn't want to be saved. And that was the beginning for Clara and Tom Smith. It was love at first sight. Tom was all of seventeen years old (plus 246). Clara was eighty-two (plus nothing).

Their relationship unfolded in the darkness of the hay loft, usually in Tom's tiny quarters. If the other cowpokes knew about it, nobody said nothing. That was the cowboy code. Live and let live. Don't poke your nose where it doesn't belong. This was the love that Tom had been seeking, true love without all the fuss and muss of flesh. Clara was right there with him.

They passed many hours, weeks, months in each other's company until they knew the other better at times than they knew themselves. But Clara was restless, not being the type to let the grass grow under her feet, and when she heard about all the young people from all over the country making their way to San Francisco to celebrate what was coming to be called the Summer of Love in 1967, Clara was anxious to join them. Tom was content with his life. More than content he was finally at peace, but when Clara badgered him to pull up roots and join her in this adventure, how could he deny her? She knew what he was and promised to accommodate his night-time travel needs. He'd come to be so dependent on her he couldn't imagine going back to his pre-Clara life.

So, one day in May of 1967, Clara and Tom hit the road, hitchhiking only at night, camping roadside by day in a thick canvass tent that permitted no light, joining up with the long train of flower children making their way to Haight-Ashbury. And this is how Tom Smith came to San Francisco, a city he would never leave.

Scratch that last line. One thing I don't need is some old-school yahoo coming to San Francisco armed with a Gurkha Kukri trying to make a name for himself by bagging the last vampire.

So, one day in May of 1967, Clara and Tom hit the road, hitchhiking only at night, camping roadside by day in a thick canvass tent that permitted no light, joining up with the long train of flower children making their way to Haight-Ashbury. And this is how Tom Smith came to San Francisco where he lived until his final move to Seattle.

Will these edits never end?

ABOUT THE AUTHOR

Kathryn Berla likes to write in a variety of genres including light fantasy, contemporary literary fiction, and even horror. Kathryn grew up in India, Syria, Europe, and Africa. Her love for experiencing new cultures runs deep, and she gives into it whenever she can. She has been an avid movie buff since childhood, and often sees the movie in her head before she writes the book. Kathryn graduated from the University of California in Berkeley with a degree in English. She lives in the San Francisco Bay Area.